S0-ABC-348

Proudly bearing the sword Excalibur, the Lady of the Lake rose up from the glistening waters . . . of Central Park Lake.

She looked like hell.

Weeds and crud had ruined her beautiful white dress. Her hair, also filled with crud, hung limply. In her jeweled crown a dead fish had somehow managed to lodge itself to stare glassy-eyed at the world.

She glared at Arthur for a moment and then, in an attempt to restore some measure of dignity, took a majestic step forward, slipped and fell flat into the mud.

Arthur reached down to help her but she waved him off, pulling herself to her feet. Using the sword to balance herself by thrusting it into the silt, she lifted one foot and pulled an empty cigarette pack off the bottom of her shoe. Then she gave the still-gleaming sword to Arthur.

"Thank you, lady," he said, and bowed to her.

She pulled a crushed beer can from the hem of her dress, and said two words in a musical voice that would have shamed the sirens of myth.

"Never again."

Knight Life

Peter David

ACE BOOKS, NEW YORK

This book is an Ace original edition,
and has never been previously published.

KNIGHT LIFE

An Ace Book / published by arrangement with
the author

PRINTING HISTORY
Ace edition / April 1987

All rights reserved.
Copyright © 1987 by Peter David.
Cover art by Hiro Kimura.
This book may not be reproduced in whole or in part,
by mimeograph or any other means, without permission.
For information address: The Berkley Publishing Group,
200 Madison Avenue, New York, New York 10016.

ISBN: 0-441-45130-6

Ace Books are published by The Berkley Publishing Group,
200 Madison Avenue, New York, New York 10016.
The name "ACE" and the "A" logo
are trademarks belonging to Charter Communications, Inc.

PRINTED IN THE UNITED STATES OF AMERICA

10   9   8   7   6   5   4   3   2

Dedicated to Myra
Because she's always
been dedicated to me

Author's Note

The author would like to cite the following books and/or authors:

Le Morte d'Arthur by Sir Thomas Mallory
The Once and Future King and The Book of Merlin by
    T. H. White
The Last Enchantment and other assorted titles by Mary
    Stewart
Tales of King Arthur by John Steinbeck
Arthur Rex by Thomas Berger

All of the above have been carefully read, or purchased, or checked out from the local library and never returned by the author of this work. In the preparation of this manuscript the author has at the very least skimmed the flap copy, sell copy, and table of contents of all of the above, plus many other titles too numerous or obscure to mention.

The author thanks all of the above for their contribution, however small, to this work. But don't expect royalties.

Chaptre the First

The apartment was dark, illuminated only by the dim flickering of the twelve-inch, black-and-white Sony that sat atop a scratched coffee table. From the glow of the picture tube one would have seen an apartment allowed to go to waste through lack of attention. The wallpaper was yellowed and peeling—there were squares and circles imprinted where various paintings or pictures had once hung. The floor was bare, the boards warped and uneven. Off to one side was a small kitchen that had a gas stove last cleaned sometime around the Hoover administration, and a refrigerator stocked with two cracked eggs, half a stale loaf of Wonder Bread, and a flat bottle of club soda. And three six-packs of beer.

The occupant of the apartment was also illuminated in the light.

On the screen an old sitcom was playing. She had seen it before. She had seen all of them before. It did not matter to Morgan. Nothing much mattered anymore.

She smiled slightly at the antics of the castaways on the screen. Somehow Gilligan was always able to make Morgan smile slightly. A buffoon, a simple jester.

Simple. She remembered when her life was simple.

She took a sip of the beer, finishing the contents of the can and tossing it off into the darkness. She thought there might be a trash can there to receive it. She didn't much care.

Morgan Le Fey hauled her corpulent body protestingly to its feet. She was clad in a faded housecoat that had once been purple, and her swollen feet were crammed into large fuzzy slippers. Her hair was still the raven color it had always been, or at least had been for as long as she could recall. She hadn't checked the roots for a few decades now. But the fine lines of her face, her sleek jaw and high cheekbones, were now sliding off into her collarbone. She had given up counting her chins, as another one seemed to spring into existence every decade, like clockwork.

As she waddled into the kitchen, her housecoat tugged at the protesting buttons, threatening to pull them all off their thin moorings.

She squinted at the dazzling (by contrast) brilliance of the refrigerator bulb, reached in and snapped another can of beer out of a half-consumed six-pack. She made her way back across the kitchen, the slippers slapping against the bottom of her feet.

As she sank back into the easy chair, resting her hands in the customary places on the arms, she watched the final credits run on this latest rerun of the adventures of the castaways. Even more than Gilligan, she empathized with the concept of castaways as a whole. She was a castaway too. Drifting, floating, on an island of isolation. That her island existed in the midst of a bustling metropolis was irrelevant.

She flipped the top off her beer can and started to drink. The cold beverage slid down her throat, basking her in a familiar warmth and haze. She patted the can lovingly. Her one friend. Her familiar.

She held up the can in a salute. "To mighty Morgan," she croaked, her voice cracking from disuse. "Here's to eternal life, and to the thrice-damned gods who showed me how to have it."

She choked then, and for the first time in a long time she really thought about what she had become. With a heart-rending sob she drew her arm back and hurled the half-empty can square into the TV which sat two yards away. The screen exploded in a shower of glass and sparks, flying out like a swarm of liberated sprites. There was a sizzling sound, and acrid smoke rose from the back of the set.

Her face sank into her hands, and Morgan Le Fey wept loudly. Her sides heaved in and out, her breath rasped in her chest. The rolls of fat that made up her body shook with the rage and frustration she released.

She cried and cursed all the fates that had brought her to this point in her life, and it was then that she resolved to put a stop to it. Existence for the sake of existence alone is no existence at all, she decided. "I am a mushroom," she said out loud. "A fungus. I have lived for far too long, and it's time I rested."

She stood again, but this time with far greater assurance, for her movements now had a purpose to them other than simple self-perpetuation. She lumbered into the kitchen, fumbled through a drawer crammed with plastic spoons from Carvel's ice cream stores and equally harmless knives from Kentucky Fried Chicken. Finally she extracted a steak knife. She blanched at the rust, then realized that rust was hardly a concern.

She sat back down in front of the TV, the knife now cradled serenely in the crook of her arm. The TV screen had miraculously mended itself. There was a crisscross of hairline fractures across it, but these too would fade in time. Not that this was any concern to Morgan either.

"One last time, old enemy," she said. Her thin, arched eyebrows reached just to the top of her head, even though her eyes were little more than slits beneath painted green lids. She fumbled in the drawer next to her for the remote control, and she started to flick the switch. Time had lost all meaning to her, and she could not recall how long it had been since she had looked in on Him. Five days? Five months? Years? She was not certain.

Once these long-distance viewings had exacted a great toll from her, physically and spiritually. She had had to use specially prepared mirrors, or magic crystals. With the advent of the diodes and catheters, however, had come a revolution in the art of magic. A one-time ensorcellment of the wires and tubes, and she could look in on Him whenever she wished. That was why she had never opted for solid-state components —she didn't trust her ability to control something as arcane as microcircuitry.

She clicked her remote to Channel 1, and the smiling face of the news anchor disappeared. In its place was the exterior of a cave. Erosion and overgrowth had altered the exterior somewhat over time, but not enough to throw her. She knew it.

And she would take the knowledge to her grave, providing that someone ever found her bloated body and tossed it into the ground for her.

She held the knife to her wrist. She should really do this in a bathtub, she remembered reading now. But she hated the water. Besides, she wanted to be here, in front of the entombed resting place of her greatest magical opponent.

She stared at the cave entrance on her TV screen. "You'd really enjoy this moment, wouldn't you, you cursed old coot? Morgan Le Fey, driven to this, by you. You knew this would happen someday. This is your doing, you reaching out from beyond the grave." She pressed the blade against the skin of her right wrist. "Damn you, Merlin," she said softly. "You've finally won."

Then she stopped.

She leaned forward, the knife, still against the inside of her wrist, forgotten now. She squinted, rubbed her eyes, and focused again.

Against the mouth of the cave rested a huge stone, covered with moss and vegetation. This stone was far more than just a dead weight. It was held in place through the magic of a woman's wiles, and there is no stronger bond than that. And though the woman, Nineve, was long gone, the magic should hold for all eternity.

The operative word here being *should*.

For Morgan now saw that the rock had moved. It had rolled ever so slightly to one side, creating an opening. An opening far too small for a man to squeeze through. But still . . . it hadn't been there before.

Responding to Morgan's merest thought, the TV screen zoomed in tight on the hole. Yes, definitely new. She had never seen it before, and she could see where the overgrown leaves had been ripped away when the stone was moved. . . .

Moved! But who had moved it?

It was more than she dared hope. The camera panned down, away from the hole which was several feet above the ground.

There were footprints. She could not determine how old. Once she would have known immediately, for once she had looked in on this spot every day. But with passing years had come passing interest, and the occasional look-see had seemed to be sufficient. Seemed to be, but clearly was not.

Yes, footprints. Barefoot. And something else, she realized. They were small. A child's. Heading one way, away from the cave.

"A child," she breathed. "Of *course*. *Of course!*"

The knife clattered to the floor as Morgan Le Fey, half sister of King Arthur Pendragon, incestuous lover of her brother, mother of the bastard Modred, tilted her head back and laughed. At first it was hardly a laugh, but more like a high-pitched cackling imitation, similar to a parrot. With each passing moment, however, it grew. Fuller. Richer. Although the abused body of Morgan still showed its deficiencies, years were already dropping from the voice.

If anyone had once dared tell her that she would be happy over the escape of her deadliest enemy, she would have erased that unfortunate person from the face of the earth. The suggestion was postively ludicrous. But so had her life become as well.

For Morgan Le Fey had come to realize that she thrived on conflict and hatred. It was as mother's milk to her. And without that her spirit had shriveled away to a small, ugly thing lost somewhere in an unkempt form.

Now her spirit soared. She spread wide her arms and a wind arose around her, blowing wide the swinging windows of her apartment. It was the first time in several years fresh air had been allowed in, and it swept through as if entering a vacuum. Fresh air filling her nostrils, Morgan became aware of the filth in which she had resided for some time. Her nose wrinkled and she shook her head.

She went to the window and stepped up onto the sill, reveling in the force of the wind she had summoned. Above her, clouds congealed, tore apart, and reknit, blackness swarming over them. Below Morgan, pedestrians ran to and fro, pulling their coats tight around them against the unexpected turn of bad weather. A few glanced up at Morgan in the window but went on about their business, jamming their hands down atop their heads to prevent their hats or wigs from blowing away.

Morgan drank it in, thriving on the chaos of the storm. She screamed over the thunder, "Merlin! Merlin, demon's son! The mighty had fallen, mage! You had fallen. I had fallen. All was gone, and you were in your hell and I was in mine." She inhaled deeply, feeling the refreshing, chilled sting of cold air

in her lungs. She reveled in the tactile sensation of her housecoat blowing all around her, the wind enveloping her flimsy
garment.

"You're back now!" she crowed. "But so am I! I have
waited these long centuries for you, Merlin. Guarding against
the day that you might return, and yet now I glory in it. For I
am alive today, Merlin! Do you hear me, old man? *Morgan Le
Fey lives!* And while I live, I *hate*! Sweet hate I have nutured
all these long decades and centuries. And it's all for you,
Merlin! All for you and your damned Arthur!

"Wherever you are, Merlin, quake in fear. I am coming for
you. I thank you for saving my life, Merlin! And I shall return
the favor a thousandfold. *I, Morgan Le Fey!*"

"Harry, what's going on?"

Harry peered through the curtains at the window of the
apartment across the way. "It's that nut, the black-haired
broad again. God, what a slob. I don't know how people let
themselves go like that."

His wife eyed his beer belly but wisely refrained from comment.

"She's shouting about some damned thing or other," he
muttered as he came to sit next to her on the couch. "Usually
she's just regular drunk. I don't know what she's on tonight,
but it must be a wowser."

"Bet she's from New York," mumbled his wife.

"What?" he asked.

She repeated it, adding, "It wouldn't surprise me in the
least."

"No?"

"No. Because New Yorkers are all crazy. They know it. The
government knows it. The whole country knows it. In New
York everyone acts like that," and she chucked a thumb
across the street in Morgan's direction. "You never know
what's going to happen."

"Yeah," said Harry. "That's why I like it."

"Well, I hate it," his wife said firmly, as if she'd just turned
down the option to buy Manhattan. "All the crazy people
there—they all deserve each other. Why, I hear tell it's not
safe to walk the streets at night there. You never know what
weird thing you'll run into next."

Chaptre the Second

Each day in life begins with the same expectations. At least each day did for Sidney Krellman, the manager of Arthur's Court.

Arthur's Court was a fashionable men's clothing store situated near Central Park. And for Sidney each day was nice and simple. He woke up in the morning. Got dressed (nattily, of course). Went into work. Acted politely to most clientele, enthusiastically to a select handful, and brushed off whatever else might exist. At the end of the day he and an assistant—it was Quigley, this particular day—would check over the day's receipts, shutter and close up the store, and leave precisely at 7:45 sharp.

Sidney Krellman expected nothing different on this particular day. It did not occur to him that this brisk November day was exactly one year before the next mayoral elections in New York City. Sidney didn't care for politics. Or elections, or mayors. Or much else except his daily routine. And he disliked intensely anything that caused a deviation from that routine.

This being the case, Sidney was going to *really* dislike what was about to happen. It disrupted his store-closing routine, threw the end of his day into a turmoil, and generally wrinkled the fabric of his well-ordered life.

It might have been different had he had some warning. If he

had known, for instance, that this evening the legends were to be fulfilled, and that Arthur, King, son of Uther Pendragon, was about to return, he would certainly have kept on extra help. Or perhaps left early. Or even gone on vacation.

As it was, he did none of these things.

At 7:30 precisely, Sidney was issuing instructions to Quigley on opening the store tomorrow morning. Sidney anticipated being late, having a dental appointment scheduled. Sidney was a short, almost billiard ball of a man (but sartorially correct), and Quigley—his young, gawky assistant manager—was his physical opposite. Sidney was waving one finger in the air, as was his habit, when there was a rap at the glass front door.

The rap derailed Sidney's train of thought, and he turned with an annoyed glance to the door. He froze in mid sentence, finger still pointed skyward, as if offering directions to a wayward duck. Quigley continued to stare at his superior, waiting for him to continue. When no continuation was forthcoming, it dawned on Quigley to follow his boss's gaze toward the front door.

The knight occupied the full space of the door. He was dressed in full armor from head to toe, the plates smooth and curving over his chest, arms, and legs. The armor was excellently made, for hardly a gap had been permitted, and even those were protected, either by small stretches of chain mail or by small upturns in the plates. A full helmet covered his head, a visor with a short blunt point in front of his face. A scabbard hung at his side—it was ornately decorated with dark stones and intercurling lines of design.

The knight stood there for a moment, as if contemplating the two men within the store. He raised his gauntleted hand and knocked again, this time a bit harder.

It was the wrong move. The metal-gloved hand went right through the glass. The glass hung there for a moment in mid-air, and then with a resounding crash gave up all molecular adhesion and shattered into thousands of pieces.

Sidney Krellman's jaw moved up and down and side to side slightly, but that was it. Quigley was not even able to handle quite that much.

The knight stood there for a moment, looking down at the destruction. Then the gauntleted hands reached up and lifted the visor of the helmet. A gentle, bearded face smiled regretfully at Sidney Krellman.

"I'm terribly sorry," he said. "I seem to have damaged your establishment."

Sidney Krellman found it odd that despite the fact that this man was fully armored, the thing he found to be far more impressive was his voice. It was low and carefully modulated. It seemed to have an age and wisdom to it that contradicted the relative youthfulness of the face. It was a compelling voice, that of a great orator, or perhaps commander of men. The lines of the face that peered out from the helmet were clean and straight. The forehead sloped slightly, and eyebrows that were a bit thick projected over eyes, which were almost black. His lips were thin and what Sidney could see of his beard was very dark, but with a few strands of conspicuous gray.

Sidney Krellman shook off the daze that had come over him and gave a small bow. "Quite all right," he replied in a voice pitched two octaves above his usual tone. He quickly corrected his pitch and continued, "It could happen to anyone."

The front of the armor rose slightly. The knight had laughed. "Anyone who was clad in such foolish armor. Do you mind if I come inside?"

"Not at all. Not at all." Sidney backed up slowly, his eyes glancing at the scabbard that hung at the knight's side. It had not yet registered on him that there was no sword in it.

The knight stepped through the bashed-in door, walking across the spotless green carpet of the men's clothing store. Glass crunched under each armored foot.

"I suppose you're wondering," said the knight, "why I'm wearing this ridiculous armor."

Sidney tried to come up with an answer that seemed safe, since he was still convinced that at any moment this armored maniac might pull out a sword and send his toupeed head sailing across the store. Sensing his boss's hesitation, Quigley brightly stepped in with the first thing that came to mind. "Armor?" he said cheerfully. "What armor?"

Sidney Krellman moaned softly and waited for the whir of sharp metal winging toward his neck.

Arthur Rex laughed softly. "Italian, I'd say from the look of it," he replied, inspecting one armored hand. "Wouldn't you say?"

"Oh absolutely," said Quigley. "You can always tell Italian armor. It has, uh . . . very narrow, pointy shoes."

"Really?" said Arthur, apparently with genuine interest.

"I'd place this armor at about, oh, fourteenth century." He tapped the chestplate and smiled at the sound. "I daresay none of *your* suits would wear for quite so long. Nevertheless I still find it clumsy. In my day we wore leathers. That's when men fought men, not metal shells fought metal shells. Tell me, young man, what's your name, please?"

"Quigley," said Quigley, and chucking a thumb at his supervisor he said, "And this is—"

"The manager," said Sidney quickly.

"Ah. Well, Quigley"—Arthur leaned against the counter, draping one arm against the cash register—"you seem to be an expert. Tell me, what think you of chain mail?"

"I tried that once," said Quigley. "Sent five dollars to five friends. I should have gotten $10,037 back, but I never saw a dime."

Arthur cocked an eyebrow, said nothing for a moment, then said, "As I was saying, this whole armor thing is something of a practical joke, played by someone who I thought a bit too old for this sort of thing. I really wasn't anticipating wandering about New York City dressed for the Crusades. I had more imagined, well, something along those lines." He inclined his head toward a three-piece suit that stood handsomely displayed on a mannequin. "Might I try that on?"

"Um . . . I don't think," said Sidney cautiously, "that it will, um, quite fit over your, um, current vestments."

"I quite agree. If you would be so kind as to help me off with these . . ."

Sidney Krellman glanced at Quigley and inclined his head. Quigley shrugged, walked over to the knight, and began to pull at the thick leather straps that held the armor on.

"Do you have experience in this sort of thing?" asked Arthur as he pulled his helmet off.

"Well, I took shop once," offered Quigley.

"Metal shop?"

"No. But I made a baseball bat with a lathe."

"You'll do."

Passersby were glancing in the windows of the store as they went about their business. Some looked at the destroyed door while others focused their interest on the man in armor who stood in the middle of the store, arms raised as high overhead as he could make them go, while the young assistant manager worked busily on removing the heavy plating. Quigley's glasses kept sliding to the end of his nose and his longish hair kept falling into his eyes, but piece by piece he got the job done. He staggered and grunted under the weight of each component of the armor, and muttered at one point, "How do you wear all this stuff?"

"With as much dignity as I can muster," replied Arthur patiently. "I can readily assure you of that."

By this point Sidney Krellman had long since dispensed with the notion of contacting the police. The last thing he wanted to do was draw the attention of the store owners to this bizarre turn of events. The shattered door he would be able to chalk up to vandals. Quigley he would be able to swear to secrecy. Then Sidney looked up and saw the pedestrians looking in through the window, and with a frown he walked over to the windows and pulled closed the folding shutters that ran along the inside of the windows. This was enough to discourage most of the idly curious.

Sidney turned and was astounded to see the knight now clad in a simple tunic and a long-sleeved and legged white undergarment, the assorted pieces of armor scattered about the store. In the armor he'd seemed immense, even threatening. Here he was under five-and-a-half feet tall.

For a moment Sidney entertained the thought of throwing the unarmed and largely unclothed man out of the store. As if Arthur sensed what was on Sidney's mind, he turned his gaze on the clothing-store manager, who promptly wilted under the pure power of Arthur's presence. He dropped his gaze to the floor, the brief fire of rebellion easily extinguished, and said, "So why don't we try that suit you had your eye on?"

Some minutes later one would never have suspected that Arthur had not always worn three-piece suits. The dark blue pinstripe fit him as if it had been tailored for him, except for being slightly tight in his broad shoulders. His hair, which was a shade lighter than his beard, hung in the back to just below the jacket collar. He had picked a cream-colored shirt and a dark red tie to complete the outfit. Although the store did not carry shoes, the mannequin had been sporting black loafers, and fortunately these, too, fit Arthur just fine.

He admired himself in the mirror, turning first right and then left, and decided finally, "They are cut quite nicely. Not at all what I'm accustomed to wearing, but—"

"Clothes make the man," burbled Quigley, "although in this case I'd say it's more the man making the clothes, Mister . . . geez, what's your name anyway?"

"I am King Arthur," said Arthur pleasantly, but then he frowned. "Oh, but perhaps I shouldn't have told you that."

"King Arthur? You mean like in Camelot and Monty Python and all that stuff?"

"Yes, friend Quigley, although I request that you do not allow my indiscretion to slip past this room."

"Hey, count on me, your highness," said Quigley.

Arthur glanced at Krellman, who nodded his assent so quickly it appeared that his head might topple from his shoulders. Krellman then tried to speak, but once again nothing particularly verbal escaped his lips. Arthur viewed the abortive efforts for a time and then said, with just a trace of impatience, "Come now, sir. If you have something to say, say it. Screw your courage to the sticking point."

"Nothing," said Sidney quickly. "I had nothing to say. Except that it is late Mister . . . Mister King Arthur. King Arthur. Your Kingness," he said, searching for the right term to assuage this madman. "If we could just close up the store and go home."

"Oh, but I haven't settled with you yet."

Sidney's voice was a mouselike squeak. "Par-par-pardon?"

"Why, yes. I assume this suit costs money, and your door that I accidentally destroyed also would amount to a sum."

"Take it! *Gratis*. Compliments of Arthur's Court, to the man who gave us our name. Quigley, get a box for Mr. King Arthur to carry his armor out—"

Arthur waved a hand in peremptory dismissal. "I wouldn't hear of it."

He began to pat the pockets of the suit, as if looking for a wallet. This, thought Sidney Krellman, was rapidly degenerating into the ridiculous. How could this man, who claimed to be a long-dead, legendary king, now be checking the pockets of a brand new suit to find a wallet. This was a question, Sidney realized, that asked and answered itself. If you thought you were King Arthur, then just about anything after that was possible.

Arthur's probing hand stopped at a vest pocket and a slow smile spread across his pleasant features. From the inside pocket he produced a small wallet, and from that he extracted a familiar platinum card.

"Do you take American Express?" he asked.

Sidney snatched it away, scowling, and studied it. His eyebrows knit and he stared, squinting at the card. Quigley looked over his shoulder. The date of issue was the current month. They stared at the name, and Quigley looked up.

"It says Arthur Penn. Your name is Arthur Penn?"

"It is?" He took the card back and examined it, turning it over as if a hidden message might be on the back. Finally he sighed and handed it back. "I suppose you're right."

Sidney quickly processed the card for the cost of the suit, not even bothering to add in the cost of the door (still preferring to stick to his story about vandals). He handed it back to Arthur, who was watching with amusement Quigley's attempts to stuff the pieces of armor into a variety of different boxes and bags.

"Don't bother, please," he said, laying a hand on Quigley's shoulder. "I assure you that if I never see the wretched stuff again, it will not trouble me at all."

A stiff wind was blowing through the destroyed door, and Arthur felt the chill even through the buttoned suit jacket. "You know, I think I might have need of an overcoat."

Sidney dashed around to a rack of coats, picked a long tan one out, ran back and gave it to Arthur. "This is perfect. It'll be just what you need."

"But—"

"Please," and his voice began to tremble, "please. Please go. I can't take this much longer."

"All right," said Arthur, a trifle befuddled. "But let me at least pay for—"

"*It's my gift to you!*"

Arthur stepped back, eyes wide. "If you put it that way, all right. I shall remember you for this kindness. . . ."

"*No!* Don't remember me. *Forget* you ever *saw* me!" His fists were clenching and unclenching.

Quigley took Arthur by the elbow. "I think you'd better go, your honor. He gets like this when things go a little . . . wrong."

"Well," said Arthur, buttoning his coat. "That's the true mark of a man. To be able to take minor variances in routine in stride. He could stand a bit of work on that score."

"Yes, sir."

"You be certain to tell him that."

"I will, sir."

"When he stops crying, that is."

"Yes, sir."

Chaptre the Third

Arthur shook his head in wonderment, tilting back leisurely on his heels so that his gaze could follow to the tops of buildings that caressed the skies. It was a cloudless night, with more than a considerable nip in the air. Arthur hardly noticed, so captivated was he by the sheer immensity of the city around him. And the thing he found more staggering than anything else was that the evening's pedestrians seemed to be utterly oblivious to the wonderment all about them. No one looked up to admire the architecture or whistle at a building height which in Arthur's time would have been considered a fantasy. Such a building should surely topple over! Nothing could possibly support it.

"How things change," he murmured. "Now these buildings are the reality, and it is I who have become the fantasy."

He jammed his hands deep into his coat pockets, feeling the comforting shape of the empty scabbard through the cloth. Only the tip was visible, peeping out every so often from the long coat, and Arthur was certain that no one could possibly spot—

There was a gentle tap on his shoulder, and he turned to look up—gods above, why was everyone so bloody tall?— into the face of a middle-aged cop. He was sizing up Arthur with a gaze perfected over years of staying alive when, in his uniform, he was a walking target. He said, "Excuse me. Might

I ask you what you're wearing under that coat?''

Arthur recognized authority when he saw it. He smiled politely. "Certainly. It's a scabbard."

"Ah." The cop smiled thinly. "Are you aware of the laws, buddy, against carrying a concealed weapon?"

Arthur's voice abruptly turned chilly as the evening air. "I am aware of a great many things, sir, the main of which is that I do not appreciate your tone of voice, nor shall I tolerate being addressed in that manner."

The officer, Owens by name, was not accustomed to any abuse either. In the station house he was known as Iron-Spine Owens. Iron-Spine had backed down from no one and nothing in his life.

His face set, he locked gazes with Arthur. For a moment, but only for a moment. Then he dropped his gaze, feeling like an impudent child. "Sorry, sir. But—"

"I know that, my good man," said Arthur with no letup. "For your further information and, if you insist, for your peace of mind, the scabbard is empty. There is no sword in it, and therefore no need to concern oneself with concealed weapons. And I might add that if mankind had not worked so hard to perfect weaponry that any fool could hide in a pocket and launch a cowardly assault from yards away, with no more skill or finesse than a diseased crow, then we wouldn't have a need for quite so many laws about concealed weapons."

Arthur shook his head. "Most insane bloody process I've ever seen. Create the weapons, *then* legislate against them. It doesn't stop in New York, you know. It pervades society. Create nuclear weapons, then try to stop them from being used. The moment they used the first one they should have stopped when they saw what they had on their hands. I certainly would have."

"Well, sir," said Owens contritely, "it's a shame you weren't around then."

"Oh, I was. But hardly in a position to do anything." He sighed. "Hopefully I shall remedy that now."

"Pardon my asking sir, but . . . are you a politician or something?"

Arthur reflected a moment and then said, "I'd have to say I fall under the category of 'or something.' Why, do I come across to you as such?"

"Well, sort of. Except you sure have the rest of them out-classed. You got a way with a phrase. Let me tell you, if you ever run for public office, you'll have my vote."

"Really? On what basis?"

"Basis?" Iron-Spine Owens laughed out loud, coarsely. "Only thing people ever vote on is gut instinct. Only ones who ever vote on stuff like issues are the intellectuals, and half the time they're too intellectual to vote in the first place."

"Yes, well . . . good evening to you then."

Owens touched the brim of his cap with his finger. "Evening to you, too, sir. Oh, sir . . . you weren't thinking of heading into the park, were you?"

Arthur looked across Fifty-ninth Street to the edge of Central Park. There were a few stray couples walking arm-in-arm along the sidewalk running around the park, but no one was actually entering it.

"That had, in fact, been my intention, yes. Why? Is there some reason I should not?"

Owens rubbed his chin thoughtfully. "Well . . . most of the time it's safe enough. Nevertheless I'd advise against it. Unless you have a way of occupying that scabbard of yours with a sword double quick."

"I'll see what I can do. Thank you for the advice."

"Good evening to you, sir."

Iron-Spine Owens spun on his heel and went on his way, whistling an aimless tune, his hands resting relaxedly behind him. It was not until he was eight blocks away that he suddenly realized he had just totally violated the Iron-Spine character he had created for himself and maintained all these years. With just a few choice words this lone, bearded man had taken Owens firmly in hand, and in moments had him rolling over and playing dead. And Owens hadn't minded!

Owens whistled softly in awe. "I don't know just what that man has going for him," he said, waiting for the light to change at the corner of Fifty-first Street and Fifth Avenue, "but whatever it is, I wish I could bottle it and sell it. I'd sure as hell make me a fortune." A woman with a dachshund on a leash looked curiously at the police officer mumbling to himself, and walked quickly away, shaking her head.

Arthur walked briskly through the park, the soles of his

shoes slapping with satisfying regularity against the blacktop. A cyclist sped by him in the opposite direction and didn't even afford him a glance.

Arthur felt his pores opening, his senses expanding to drink in the greenery around him. This was something to which he had an easier time relating. This wood-and-leaf forest was something that came far more naturally to him than the brick, steel, and concrete forest that loomed all around, hemming in the park at all sides. This brought back pleasant memories of home. . . .

Home? What was home to him now? He had no friends, no loved ones. No family. Only descendants, and even they were completely screwed up. Held in high esteem by the modern British, Arthur had in his day actually fought *against* the ancestors of the modern-day Englishman. But a lot could be forgiven and forgotten in over a dozen centuries, he decided.

Camelot long gone, lost in the mist of time and memories.

Gwenyfar . . . how are they spelling it now? he wondered. Guinevere, yes. His queen, long gone.

He had survived. All were gone, but he had survived. Or were they? None of the others had been locked away in an enchanted cave all this time, of course . . . had they? But no, that was impossible. Only Arthur and Merlin had survived, and Merlin would certainly have told Arthur if any of his latter-day companions were still with them. Wouldn't he?

So lost in thought was Arthur as he made his way through the park that he failed to notice the two men lurking in the bushes.

Men might be too charitable a word. With their wild manes of black hair and their equally scraggly beards, they were of an indeterminate age. They, and others like them, were the primary reason that people rarely walked along in Central Park at night.

Once upon a time there had been three of them. Much of what was real and what was not floated in and out for the trio, and there had only been a handful of things that they agreed upon that absolutely, truly existed. Artificial stimulants headed the list, followed by money. Then came superheroes— after all, in the whole world there had to be at least one, *somewhere*. And right after superheroes came Marx Brothers films. Everything else, from the name of the president to fast food, was nebulous in what passed for their minds. In honor of the one group of actors who absolutely truly existed, the three took the names of Chico, Groucho, and Harpo. Fortunately they did not have a fourth in the group, so nobody had to be Gummo. Unfortunately, somewhere in the intervening years Harpo disappeared into the ozone. They were never sure just where he went. They were just sort of wandering around one day and realized that he was gone. They adjusted to it, but kept their own respective names, partially out of homage to their vanished partner but mostly because, after a great deal of thought-searching, they could not manage to remember what their original names had been.

The taller one, Chico, stood slowly, disentangling his beard from the snarl of the branches. "There he goes," he murmured. "You see him?"

Groucho nodded and chewed on the remains of a two-day-old stale pretzel. He stood as well, coming just to Chico's shoulder. He wiped his large nose expansively with his shirt-sleeve but said nothing. Talking had never been his strong suit. Also, he wasn't so sharp on conscious thought either.

They were dressed quite similarly, in dark sweatshirts and tattered jeans with holes in the knees. Chico was also wearing battered basketball Keds and a thin windbreaker. In his social strata this alone was enough to qualify him for the best-dressed list.

Chico said, "Look at him. Like he's got the whole world for his oyster. He must have enough on him to keep us goin' for a few days, at least. Geez, he must be from out of town. C'mon."

He and his partner, or what there was of him, stepped out of the bushes. Chico looked down and scowled, "Who told you not to wear shoes, you idiot. Geez, aren't your feet cold?"

Groucho looked at him blankly. "Feet?"

The two ill-equipped, ill-advised, and generally just plain ill muggers found themselves quickly at a disadvantage. Their intended victim was walking quite quickly, and they felt compelled to remain in the background. The general intention was not to be spotted by the victim until it was too late.

The reason this didn't work was twofold.

To begin with, it was almost impossible to sneak up on King Arthur. The warrior's sixth sense he possessed warned him that several bad-intentioned but inept gentlemen were pursuing him, but he made no effort to ward them off. They seemed harmless enough.

Then there was their own paranoia. They insisted on taking refuge behind trees and shrubbery every time they thought, even for a moment, that they might be detected. These brilliant attempts at camouflage consisted of noisily rustling bushes or tripping over projecting roots. Such endeavors were usually accompanied by colorful profanity and frantic shushing. Arthur smiled but did nothing to discourage them. In a perverse sort of way he was very curious as to how they would react to the events which would shortly transpire.

At one point Groucho and Chico were almost within striking distance, but almost out of nowhere a police car materialized. It prompted them to dive headlong into the bushes to avoid detection. When the police car drove on past, they emerged cut and bleeding, and Groucho wiped at his nose and asked if they could go home now.

"That's it," growled Chico. "We're endin' this right now."

They scuttled ahead but found, much to their chagrin, that they had lost their quarry at the fork in the road. Trusting to his luck, which had not served in good stead for over a decade, Chico pulled his partner to the right and walked as quickly as he could.

Farther on down the road, Arthur watched from the shadows, and when he saw them coming, stepped back out onto the path. If they had guessed wrong, he'd been prepared to clear his throat loudly to guide them on their way. He began to walk, paused momentarily and cast a glance over his left shoulder. There was the expected crash and curses as the two leaped into the bushes once again. Arthur laughed to himself. He hadn't had this much fun in centuries.

The road angled down, and within a few more moments Arthur stood at the edge of Central Park Lake. His nostrils flared. He could smell the magic in the air, like a faint aroma after a barbecue. It was a pleasant scent, a familiar one. After all, he had lived with it for more years than any man could rightly expect to live.

He looked out across the lake and waited. It would be here, he knew. It had to be. All he had to do was wait. . . .

The stillness of the night air hung over him. Faintly he heard an ambulance siren, or perhaps a police car. Closer, he felt the small animal life all around him. The creatures of the woods had tensed as well. They, too, sensed it.

Arthur let his breath out slowly and mist filled the air in front of him. It was chilly, rapidly approaching thirty-two degrees—the point at which water freezes.

Which did nothing to explain why the middle of Central Park Lake was beginning to boil.

Arthur stared in rapt attention as the water in the center of the lake bubbled, swirled, and undulated, as if a volcano were about to leap forth, spewing lava into the park. Then, somehow, the water folded in on itself, creating a small whirlpool.

Now there were no nearby sounds of forest animals scavenging for the last scraps of food, or faraway sounds of ambulance sirens. All of New York City had shut down, leaving only the noises of the churning water.

It was then that it emerged from the center of the lake. Arthur's eyes widened, and for one moment he was no longer Arthur Rex. He was Arthur the wondering boy, dazzled and stunned by the wonders that were his to witness.

At first only its tip was visible, but then it rose, straight, proud, all that was noble and great and wondrous. The tip of the blade pointed toward the moon, as if it would cleave it in two. The blade itself gleamed like a beacon in the night. There was no light source for the sword to be reflecting from, for the moon had darted behind a cloud in fear. The sword was glowing from the intensity of its strength and power and knowledge that it was justice incarnate, and that after a slumber of uncounted years its time had again come.

After the blade broke the surface, the hilt was visible, and holding the sword was a single strong, yet feminine hand, wearing several rings that bore jewels sparkling with the blue-green color of the ocean.

It was a moment frozen out of time . . . another time . . . as the man at the lake's edge watched the entire scene, unmoving but not unmoved.

Slowly the hand began to glide toward him, bringing its proud burden straight and true. As it neared Arthur, the water receded as more and more of the graceful arm was revealed.

Within moments the Lady of the Lake stood mere feet away from Arthur, the water reaching the hem of her garment.

She looked like hell.

Weeds and crud had ruined her beautiful white dress. Her

hair, also filled with crud, hung limply. In her jeweled crown a
dead fish had somehow managed to lodge itself to stare glassy-
eyed at the world. She pulled another dead fish, plus an orange rind, out of the cleavage of her dress while the man on
shore glanced away in mild embarrassment.

She glared at him for a moment and then, in an attempt to
restore some measure of dignity, took a majestic step forward,
slipped, and fell flat into the mud.

Arthur reached down to help her but she waved him off,
pulling herself to her feet. Using the sword to balance herself
by thrusting it into the silt, she lifted one foot and pulled an
empty cigarette pack off the bottom of her shoe. While one
hand made vague attempts to wipe off the sludge, with the
other she gave the still-gleaming sword to the man on shore.

"Thank you, lady," he said, and bowed to her.

She pulled a crushed beer can from the hem of her dress and
said two words in a musical voice that would have shamed the
sirens of myth.

"Never again."

And with that the Lady of the Lake turned and trudged
slowly back as the roiling waters reached out to receive her.

Carefully Arthur examined his sword. They were two old
friends, reunited at last. It gleamed in his hand, happy to see
him.

He stepped over to a large, dead tree and swung at a low
branch. The branch was as thick as the arms of two men, but
the glowing sword passed through it without so much as slow-
ing down. As if startled that it could so easily be severed, the
branch hung there for a moment before thudding to the
ground.

He heard the rustling behind him and he spun. Automatically he grabbed the hilt with both hands, holding the sword
Excalibur in such a manner as to be both offensive and defen-
sive. His eyes glittered in the dimness. "Who?" he called out.
"Who is there?"

But he knew the answer even before they stumbled forward.
In the wonderment of it all he had completely forgotten about
his two would-be assailants. He was fortunate, he realized,
that they were as incompetent as they were. Had they been
even mildly formidable, he would have left himself foolishly
vulnerable.

As it was, they stumbled out with eyes like saucers. Chico

came right to Arthur's feet and then, to the returned king's surprise, the scruffy skulker dropped to one knee. Groucho looked down at him curiously. Without returning the glance Chico reached to his partner's pants leg and pulled him down also. Groucho's knees crunched slightly as he hit the ground.

Arthur lowered Excalibur, holding the pommel with one hand and letting the blade rest in his palm. "May I help you?"

"We swear," said Chico fervently.

This came as no surprise to Arthur, but he waited with polite curiosity to see if that was the end of the pronouncement. It wasn't.

"We swear our undying allegiance to the man with the Day-Glo sword and the submersible girlfriend."

King Arthur gave a little nod of his head. "Thank you. That's very kind."

There was a long pause, and then Arthur said, "Is that it?"

Chico looked up at him as if Arthur were a drooling idiot. "We're waiting for you to knight us."

Arthur suppressed a cough. "When hell freezes over," he said.

Chico gave this some thought. Finally he nodded. "All right," he said agreeably. "We'll wait. Won't we?" He nudged Groucho in the ribs.

Groucho stared at him forlornly. "My feet are cold," he sniffled.

They left the park together, their feet crunching on the gravel of the path beneath their feet.

Chaptre the Fourth

The young woman stepped out of the shower, now refreshed and prepared to face the new day that was shining so nauseatingly through the bathroom window. It was the bathroom's only source of illumination, the fluorescents having burnt out some time ago. There had been no money to buy new ones.

She ran the towel over her slim body, rubbing it briskly across her back. Here in the womblike security of the bathroom, the day didn't seem quite so bad. She had just done the shower breast examination that she always dreaded, and was pleased to have found no lump in evidence. So she had her health, knock wood. And even better, she had a job interview this morning.

She wrapped the light blue terry-cloth towel around her body, and another towel around her strawberry-blond hair. She kept it short and manageable enough that drying it took only a few minutes. She was not one for wasting a lot of time on external frivolities.

She wrinkled her nose at herself in the mirror. She hated her face because it was perfect. The nose was just right. The eyes were just the right space apart, the eyebrows just the right thickness. Her cheekbones were not too high or defined. Her skin displayed no mars or blemishes. She was, on the whole, very attractive, as far as most people were concerned. But she did not agree. She longed for some distinguishing feature to give her face the character she felt it lacked. All the truly elegant women, she believed, had some feature you could hang a description on. A majestic profile caused by highly arched eyebrows, or a nose that was a tad too long—that was what she wanted.

She had even gone to a plastic surgeon once. He had laughed at her. Laughed! He told her that his patients would kill for looks like hers. He'd advised against unnecessary surgery, and told her to go home for a week or so and think it over. She had never gotten the nerve to go back.

She padded quietly into the living room which doubled as an office. She found him—her boyfriend—as she knew she would. He was slumped over his typewriter, his head resting comfortably on the keyboard of the battered Smith-Corona manual. She ran her fingers through his greasy black hair and whispered, "Hon? Honey, go to bed. You really should go to bed."

He grunted as he stood, balancing himself against the table. His eyes did not open as she took him firmly by the shoulder and steered him toward the bed. He passed an open window and snarled, and she noticed with distress that he was developing a most unhealthy pallor.

"Hon, have you considered trying to get outside a bit more?" she said carefully. She was treading on tricky ground —the last time she'd broached such a subject, he had construed it as a criticism of him, and worse, an implication that he should get a job. "How can I get a job?" he'd screamed at the time. "I have my work!" He had then gone into a silent tantrum that lasted three days. It had been three very peaceful days for her.

This time he barely uttered a reply before collapsing onto the couch. It wasn't the bed, but she decided to leave him there. It wasn't worth the aggravation somehow, and besides, she had to get to the interview.

She had to get the job. She just had to. If for no other reason than that, within two days, the employment agencies would no longer be able to get in touch with her. The phone company would be disconnecting them then.

She let the towel drop to the ground as she looked at the small assortment of clothes that hung in her closet. She heard a stirring in the living room, and for one moment fantasized that he was waking up. That he would come into the room, see her standing there as she was, naked, her hair wet, her body slim and supple. That he would take her in his arms and make wild, intense love to her.

He snorted and turned over on the couch.

She hoped against hope there would be further noise, but there wasn't. So she allowed herself the luxury of sitting down on the threadbare bedspread and sobbing for five minutes. Then she dressed quickly and quietly, went back into the bathroom, washed the tears from her face as best she could, and let herself out of the apartment. The soft click of the door roused the man sleeping on the couch only briefly.

She looked up at the small office building on Twenty-eighth and Broadway. The words Camelot Building were stenciled in fading gilt letters on the glass above the entrance. An ironic name, she mused, for Camelot was a place of pageantry and legend. This slightly rundown building was hardly that.

The guard at the front desk was sixty if he was a day. A cigarette hung from between cracked lips as he said, "Can I help you, miss?"

She had been looking at the directory on the wall, and turned to him now. "Yes. I'm trying to find the offices of a Mr. Arthur Penn."

He looked blank for a moment, and she felt her hopes sink. She wasn't even going to get out of the starting gate on this one. Then his face cleared and he said, "Right. New fella. Thirteenth floor."

"I thought buildings didn't have thirteenth floors."

The guard shrugged. "Fellow who built this place wasn't a superstitious sort."

"Oh, really?" The guard looked old enough to have been there when the building was first constructed.

"Yeah. And he was a lucky fella too. He was fortunate enough to see his work completed." He coughed. "Day after, he got hit by a truck. You can go on up."

"Gee, thanks."

"Main elevator's out. Better use the freight 'round back."

The freight elevator was a rickety affair that moved up the shaft with a maximum of screeching and clanking. She felt out of place, neatly pressed and dressed, wearing high-heel shoes and trapped in a huge elevator with metal walls and floor. A dying fluorescent bulb lit the elevator, and she felt as if she were being carted up to her execution.

When the doors opened on the thirteenth floor, she stepped out gratefully and the elevator bounced up and down like a yo-yo. As it closed behind her with a thud like a guillotine blade descending, she walked out into the main corridor, and what she saw astounded her.

The offices of Arthur Penn were beautifully put together, but far from modernistic. All the furniture was antiques, solid, dependable pieces everywhere she looked. The walls were paneled in knotty pine. The carpeting was a deep plush in royal blue.

Her breath taken by the extreme contrast between this office and the rest of the building, she started to wander about until a firm voice called her up short, saying, "Can I help you?"

She looked around and saw a fierce-looking receptionist seated at a desk, and she wondered how she had missed the receptionist the first time. "Oh, yes, I'm sorry. I have an appointment. An appointment with Mr. Penn."

The receptionist glanced down at a calendar on the edge of her uncluttered desk and asked, "You're Gwen?"

Gwen nodded.

The receptionist seemed slightly mollified by the fact that this person was supposed to be here, but still looked regretful that she was not going to have an opportunity to give someone the heave-ho. She said, "Very well. Take a seat, please. Mr. Penn will be with you shortly."

"Thank you."

Gwen sat in an ornately carved chair and looked down at a coffee table next to her, on which several recent news magazines rested. She started to reach for one but then said, "Would you like me to fill out a form or something?"

"No. That won't be necessary."

"Oh. But how will the woman in personnel know anything about me?"

Looking up from the book she was trying to read, the receptionist snorted in annoyance. "We don't have a personnel department. Mr. Penn himself will see you and decide either yes or no. All right?"

"Yes. All right," said Gwen, feeling completely cowed.

"Any more questions?"

"No, ma'am."

The receptionist went back to her book. What appeared to

be an unspeakably long time passed, and finally Gwen ventured in a small voice, "Nice weather we're having, isn't it?"

She'd barely gotten the words out when thunder rumbled from outside and rain smacked in huge droplets against the single office window. Gwen glanced heavenward.

"He will see you now," said the receptionist abruptly.

"Who will?" said Gwen, but quickly recovered. She stood and said, "Well, thank you. Thank you very much." She smoothed her denim skirt. "You've been very kind."

"No, I haven't," was the tart response. "I've treated you like garbage."

"I beg your—"

"You let people walk over you, dear, you'll never get anywhere." She stabbed a finger at Gwen. "I bet your personal relationships have the success rate of buggy-whip manufacturers, right?"

Gwen drew herself up to her full height. "Now I don't think that's any of your—"

"You don't think? Hmph. I bet." The portly woman chucked a thumb at a closed office door. "Go in. He's expecting you. He's been expecting you for ages. And for pity's sake, don't let yourself be used as a doormat. You've got too pretty a face to let it be filled with shoeprints."

And with that she stared down at her book again. Silently Gwen walked past her, completely confused. She went right up to the door, then swung about on her heel to face the receptionist.

There was no one there.

Gwen's eyebrows knit in confusion. She walked back to the desk, looked around. Nothing. Under the desk was nothing. But the receptionist hadn't gone out the door—it had creaked horrendously when Gwen had entered; she would have heard an exit. Out of curiosity she rested a hand on the cushion of the seat behind the desk. It was cool, as if no one had sat there all day.

Gwen assessed the situation.

"Oooookaydokay," she said finally, went quickly to the office door that the receptionist had indicated, and swung it open.

She was a little surprised to see a bearded man deep in discussion with an eight-year-old boy. They were speaking in low, intense tones, and it was quite clear to Gwen that there was none of the typical adult condescension in the man as he argued with the boy. Not the slightest. Apparently this Arthur Penn, if that was who this in fact happened to be, treated everyone as an equal.

Arthur didn't notice her, and it took the boy's abrupt indication by way of a fierce gesture in her direction before Gwen was even sure that she would ever be noticed at all.

She was seating herself on a large chesterfield couch as Arthur was saying petulantly, "Honestly, Merlin, sometimes you treat me as if I'm a child."

"Arthur, we have a guest."

"I am perfectly capable of making decisions and watching out for . . . pardon?"

"A guest." The boy was skinny, his hands too large for his arms, his feet too large for his legs. His silken brown hair was longish in the back, and his ears virtually stuck out at right angles to his head. He was nattily attired in dark blue slacks, shirt, striped tie, and a blazer with a little sword emblem on the pocket. Bizarrely, the man's clothing was identical, but the boy looked better in it.

Arthur turned, and the moment he saw Gwen, he smiled. Merlin, on the other hand, frowned deeply.

Gwen found herself staring deeply into Arthur's eyes. She had never seen such dark eyes, she thought. Dark as a bottomless pit, which she would willingly plunge into. . . .

She tore her gaze from him and swung over to the boy he'd called Merlin.

And stifled a gasp.

It was like looking at two different people in the same body. The lines of the boy's face were youthful enough, but his eyes were like an old man's, smoldering with wisdom of ages and resentment when he looked at her. He frightened her terribly, and she stared down at her shoes.

Arthur appeared oblivious to her thoughts. "How unforgivably rude of me," he said. "You're the young woman who was sent over by the employment office."

"That's right," she said quietly.

Arthur regarded her for a time and then said, "Is there something particularly intriguing about your feet, my dear?"

She looked up, her cheeks coloring. "I'm sorry. I just—"

"What is your name, child?"

The question had been asked by the eight-year-old boy, and

the phrasing was, at the very least, extraordinary. She gaped openly at him. "My what?"

"Nom de guerre. Moniker. Name."

"Oh, name!"

Merlin let out a sigh as she stammered out, "Gwendolyne."

"What a lovely name," said Arthur, and Gwen looked up to see that Arthur was staring at her. He saw her noticing, but did not look away. His stare was wonderfully open, and unembarrassed. "Forgive me for staring so, but you remind me a great deal of someone I once knew—"

"Arthur," said the boy warningly, "what were we *just* discussing?"

"Merlin, *please*. My apologies, Gwendolyne. I am Arthur Pendr— Arthur Penn. My associate"—he chuckled slightly on the word—"is Merlin."

"Last name?" asked Gwen.

"Last one *I* intend to use," snapped Merlin.

"As you know," continued Arthur, "I am in the market to hire a personal secretary. This may not seem necessary now, but I assure you in the months to come this office will become quite busy. I would like to know all about your background, everything you've done in the past several years. We have several people to see, so I'll tell you right now that it may be a week or two before we can let you and your agency know for certain. Stop glowering, Merlin. You'll get crows' feet. Remember the last time that happened, you couldn't walk properly for days."

Gwen laughed, but Arthur stared at her with an upraised eyebrow and said, "Was something funny?"

"No. Not at all. I understand. Find out about me, more people to see, a week or two for response. Got it."

"Fine then. Let's begin." Arthur pulled around a comfortable chair and seated himself across from Gwen. He leaned back, steepled his long fingers, and said, "So let's start, miss . . . I'm sorry, Gwen, I didn't catch your last name."

"DeVere," she said. "Gwen DeVere."

"You start on Monday," said Arthur.

Merlin, seated on the desktop, moaned.

When Gwen DeVere returned home, the apartment seemed

a little less gloomy, and as she marched in the door she called out, "Lance, I got it!"

She stood in the doorway, dripping little puddles at her feet.

There was no response. She sighed, the wind slightly taken out of her sails. She should have known. It was raining heavily, and Lance only went out when it was a downpour such as this. He got inspiration from foul weather, he said. He had once filled a cup with rainwater, held it in front of her and informed her that an entire allegory of mankind could be found in that glass of precipitation. When she'd said she only saw rainwater, he'd emptied the contents on her head.

She thought about what the phantom receptionist had said, and went into the bathroom, her feet squishing in her shoes.

A few minutes later, wrapped in a towel, she went to the window and looked out at the street. It was covered with garbage, and derelicts were huddling in doorways for shelter. There was a constant tension in the neighborhood, a tension that she supposed was natural in the city. But it wasn't natural to her, and she wasn't going to live with it if she could help it. Perhaps, once she'd been working steadily for a while, they could afford to move out to a nicer area. Maybe someplace out in Brooklyn, or maybe even the Island.

If only Lance would get a job.

But his writing always came first.

She glanced over at his work area, for it could hardly be called a desk. The crumpled paper was gaining altitude. She reached over, pulled one wad from the stack, and uncrumpled it. It had one sentence typed across the middle—"All work and no play makes Jack a dull boy"—and she cursed the day she'd taken him to see *The Shining*.

If only Lance would get a job.

If only she could leave him.

But he was all she had.

She flopped down onto the bed, reached over and snapped on the small, black-and-white TV. She recognized the old movie as soon as it came on—Danny Kaye in *The Court Jester*.

Knights and knighthood. Those were the days. Chivalry. Women were demigods back then, she thought, and men their protectors. Now it's everyone for themselves.

She reached over to the bureau, opened her purse and dug

through it. Eight dollars and change. What the hell. She
reached over to phone for a pizza, figuring it would arrive two
hours later, cold and soggy. But it wasn't really dinnertime for
two hours yet, anyway, and she could heat it up.

And maybe the pizza guy would come riding up on a silver
charger, balancing the pie on a gleaming shield. . . .

Late into the night the offices in the Camelot Building's
thirteenth floor blazed with light.

"You're out of your mind. You know that, don't you? Ten
centuries to contemplate, and you're no smarter now, Wart,
than you were then."

Arthur had removed his coat and tie and was sitting in shirt-
sleeves, watching Merlin stalk the room like a cat tracking
down a mouse. From his reclining position on the couch he
called, "Now Merlin, I think you're exaggerating a bit."

The lad turned on him. "You think?" he said in a voice
ringing with authority despite its boyishness. "Who told you
to think!?"

Arthur's voice was sharp as he said, "I caution you, Merlin.
You will not address me in that manner. I am still your—"

Merlin turned, placing his hands defiantly on his narrow
hips. "My what? Finish the sentence. My king? Well huzzah,
Your Majesty," and he genuflected mockingly. "You rule a
kingdom of one . . . unless you planned to return and lay claim
as king of all the Britons. I can just see it!" He rubbed his
hands together, relishing a good laugh, as Arthur shifted
uncomfortably on the couch. "I wonder how they would
react, those ineffectual, impotent figureheads who do nothing
for the populace except provide them with tidbits to gossip
about in taverns at teatime. There you'll be, presenting yourself as the once and future king. What the bloody hell do you
think will happen? Do you think the queen is liable to step
down and say, 'Good of you to show, old sod. We've spent
centuries keeping your place warm. Have the throne.' Perhaps
they'll revoke Magna Carta for you. That would be a sweet
thing. Disband the House of Commons, House of Lords, put
you in charge of the entire affair? Eh?" He slammed a small
fist on a table, jiggling an ashtray. "What are the imperial
thoughts, Arthur? Tell me, oh king of nothing!"

They glared at each other for a long moment. Then, finally,
Arthur's eyes softened slightly and he said, "All right. They

can keep the House of Commons. How does that strike you?''

Merlin laughed lightly. "Ah, Arthur, you madman. I should let you go in and try it. Either they'd lock you up, or maybe, by God, maybe they would make you king.''

Arthur stood, smiling, and started to pace the office. His hands were folded behind his back. "Oh, Merlin," he sighed, "what are we doing here? Perhaps the time is not right for us.''

"What would you then? A return to the cave?"

"It has crossed my mind."

"Well uncross it. Not the right time for you? Don't be absurd. Look around you. Go into a bookstore, what do you see? Dozens of books on you. Fact, fiction, and everything in between. There have been countless movies about you.'' Now he was ticking off items on his fingers. "There are TV programs. Broadway shows. Buildings and businesses named after you and Camelot. People dress as knights and stage mock jousts and battles. There's a video game with a knight slaying a dragon.''

"So knighthood has become a valuable entertainment tool. So what?''

"Life reflects in its art, Art. And also remember—the fondest times this country remembers, in its recent political history, is a presidency which has come to be known as Camelot.''

"Camelot," echoed Arthur.

Merlin nodded. "I know it sounds a bit bizarre. But don't you see, Arthur,'' and the king stopped his pacing, "the time is ripe for your return. More than ripe—the seeds are bursting forth from their fruits. They need you, Arthur, to show them the way.''

Arthur half smiled. "You're sounding messianic this evening, Merlin.''

"Hardly. Merely stating the facts.''

"But, dammit all, what am I supposed to do? You say they want me. But they don't want a king. . . .''

"They want a leader, and you're certainly that.''

"But who would I lead? Shall I start a cult following?''

Merlin shook his head mournfully. "Arthur, Arthur, you have to learn to think on a larger scale, the way you used to. Realize, then, that if you are to do any good, you must rule again. And you must rule, or lead, in a country that has clout.''

"And I must go about it in a civilized manner," said Arthur sternly. "That means no military junta in a banana republic." He abruptly snapped his fingers. "But now, Merlin, let us say I could master the electoral system of this country and become their . . . not prime minister—president! That's it."

Merlin gave an approving nod. "Very good, Wart."

Arthur sat on the edge of the Chesterfield couch, leaning forward excitedly. "I haven't been idle all this time, you know. The animals in the cave with me, they brought me information from the outside world. I kept abreast of matters, for I knew that when I returned I would do no one any good as a clanking anachronism. And yet, for all my careful preparations, I was never altogether certain what I was preparing *for*.

"But I know now." He bounced excitedly to his feet and went to a window, looking out over the city. "Merlin, by all the gods that's *it*! I shall become President of the Soviet Union of America."

Chaptre the Fifth

The *V* had burnt out in the Vacancy sign that hung outside the beat-up roadside motel situated just off of the interstate. The signs posted nearby had promised waterbeds and triple-X-rated films in the room. Just the sort of thing the average passing traveler would be looking for.

Morgan was passing, and a traveler, but she was certainly far from average.

When she'd checked in, the desk clerk had gaped at her openly. Part of her was tempted to put him in her place, but another part was flattered by the attention, and it was this aspect of her that saved the clerk's life. The balding, potbellied man was able to go home that evening alive, his brain functioning normally, carrying secret fantasies acted out with the stunning woman who had checked in at the scummy little motel he managed.

He had no idea that weeks earlier Morgan Le Fey would hardly have turned any heads. Indeed, she might have turned a few stomachs. But the excess weight she'd been carting with her all this time had slid away like melting butter. All the extra chins had vanished into memory, leaving her with the one jutting chin that stuck out so proudly. The raven-black hair was black through and through—no gray at the roots—and her feet, once swollen and cracked, were now slim and strong.

She was nude now, admiring herself in the full-length mir-

ror that hung on the wall of her room. She admired the con-
tours of her muscular body and was filled with disgust at the
lethargic lump she had once been.

But that loathsome creature was long gone. And Morgan Le
Fey was back in business.

The naked sorceress rolled back the threadbare rug, bracing
it with her foot against the wall. Then she padded back to the
bare area and removed a piece of chalk from the pocket of her
long black coat. She knelt down, then, and brushing strands
of hair from her face, carefully traced a circle with a five-
pointed star enclosed within. She then reached into her beat-
up duffel bag and extracted five black candles, fondling the
length of them almost sexually. She placed one at each point
where the star touched the circle and then lit them.

She stepped back, admired her handiwork, and smiled.

She rolled the television set near to the circle and sat down
facing it. Her bare rump was chilled by the floor but she ignored it, busying herself with lighting each of the five candles.
When they were finally lit, she reached over and snapped on
the television.

The screen of the color set flickered to life. A couple madly
rutted on the screen, panting like twin locomotives. Morgan
frowned in a distant, irritated manner, and waved a hand as if
brushing a flea away. The picture vanished from the screen,
replaced by blankness.

Morgan concentrated, reaching out with her mind and tracing the waves of magic that filled the air around her. She'd
been doing this regularly. She had gone from town to town,
city to city, trying to discover a mystical trace of Merlin. It had
proven to be frustrating. Merlin had covered his tracks too
well. If she'd begun the trace from the moment when he'd escaped from his centuries-long confinement, she could have
picked up on it in no time. But this was no longer possible.
Just as a fox can cover his trail and scent given time, so had
Merlin been able to erase any trace of his person.

If Merlin had been practicing magic lately, however, he
would most certainly have been tapping into the magic bands
of energy that encompassed the earth. An adept was able to
detect them, pale ribbonlike trails that filled the air. Had
Merlin been using his sorcerous powers, Morgan should have
been able to track him down along those mystical bands as if
she were tracing a telephone call.

But she had found nothing. Which either meant that he had been using no magic lately, or more disturbing, that he'd discovered a means by which to cover any trace of magic use. And if it were the latter case, Morgan would certainly have her work cut out for her.

She found a faint whiff of magic along one stream and immediately ran it back to its source. The TV screen flickered, and then the image of a young girl appeared. She was a teenager, naked as was Morgan, seated in what appeared to be the middle of her high school's athletic field. She was chanting quietly to herself and burning a photograph of a handsome young man. The candle was white.

Morgan pursed her lips. Amateurs dabbling in love spells. This was the sort of tripe she'd been unearthing in her searches these past weeks. Where the devil was Merlin? Where—

The screen suddenly went black, and Morgan jumped slightly, startled. At the same time she knew instinctively what had caused it. And so she waited.

And eventually it came.

The screen became a picture of an office with antique furniture. And there, seated in a large easy chair, was a boy looking for all the world like a pint-sized Alistair Cooke. His feet dangled several inches above the ground; his hands were interlaced behind his head. He had a smile on his lips which was not mirrored in his eyes.

He was looking straight at her as he said, "Hello, Morgan. You're looking well-preserved these days."

She inclined her head in acknowledgment. "Thank you, Merlin. You're too kind."

"I know." He studied her for a moment. "You're not surprised to see me?"

In truth she was very disconcerted. It had not occurred to her that Merlin's power would be so great that he would detect her attempts to find him; that he would turn the tables back on her, apparently without effort. He did not seem to have undertaken any conjurations. He had simply taken command of her equipment, commandeered her. Could his power really have grown so? Was everything so effortless for him now? If it were true, he would be far more than formidable. He would be unbeatable.

All of this passed through her mind in a moment, and in the next moment she said, "No. I'm not at all surprised. Your overwhelming ego would only allow you to perform some such stunt as this.''

"Ah, how well you know me.''

"I knew Merlin the man, not Merlin the tot,'' she said airily. "I had thought the legends exaggerated. I see now they were not. You do indeed age backward.''

He nodded. "Just so. And, intriguingly enough, I become more powerful as well. It's quite a combination, Morgan: the energy and drive of youth combined with the wisdom and skill of an older man. An unbeatable combination, wouldn't you say, Morgan?''

She leaned back, uncaring of her nudity. Her long hair hung discreetly over her breasts. "*You* would certainly say so, Merlin. Unless you let yourself be overwhelmed by your staggering sense of self-complacency. I will admit I'm impressed. Magic wards were placed all around the cave in which you were imprisoned long centuries ago. How did you get through them? Even at the height of your power—''

"Remember what I taught you, Morgan. Wards are nothing more than mystic prison bars. These were small enough to contain any man. However, sliding between the ward bars in a child's body was quite simple, really.''

"So you simply allowed time to take its course.''

"Quite true.'' Merlin slid forward, alighting on his feet, and came "closer" to the screen. "And I'm sure you realize that I subsequently arranged for Arthur's release.''

"Time off for good behavior, no doubt.''

This time Merlin did not even try to smile. "Now listen carefully, Morgan. I did not have to contact you this way. I can assure you that mystically you would never have found us. However, before too long Arthur is going to be in the newspapers. Rather than give you the satisfaction of locating us, I decided to expend the smallest aspect of my power to issue you a warning.''

She raised an eyebrow. "Warning, is it?''

"It is. Arthur will be running for mayor of New York City. As I said, you would undoubtedly read of this in the newspapers, for Arthur is destined to be quite a controversial candidate. I would not wish you to think for even a moment that we were living in fear of your discovering us. So I give you our city of operations ahead of time, secure in the knowledge that there is not a damned thing you can do to deter us.''

She frowned. "Arthur? Mayor? I would think that president would be more appropriate."

Merlin shook his head and his image flickered on the screen. "You and Arthur, half brother and half sister, thinking alike. That was Arthur's first inclination. But he has too much he has yet to learn, including," he said ruefully, "the name of this country. But that is neither here nor there. A complete unknown cannot come sweeping into the greatest office in the land from nowhere. He has to establish a political track record. New York is a highly visible city. And they could really use him. So," he concluded, "mayor of New York it is. It's inevitable, so don't even think about averting it. You do not have anyone to aid you any more, Morgan. Modred is long-gone bones. You command no legions of hell—human, mystic, or otherwise. It is just you, rusty in the use of your powers, versus me at the height of mine. You might say I've been working out."

"Are you trying to scare me, Merlin?"

"Trying? No. I believe I've succeeded. Stay out of my way, Morgan, or prepare to suffer dearly."

Morgan opened her mouth to reply, when sparks began to fly from the television. She dove for cover and ducked as, with a low hum followed by heavy crackling and smoke, the TV screen blew outward, spraying glass all over the inside of the hotel room. It flew with enough velocity to embed itself in the wall, in the carpet, and if Morgan had presented a target, in Morgan herself. She, however, had moved quickly enough to knock over and hide behind a coffee table, and so was spared the inconvenience of having her skin ripped to shreds.

She waited until she was certain that the violence was over. Slowly she raised her head, picking a few shards of glass out of her hair. She looked around. Gray smoke was rising from the now silent television. There was faint crackling in the air, and her nose wrinkled at the acrid odor. She stood fully and then slowly, daintily, picked her way across the floor. She stood in front of the television and, somewhat unnecessarily, turned it off. Then she padded across to the telephone, picked it up, and waited impatiently for an outside line.

When it came she dialed a long-distance number quickly, efficiently. Her face was grim, but her spirits were soaring. She felt the blood pulsing in her veins for the first time in centuries. There was almost a sexual thrill, she thought, matching wits and powers with Merlin. She had been little better than dead all these decades. How had she survived all this time? she wondered, as a phone rang at the other end. How could she possibly have—

The phone was picked up and a slightly whiny male voice said, "Yeah?"

Her eyes sparkled as she said, "He's contacted me. They're in New York."

"They're in New York?!" The voice was incredulous. "But I'm in New York! How could I not have known?"

"Because you're a great bloody twit. I'm on my way up there now." She paused, frowning. "We have only one thing going for us. Merlin is not as all-knowing as he believes himself to be. He thinks you do not exist, Modred. He thinks I am on my own. It may prove to be his fatal mistake."

"Fatal?" There was an audible gulp. "You mean like dead?"

She sighed, and hung up without another word. Then she leaned back on the bed, brushed away pieces of glass, and closed her eyes.

"Great bloody twit," she muttered. "This is going to be tougher than I thought."

Chaptre the Sixth

"You're late."

Gwen stopped in the doorway, openly surprised. Lance was seated at the kitchen table, his chair tilted back against the wall. He looked impatient, even huffy. And she realized with a shock that it had been ages since she'd really taken a look at him, so rarely had he been around these days.

He pushed his thick glasses back up on the bridge of his nose. The unhealthy pallor he'd acquired had not improved. In addition his lips were dry and cracked. The blue check shirt he'd worn for four days straight was taking on a life of its own. His jeans were threadbare at the knees, and his socks were standing over in the corner, retaining the shape of his feet from memory.

"Lance," she managed to get out. She glanced at her watch. "Am I really that late? It's only a little after six."

He tapped a bony forefinger on the tabletop. "I expect dinner by six P.M. sharp."

She looked askance at him as she removed her coat and hung it on a hook near the door. "Since when, Lance?"

"Since when what?"

"Since when do you expect your dinner at six P.M. sharp. You're usually not home then. And even if you are, you might be asleep, like as not."

"Are you criticizing me?" He'd spoken in a tone that was guaranteed to make her back down, to force her into a sniveling apology. But as she crossed the room and sat down across from him, he realized with a distant sort of surprise that such an apology was not to be forthcoming.

"I am not criticizing you," she said slowly, thoughtfully. "If you have a regular schedule you'd like to maintain, I'll be more than happy to aid in maintaining it. But don't try to change things on me and then get mad because I can't read your mind."

His eyes narrowed wolfishly. "I don't think," he decided, "that I like your attitude." He had tilted the chair forward, and now tilted it back, interlacing his fingers in a gesture he imagined made him look very authoritative. "I think you should give up your job."

Her eyes widened. "Stop working for Art? Are you nuts?" Her voice went up an octave. "He's the best thing that's ever happened to me! The past two weeks I've been working for him have been—"

He wasn't listening anymore. "Wait a minute. Best thing? What about me? I thought *I* was ostensibly the best thing that's ever happened to you."

She huffed in irritation. "Well, of *course* you are, but I'm talking about two different things."

"Best thing means best thing. It doesn't mean anything else." He stood up, swaying slightly, and it was only then that Gwen realized he had a few drinks in him. The alcohol was easily discernible in the air now. "I should know. I'm a writer."

"So you say," she replied, and immediately wished she could have bitten her tongue off. She stood quickly and started to head for the bedroom when Lance's hand clamped on her shoulder. She turned and faced him, and his eyes were smoldering.

"What do you mean by that?" He spoke in a voice that was low and ugly. *"What do you mean?"*

"Nothing, Lance. I—"

"What do you mean?"

She whimpered and pulled back ineffectually. With an angry snarl he shoved her away and drew himself up to his full height. "You seem to forget our college days, Gwen. You looked up to me then, remember?''

"I still look up to you, Lance." Gwen backed up slowly, until she bumped into a wall and could go no farther. She waited, panic stricken, for Lance to advance on her, but he did not.

Instead he said, "Remember those days, huh? I was somebody then. All the English teachers knew me. They said they wished I'd never leave."

They said they thought you'd never leave, Gwen wanted to scream at him. You flunked bonehead English, twice. Creative writing teachers said you were incomprehensible. She thought all of this, but didn't say it. Instead she said, "I remember, Lance. I remember. Lance, I can't quit my job. We need the money. And Arthur's going to be the next mayor. You'll see. . . ."

Lance guffawed and waved his hands about as he spoke. He bumped the single bulb that hung overhead in the kitchen, and it tossed up wildly distorted shadows on the wall. "Mayor, is he? Has he been out canvassing for votes? Has he even got the signatures of people who say they want him to run for mayor? Gwen, the man is a loser. You always hook yourself up with losers. You have a streak of self-abuse that . . ."

His voice trailed off as he realized she was looking at him in an assessing manner, and he realized also exactly who he had described so accurately. With a snarl he stormed over to the front door of the apartment, yanked it open, and barreled out into the hallway, down the stairs to the next landing, and eventually out the door of the building.

In the past Gwen would have chased him down the stairs, risking a battering of life and limb just to throw her arms about his legs and get him to come back. But this time she watched him go. He stopped at street level and looked up at the window. She glanced down at him briefly, then turned away.

With a roar he pushed his way into the crowd and vanished from Gwen's sight . . . had she been looking, of course.

Instead she was looking elsewhere—at the shape and course of her own life.

All she knew was one thing—that over the past several years she'd been living in limbo. A lady in waiting. Waiting for Lance to complete his book and sell it (he'd made it sound so easy!). Waiting for her life to take some direction.

A lady in waiting.

She pulled herself up with a smile. That's what she liked about Arthur Penn, she decided. He didn't make her feel like a lady in waiting. He made her feel like a queen.

Chaptre the Seventh

The couple was walking briskly down Fifth Avenue near the park, the woman's heels clacking merrily on the cobblestones, when the mugger leaped from behind a tree.

Instinctively the man pushed the woman behind him. His desperate gaze revealed, naturally, that there was not a policeman in sight, so he pulled together the shards of his shattered nerve and held up his fists.

The mugger stared at them for a moment, puzzled, and then slapped his forehead with the palm of his hand in self-reproachment. "Right!" said Chico. "Money! You think I want money!"

The man, who was somewhat portly and in his late fifties, peered over the tops of his fists. "You . . . you don't?"

"Nah! I mean, in the vast, general socioeconomic strata of the world, yeah, sure I want money. I mean, it makes the world go around." He paused. "Or maybe that's gravity or something."

"Yes. Well. We have to be going."

"Fine. Well, you have a nice day."

"You bet. Same to you."

"Real soon."

The couple was slowly backing down the street. Chico stood there, waving the filthy fingers of a filthy hand, his beat-up army poncho blowing in the breeze. They turned quickly then, but had only taken several steps when a voice screamed out from behind them, *"Hey!"*

"This is it, Harold," muttered the woman. "We're going to die now."

Chico came barreling around them and faced them for a moment, his shaggy head shifting its gaze from one of them to the other. Then he thrust a clipboard forward. "I'm getting signatures for an election."

Harold looked at him incredulously. "What . . ." He cleared his throat, "What are you running for?"

"Who, me? Oh, geez, no. It's for mayor. I'm helping one hell of a guy become mayor of the city."

"Which . . . which city?"

Chico paused a moment and frowned. "Holy geez, I never asked. You think it's this one?"

"With my luck," muttered the woman.

"Look, we don't want any trouble," Harold began again. He noted the fact that people were walking right past without offering any aid to two older people, obviously in distress. Indeed, they seemed to pick up their pace. "If you want me to sign this—"

"Harold!"

"Hey, man, you're great." Chico thrust the clipboard forward once again, and this time Harold took it, holding it gingerly between his fingers.

"Um," Harold said, and patted down his pockets. "I, uh, I don't seem to have a pen."

"Not to worry," said Chico, who patted all the pockets in his limply hanging poncho and then in his tattered pants. With a frown he checked the hair behind his ears and then his beard. It was from that unchecked growth of facial hair that he finally extracted a Bic pen and extended it to the couple.

"I'm going to be sick," said Alice between clenched teeth. "I swear, God as my witness, I'm going to be sick."

"Shut up, Alice," muttered Harold as he took the pen and signed the petition. "Maybe you would have preferred it if he had assaulted your virtue."

Chico and Alice exchanged glances. Neither seemed particularly enthused with the idea.

"Harold!" she said after a moment. "You're putting our address!"

"Yes. So?"

"So . . ." Her eyes narrowed as she inclined her head toward Chico. "What if he tries to, you know, come to the house."

"Oh, I'd never do that," said Chico. Then he gave the matter some thought. "Unless you invited me."

Harold tried to smile pleasantly. What he achieved was the look of a man passing a kidney stone, but he continued valiantly, "What a . . . what a marvelous idea. We have to do that, real soon."

"When?"

"What?"

"When do you want me to come over?" He looked eagerly from one of them to the other.

"I'm . . . I'm not sure. It's going to be pretty hectic for us, too hectic to make social plans."

"Oh." Chico looked crestfallen, but he brightened up. "Well, I'll give you a call, okay?" He smiled ingratiatingly.

"Okay. You bet."

They walked at double-time down the street. Chico watched them go, and when they were almost out of earshot he screamed, "Are we talking dinner or just coffee and cake here?"

He shrugged when he got no response, and looked down proudly at his first signature. Only a few thousand more and he could knock off for the day.

Then he reached into his beard and moaned. "Crud! The sons of bitches took my pen." He shook his head in disillusionment. "You just can't trust anyone these days. There's freaks everywhere."

Professor Carol Kalish, noted geologist, was emerging from the depths of the New York University subway stop on the BMT when a shadowy figure materialized in front of her.

In one hand was a switchblade. In the other was a clipboard.

"Hello," growled Groucho. "I'd like your support for Arthur Penn, who would like to run as an independent for mayor of New York City. Sign this or I'll cut your fucking heart out."

Groucho collected 117 signatures. Before lunch. Without breaking a sweat.

*　　*　　*

Up in Duffy Square, in the heart of the Broadway theater district, Arthur Penn stood on a street corner near a Howard Johnson's and felt extremely forelorn.

A likely looking pair of elderly women approached him, and he started to say, in a very chatty and personable manner, "Hello, my name is Arthur Penn and I would like your support in my candidacy for mayor. . . ." which was more or less the phrasing that Merlin had told him to use. But the couple picked up their pace and stared straight ahead. His voice trailed off as Arthur realized with a shock that they were ignoring him. But then he thought maybe they simply had not heard him. The elderly were notorious for being hard of hearing. Yes, that may very well be it.

So the next time a youngish, businessman looking sort approached him, he began his approach again of "Hello, my name is . . ." But again he got no further than stating his raison d'être before this chap, too, was out of earshot.

No. It was not possible. People of any age could never be so unspeakably rude as to ignore someone who was point-blank addressing them. Could they?

Arthur checked his appearance in the reflection in the display window of the Howard Johnson's. No, his suit was well cut and smart, his grooming immaculate.

It started to sink in on him that everything that Merlin had said to him very early this morning, before he'd gone out canvassing, had been absolutely correct.

He had remembered being thunderstruck by the concept that Merlin had introduced to him, there in their office at the Camelot Building.

"Is it possible," he had asked with naivety astounding in a man nearly a millennium old, "that there might be some people who won't vote for me?"

Merlin stared at Arthur, looking so modern in the dress pants and shirt and yet so innocent of the world around him. What in the name of all the gods had he thrust the king into? he wondered. Maybe he *should* let him go back to the cave. But the boy wizard put the thought from his mind and concentrated on the issue at hand. "Yes." He laughed tersely. "There is an outside chance."

"But who would not vote for me?"

"People who would want to examine your record of past achievements, for one."

"But my achievements are legend— Oh, I see." He slumped against his desk, his hands in his pockets. "I see the problem."

"Yes. Understand, Arthur, in this form my power is a force to be reckoned with. I can conjure up credit cards. I can create things like Social Security numbers, drivers licenses—although for pity's sake take a few lessons first—and I can put records of your birth in Bethlehem . . ."

"How very messianic."

". . . Pennsylvania," Merlin continued. "I can conjure up a history of military service for you. I can, essentially, create an identity for you, Arthur Penn, but I cannot alter by sheer force of will the entire public consciousness. I can't *make* people like you. That will be your task."

And now Arthur, with the words ringing in his ears, was starting to wonder whether it was a task he was up to.

For the first time he turned and saw, really saw, the hustle and bustle of the area around him. It was a nippy day, but the sun was shining brightly. It was twelve-thirty, the height of the lunch hour. Furthermore it was a Wednesday, which meant many people were out looking to pick up matinee tickets to shows.

Arthur was not prepared for it, for the pulse of the humanity around him. Every blessed one of the passing people was in a hurry, as if (although the comparison didn't occur to him) they had an inner spring mechanism unwinding at an incredible rate.

It had not dawned on him at first that it had any direct bearing on him. Well, of course it did, he now realized. He couldn't expect people to stop in their tracks for him. He had to attempt to adapt himself to their speed. He had to be flexible, after all. The wise man—the civilized man—knew when to be firm and when to adapt.

So he began to speak, faster and faster, and soon the words were tumbling one over the other, like cars piling high on a crashing locomotive. Hellomynameisarthurpennandiwould-likeyour . . ." The only evidence that he was having any sort of effect at all was that now the people were walking faster to avoid hearing him.

Abruptly he stopped talking. His lips thinned and his brow clouded. He looked across the street and noticed that in a traffic island there was a mob of people, all milling around in

loosely formed lines. Reaching out, Arthur stopped the first
passerby, a delivery boy carrying somebody's called-in lunch.

"What is the purpose of that gathering?" asked Arthur.

"Look, asshole, I'm runnin' late and I can't—
uuuhhnnnff!"

Arthur had grabbed a handful of the boy's windbreaker,
and despite the fact that he and the teenager were the same
height, effortlessly lifted him into the air.

The boy's eyes bugged out, not from lack of breath so much
as from pure astonishment.

"I will be ignored *no longer!*" thundered Arthur. But then
he saw the lack of color in the boy's face, and immediately his
anger lessened as he chided himself. "Is this what it has come
to then, Pendragon? Threatening hapless errand boys?" With
that he lowered the boy gently to the ground. "Art well, lad?"

"My . . ." He gulped once, afraid to say the wrong thing
and set his captor off again. "My name's not Art. But I'm
okay, yeah."

"I have been at this for much of the day, and the paltry few
signatures that I have accrued—blast their eyes!" He smashed
a fist against a nearby wall. "That *I* should have to endure this
just so that I can offer them my aid. The leadership I should
be given by right I have to scrabble for . . . but that's no concern of yours, lad. However, I still await an answer to my
original query—the purpose of yon gathering."

"That's the TKTS line," said the boy, pronouncing each
letter individually. "People stand there on line and can buy
tickets for half price to—"

And now Arthur exploded. "*That* they have time for? By
Vortigern, they make time to await tickets for entertainment
purposes and yet cannot spare as much as half a minute on
topics that could alter the face of this city . . . of this nation!
Gods!"

Without heed to the traffic around him, Arthur stormed
across the street. Cars screeching to a halt mere inches from
him did not even catch his notice. Horns blasting didn't faze
him.

He reached the TKTS mob and elbowed his way through,
earning shouts and curses from his would-be constituency.

Arthur found himself at the base of a statue that was labeled
Father Patrick Duffy. With quick, sure movements he scaled

it, and moments later was shoulder to shoulder with the fighting priest from World War I.

A few people glanced at him and then turned away. The rest ignored him completely.

His jaw dropped to somewhere around his ankles. This was it. He'd had it. He reached across, with one arm still wrapped around the statue, to his left hip.

He felt it there—the pommel, and then the hilt of Excalibur. He had point-blank refused to go out onto the street without the comfortable weight of the enchanted sword by his side. So Merlin had added a further enchantment by rendering the blade invisible as long as it remained in the scabbard.

Arthur pulled on the sword and it slid from the scabbard with noiseless ease. Excalibur sparkled in the sun and Arthur thrilled to the weight, to the joy of it.

"My arm is whole again," he whispered reverently. Then he swung the sword back, brought it around, and smacked the flat of the blade against the statue.

The clang was on par with a Chinese gong.

It finally got their attention.

"All right," he shouted. With practiced smoothness he had already returned Excalibur to its sheath, returning it to invisibility as well. "I have had enough. Enough of this street-corner posturing! Enough of these games. By the gods you will listen. Turn away from the mindless frivolities with which you occupy yourselves and turn your attentions to where it will do some good. I am running for mayor of this city!" He saw their reactions and added, "Yes, that's what this is all about. I see it in your faces. This is why I want a moment of your precious time."

"You don't have to get insulting," shouted someone in the crowd.

Arthur laughed. "I? When every common grunge thinks nothing of treating me as if I were a nonentity, to be snubbed and ignored at their discretion? I merely call a halt to the insults that have been dealt me this day." He held up a clipboard, and the sheets of paper affixed to it rustled noisily in the breeze. "Do you see these?" Without pausing for a response he continued, "These are petitions. In this free society not just anyone can declare himself a candidate for office. I have to obtain ten thousand signatures, which actually means that I have to have twice that number, since it is generally assumed that half of you will be bloody liars. So I'm going to want every one of you to affix your signature to this most noble document. Is that clear?"

The question came from the crowd. Arthur did not see who asked it. The only thing that he noticed was that the voice was slightly nasal, almost tremulous. But the question was cutting in its simplicity. "Why should we vote for you?"

Arthur looked around. "What?"

There was a ripple of laughter from the crowd at his bewilderment.

"You haven't even told us your name!"

"I am Arthur. Arthur Penn." He could have kicked himself for the brainless oversight.

"Why should we vote for you, Arthur Penn?"

Arthur would have felt more at ease if he could have found who in the world was addressing the questions to him. But it was an anonymous face, one he simply could not locate (although the voice was greatly disturbing to him). "Because . . ." he began, wishing frantically that Merlin had tutored him better. But then Merlin had not been aware that Arthur was going to take his first shot at addressing crowds at a completely impromptu political rally.

At that moment Merlin was not too far away. At Bryant Park, behind the Forty-second Street Library, the wizard was watching an old drunk, watching as he rocked slowly back and forth against the cold, his coat pulled tightly around him.

Merlin shook his head. "Pitiful. Simply pitiful." Hands buried deep in his New York Mets sweat jacket, Merlin walked over to the derelict and dropped down onto the cold stone step beside him. He wrinkled his nose at the stench.

At first the drunk didn't even notice him, but was content to rub the bottle with his cracked and blistered hands. Eventually, however, he became aware of a presence next to him, and he turned bleary eyes on Merlin. It took him several moments to focus, and when he did, he snorted.

He was a black man of indeterminate age. His wool cap obscured much of his head, although a few tufts of curly white hair stuck out. Much of his face was likewise hidden behind the turned-up collar of his coat. His eyes were bloodshot.

"Youakid." Three words into one.

After a moment of meeting his gaze, Merlin turned and looked straight ahead. "Looks can be deceiving," he observed.

"You got money on you?"

"No."

"Parents care where y'are?"

"No."

"You a kid, all right. Ain't no doubt."

Merlin winced. "Why must you talk like that? You're perfectly capable of proper grammar if you so desire."

This time the drunk looked at him more carefully. "You're a smartass kid, besides," he finally concluded.

"Probably." His rump becoming chilled by the cold stone, Merlin shifted his position and sat on his gloved hands. "My name is Merlin."

His words were accompanied by little puffs of mist. The weather was turning even colder.

"Merlin? Like the football player?"

"More like the wizard, actually."

The drunk proferred his almost empty bottle, wrapped in a brown paper bag. "You want some lifeblood, little wizard? Not much left, I'm sorry to say. . . ."

"It's full," said Merlin quietly.

The drunk laughed, a wheezy, phlegm-filled laugh that became a hacking cough within moments. When the fit subsided he told Merlin, "If there's something I always know, little wizard, it's how much I got in this here—"

He hesitated, because suddenly the bottle felt heavy. He slid the bag down and saw the top of the liquid sloshing about less than an inch from the mouth of the bottle. He shook his head. "Ooookay."

Merlin finally stood and stepped down two steps so that he was on eye level with the drunk. His thick brown hair blew in the wind. "Enjoy it, Percy." The drunk's eyes narrowed, but Merlin didn't pause. "It's the last you're going to be having for a time—ever, with any luck. We're going to sober you up and put you back in harness."

Percy shook his head and waggled a finger. "I ain't no horse."

"No. You're not. If you were a horse, we'd simply shoot you and put you out of your misery."

"You ever learn not to talk to y'elders that way?"

For the first time Merlin threw his head back and laughed. He himself did not like his laugh—it was far too squeaky and childish to suit him. But in this instance he could not help himself. "Percy," he said. "How old do you think I am?"

He shrugged. "Dunno. Eight, nine, I guess. Sure not old enough to be—"

"Eight or nine. Guess again. Guess a couple of hundred times that and you'll be on the right track. Percy, I'm going to tell you this because if you decide to stay in the gutter, no one will care what you say, and if you come now with me, you won't want to tell anybody. I am Merlin, Percy."

"Yeah. So?"

"The original Merlin. King Arthur's Merlin."

Again Percy laughed, this time managing to stop before a coughing fit racked his lungs. "Don't gimme that. Merlin's an old man with a beard and a pointy hat. I seen pictures. You sure ain't no old man."

"I was once." He wiped at his nose with the sleeve of his sweat jacket. "You will not find this simple to comprehend, Percy, but I live backward in time. In another fifteen centuries —by my reckoning, not yours—I shall be an old man. The price of immortality. It's difficult to maintain the form of an old man for an excessively long time, which is what would have been required had I aged as other men—had I been spawned as other men, Mary Stewart notwithstanding. But to age backward, to be forever becoming younger—I can maintain this body for decades, centuries to come. When I said fifteen centuries by my reckoning, I meant backward to the fifth century. Forward into the twenty-fifth century I shall be much as you see me now . . . if not a tad younger.

He held out a hand. "Come with me, Percy. Let's go somewhere and talk. We can use you."

Slowly Percy shook his head. "You are without a doubt the smoothest talkin' little so-and-so I ever met. You really expect me to believe all that?"

"Not at first," Merlin admitted. "But you will, you will."

"No—"

"Percy, look around you. Look at this place. The leaves are disappeared from the trees. Winter is hard upon us. All that's left for you to do is huddle and shiver on cold, uncaring stone stairs. And when the winds blow hard, the best you can hope for is to find shelter in that pile of garbage over there; human refuse blending in with the rest of the trash." He leaned forward, his small fists clenched and his voice pleading. "Would you refuse belief in me, Percy, to cling to this pitiful reality?"

His face almost vanished into his coat, Percy was silent for such a long time that Merlin almost thought he'd fallen asleep. In that case Merlin would have left him to rot. But finally Percy said, in a low and resigned voice, "It's my life, little wizard. Why not let me live it?"

"Because it's not a life. And it's not living."

Percy was silent.

Merlin told him, "I need someone with your skills, Percy. You were among the best. I know what you were, Percy. Before the Grail."

Percy looked up at him.

"Come," said Merlin. "We'll talk."

"Okay."

They left the park together.

"Are you Democrat or GOP?" came the whining voice again.

Arthur felt terribly exposed and vulnerable, up high on the statue in Duffy Square. "I'm an independent," he called. "I subscribe to no party line save for the dictates of my conscience."

There were shouts of "Whoa!" and the like from the crowd, and Arthur was unsure of the spirit in which they were made. He waved tentatively.

"How do you stand on the issues?"

Arthur visored his eyes. "Would you mind stepping forward, please, so I can see who I am addressing?"

The crowd parted slightly, and Arthur finally spotted him.

Their gazes locked. They analyzed each other, scrutinized carefully. Arthur wasn't quite sure what to make of him. He was about Arthur's height, but slimmer. His black hair was receding and came to a widow's peak on his forehead, giving him a satanic look. To further the image he wore a Vandyke beard that came to a neat point. His eyes were foxlike. And he immediately said, "How do you feel about capital punishment?"

Arthur recalled that this was a topic of some controversy. In the newspaper headlines that very day there had been news of the legislature once again waffling on how best to approach the touchy subject. On the one hand there was that part of the electorate who felt that they did not want people capable of taking a life without compunction walking the streets. The alarming number of murders by those who had been tried and convicted earlier and were now free was setting a great many people on edge.

But another sizable group felt that the state had no right to take a life, and that it made those who condoned capital punishment no better than the criminals they were condemning. Just put them away in jail for life. But jails were overcrowded and life was really only twenty-five years. . . .

Arthur realized they were waiting for an answer, and only one seemed practical, and civilized, to him.

"There was a time," he said, "not so long ago at that, when merely insulting the aggrieved party was enough to warrant death on the field of honor. Certainly that is a bit extreme nowadays." He was pleased at the laughter this prompted. "I do favor allowing the death penalty in instances of murder." This got applause from some, frowns from others. That was expected. This, however, they would not be expecting. "However, I do not feel that it should be up to the state to decree whether a man live or die."

The crowd looked puzzled, and someone—a girl with an NYU sweatshirt—called, "Well, then, who?"

"The injured party," he said.

There was silence of disbelief.

"You mean the victim?" asked the girl.

Arthur laughed loudly, and several others, uncertain, joined in. "Hardly," he said. "The problem with the criminal justice system is that it ignores the wants and desires of the people, leaving the matter to lawyers and their tricks of the trade, and the judges."

There were a number of nods of approval, and murmurs that did not sound the least bit hostile. The bearded man who had posed the question watched carefully with his ferretlike eyes as Arthur warmed to his topic. "Now I'm not advocating a return to trial by combat, because then the aggrieved party doesn't win—rather, the party with the biggest sword. The justice system is the sword arm of the injured. But when it comes to actually deciding upon death, it should be the survivors of the victim who actually make the determination, not a judge whose life had not been permanently affected."

A sharp wind came up and he clutched more tightly onto the statue for fear of being blown off. Then the wind switched about, carrying his words out to all the crowd—a crowd that had grown considerably beyond merely those people waiting for tickets.

And his voice rang out, strong and clear. "If a woman has her husband taken from her, it should be up to her to decide whether the man who did the deed should live to see another sun or not, for it is the woman, not the judge and not the state, who must come home to an empty bed!"

The crowd went wild, for they had never heard a reply to this often-asked question quite like this one. They were thrilled by its novelty.

Someone shouted, "Aren't you just passing the buck?"

Arthur didn't even try to locate the individual but addressed the crowd, even those who may not have heard the question. "Is advocating a true trial for the people passing the buck? On the contrary, it's the perfect solution. No one will be able to feel that a proper sentence has not been meted out, for it will be the sentence of the people whose lives had been hurt the most by the criminal's actions." Raising a fist proudly, he unashamedly mixed up quotes as he declared, "Trial by jury of the people, by the people and for the people!"

Traffic didn't move for an hour.

Chaptre the Eighth

It was sometime later when the ferret-eyed, bearded man from the crowd entered the Eighth Avenue Health Club and made his way down to the racquetball courts.

He slid through empty seats mounted on tiers, moving down as close as he was allowed to the actual court. A large piece of Plexiglas separated him from the two men aggressively battling it out for final points on the court. One man was tall, lean, a sharp and accurate player. The other man was much shorter, heavyset, with a beer belly he liked to smack affectionately and refer to as his "old hanger-on." His legs were spindly and looked as if every sudden shift in direction might cause them to break like twigs. His thin blond hair was tied off in a sweat-soaked bandanna, and his LaCoste shirt was plastered to his chest. The first man was, by contrast, calm and self-possessed. His opponent was on the ropes, and he had barely broken a sweat.

The bearded spectator rolled his eyes as the heavyset man lunged at the ball and missed it by the width of several states. He thought to himself, as the two players shook hands, See if you can pick the likely candidate for mayor, and groaned silently.

The beer-bellied man turned and spotted him. "Moe!" he called cheerfully, waving a beefy hand. "Come to see your next mayor in action?"

Moe managed a grimace and a nod. "You bet, Bernie. You bet."

The exceptionally jovial (exceptionally, considering he'd just been slaughtered at racquetball) Bernard B. Bittberg dragged his opponent by the shoulder. "Moe, you gotta meet one of the top eleven players I ever met. This is Ronnie Cordoba. Ronnie, this is Moe Dredd, one of the top three P.R. hacks I ever met. Ronnie, Moe. Moe, Ronnie."

Moe reluctantly extended his hand and felt several fingers crack in Ronnie's grip. He grimaced again, and gingerly unwrapped the remnants of his hand. "Bernie, we have to talk."

"So we'll talk. We're talking."

"I think he means just the two of you," said Ron. "I'll be shuffling off to the locker room."

Bet he tosses a salute, thought Moe.

Ronnie smiled a perfect smile and tossed a salute before turning his broad back and trotting away, arms held perfectly for jogging.

"So what's to talk?" said Bernie. "Newspapers already start giving their endorsements for me?" He grinned broadly, displaying teeth dirty from cigar smoke. "I got it sewn up, even before the primaries. They know that. I know that. We all know that."

Moe said, "Bernie, sit down."

Bernie looked at him oddly and stroked the faint stubble on his cheeks. "Whaddaya mean, sit down?"

Moe sat and patted one of the solid wood fold-out chairs next to him. Bernard B. Bittberg sat down. He drummed his fingers on his knee impatiently.

"Bernie," said Moe slowly, "I agree with you that you have the Democratic nomination sewn up. With the incumbent mayor leaving politics to go into show business, it leaves a clear path for you. You've got your years of being City Council head. You've got your high-profile participations in well-covered charity stunts and your seat in the Macy's Thanksgiving Day parade, and all of that. You've got great TV presence, an aggressive stand that lots of New Yorkers find easy to handle—"

"Moe," said Bernie cannily, "you didn't want to talk to me to tell me all these wonderful things about me."

"This is true," said Moe, lowering his gaze. "What I'm saying is that you may have your work cut out for you after the primaries."

"After?" He eyed Moe suspiciously. "You trying to tell me you think the Republicans really have a prayer?"

"No."

His eyes widened and he whispered, "The Commies?"

"No. Not the Commies."

He sat back and spread his hands questioningly. "Well then, who. . . ?"

"There's an independent candidate—"

Bernard laughed hoarsely and shook his head. "You're kidding me, right? An independent candidate? Some schmuck who puts up his own soapbox and starts pontificating to the public? Bullshit! I do not for one minute—"

"Bernie," and Moe's tone as always was unpleasant, "you pay me quite handsomely for giving my advice, and I am telling you now," he waved a thin finger threateningly, "that if you do not listen to what I'm telling you, you will have thrown your money on me away."

Bernie leaned back in the chair. He stroked his chin some more and then said, "All right, Moe. So who is this wunderkind you're so concerned about?"

Moe cleared his throat, covering a sigh of relief. He had finally gotten Bernie to listen to him. That was three quarters of the battle right there. "His name is Arthur Penn," he said.

Bernie rolled the name around in his mouth and finally shook his head. "Never heard of him."

"Neither have I. Neither has anybody else. But you're going to. The man's totally unhinged."

"*What?*"

"He says strange things that, in a bizarre, roundabout way make some sort of sense. When he doesn't know an answer to a question, he says weird things like . . . like . . ."

"Like what?" asked Bernie. "Like, 'We have that topic under careful consideration and plan to address it in the near future.' "

"No. He just says he doesn't know."

"What?"

"That's right."

The blood drained from Bernie's face. "The man's a lunatic!"

"That's not all. I happened to be in a crowd over by TKTS

today. He climbed up on a statue and started speech making. The crowd clustered to him like nothing I've ever seen. Bernie, it was frightening. They weren't just standing there. After less than a minute it was clear to me that they were actually *listening*. Hanging on his every word. Anyone who came within earshot of his voice was mesmerized instantly. I immediately started tossing a few random questions at him, kind of hoping to see how badly he would botch it. So instead he started giving these looney-tune answers, and the crowd ate it up."

"Loony-tune answers? What answers? What sort of questions?"

Moe told him, and Bernie's eyes widened so that they threatened to explode from his head.

"What is he, *nuts*? You didn't tell me he was totally unhinged."

"Actually, I d—"

But Bernie wasn't listening now. He was pacing angrily back and forth, up and down the narrow stairway that led up the aisle between seats. "Allowing the people to pass sentence. That's nuts! Sentences are passed in accordance with the laws of this state. Certain crimes demand certain sentences. The angered or bereaved victim can't begin to grasp the subtleties, the complexities of passing a—"

"Bernie," said Moe impatiently. "I know that. You know that. For all I know, even Arthur Penn knows that. But the people don't."

"But the people don't run the courts!"

"True enough. But they run the polling booths. And if they find this Penn's sideways view of the world attractive, they might say so come election day. New York is a city of nonconformers. Our television ratings never match. Our buildings don't vaguely resemble each other in style. New Yorkers are rude in situations where others are polite, and polite in situations where Mister Rogers would bite your head off. They might just buy and slice this crock of baloney."

Bernie had barely listened. He was too busy shaking his head, saying, "The laws dictate the punishment that should fit the crime. Can't he see that? It's impossible."

"I'm telling you right now that if that little matter were brought to his attention, his immediate reaction would be, 'Well, let's change the law.' "

Bernie scratched his head. "So how do you figure we deal with this nutcase?"

"Frankly, I'm not dead sure yet. I think we can only take a wait-and-see attitude for now." Moe interlaced his fingers and crossed his legs almost daintily. "I mean, we shouldn't start attacking his positions yet. All that will do is give him publicity. Hell, maybe that's what he's hoping for."

"Too bad," muttered Bernie. "I'd like to take this guy apart in public."

"You may yet get your chance, if he sticks around. Which, I have a sick feeling, he's going to do."

Bernie was struck by a thought. "Hey, Moe, about that thing with people deciding the sentence . . . I mean, what if they got together and decided to bring back tar and feathering?"

"With the crime rate what it is?" Moe snorted. "You could start heating enough tar to fill every pothole in New York and it wouldn't be enough to satisfy the demand." His nose wrinkled slightly. "Go hit the showers, Bernie. With the sweat you worked up, you're starting to smell like New Jersey."

Chaptre the Ninth

Arthur grabbed up the telephone before the first ring had ended. "Hello, yes? Merlin!"

Merlin's voice was overwhelmed by traffic noises in the background. "Calm down, Arthur. You're not getting a call from the messiah, after all."

"Merlin, where the devil have you been?" The excitement in his voice was unkingly, but he didn't care a bit. "I haven't seen you in over a week. I have so much to tell you! Where are you? What are you doing? What are you up to?"

"Arthur, please! I don't understand. What's been happening? I mean, you've just been out getting signatures, haven't you? What could be so exciting about that? It's—"

"Oh, no, Merlin! It's gone beyond that. Way beyond that."

Merlin sounded extremely wary. "What are you talking about?" he said slowly.

Arthur sat back in his throne. Surrounded by the walls of his castle, he felt power surging through his body and spirit. "I," he said proudly, "have been politicking."

"You've been what!"

"Making speeches. That sort of—"

"For pity's sake, Wart, who told you to do that?"

Arthur frowned. "I don't think I like the tone of your voice, Merlin."

"Tone of my—Arthur, what in the name of the gods have you been saying to the people? How did this start?"

"It began the first day I was out," said Arthur cheerily, as if relating the details of a thrilling game of cricket. "People were ignoring me, so I . . ."

He described the proceedings.

"Are you out of your mind?"

Feeling somewhat crestfallen, Arthur said, "No, I don't think so. But—"

"We were to rehearse everything you were going to be saying. Have you forgotten all of that?"

"No," said Arthur. "No, I haven't." And his voice took on an edge hard as steel as he said, "But I think you're forgetting who is going to be the next mayor of this state."

"City, you great barbarian oaf! Not state! You—"

Arthur slammed the phone down.

He got up and walked out of the throne room as the phone started to ring again. It rang a dozen times, and he finally came back in. The hem of his purple velvet dressing gown swished around on the floor, stirring up dust, and he made a mental note to get the place swept. He let it ring another few times before he picked it up, but before he could get a word out Merlin said, sounding very small, "I'm sorry, Arthur."

Arthur hesitated, his eyes wide. His grip on the phone relaxed marginally. "Merlin," he said softly, "I think this is the first time you've ever apologized to me. About anything."

"I don't intend to make it a habit. And the only thing I'm apologizing for is the barbarian remark. Everything else stands. You're supposed to follow the script I've laid out."

"I'm not an actor, Merlin. I'm . . . a politician."

"Same difference. Listen, I'll be seeing you in a day or so. And I've got a new member for our group. He's going to be our accountant."

"Good man?"

"One of the best. Utterly dedicated."

"Where have you been for the past week or so?"

"Sobering him up and cleaning him off."

Arthur laughed. "What a sense of humor you have, Merlin. What did you do, pick him up off the street?"

"More or less."

Arthur nodded slowly. "Um, Merlin—I'm going to assume

you know what you're doing. What's the fellow's name anyway?"

"Vale. Percy Vale."

Arthur's mouth opened and closed for a moment. Then he said carefully, "Merlin, I have to ask you. Percy Vale . . ."

"Yes?"

"Gwen DeVere . . ."

"Your point, Arthur?"

"Have you, well, noticed a pattern?"

"Pattern?" There was a lengthy pause, and Arthur wondered if Merlin was still on the line before he heard the wizard say, "What pattern?"

"Those names sound like—"

"Bosh. What's in a name, Arthur? See you soon." The line was abruptly cut off.

Percy Vale bore little superficial resemblance to the man Merlin had found on the library a week ago. He was now dressed in a straight-arrow, three-piece, black pinstripe suit. There was no trace of liquor on his breath, although it had left a haunted look in his eyes. He was neatly groomed, his fingernails trimmed. His eyes were bloodshot, but Visine would take that away in time. A cup of black coffee sat in front of him.

"You promised me, Merlin."

Merlin sat across from him, the remains of his breakfast all around him. Percy had had toast. Merlin had put away steak and eggs and was on his third cup of coffee. The waitress kept giving him looks every time she walked by. He ignored them; he was used to it.

"Yes, I know I promised you, Percy."

"You said that if I sobered up, you'd tell me who I am. You told me you'd explain why I got this emptiness in my gut and I always gotta fill it with booze."

Merlin sipped his coffee. "You were once a knight," he said so quietly that Percy had to strain his ears to hear him. "A knight of the Round Table."

Percy stared at him and then leaned back. "Bull-sheet. No black man ever sat at no Round Table. You mean with King Arthur and them? No way."

"Oh, you were not black at the time," Merlin said with a dismissive wave. "You have to learn to look beyond the present. Yours is an eternal spirit, Percy. You have always existed. You always will. Sometimes you will be white, sometimes yellow, sometimes male and sometimes female. You are a symbol.''

"What, you mean one of those big round things you clang?"

Merlin winced. "Symbol. Not cymbal. Symbol as in representing something. You are an incarnation, Percy. An incarnation of a human ideal.''

"Man, that is the biggest crock of—"

"In this case that ideal is dedication to a goal. You are not aware of it, Percy, but in a time past you sought the Holy Grail.''

"The what?"

Merlin pursed his lips. "In the time of Camelot there came a period of discontent. The knights became bored with the ideal of chivalry and civilization. Arthur had achieved a goal, namely the use of the power of knighthood for something other than hacking enemies into small bits of meat. Men were treating men like human beings, and women like chattel that needed protection, which was a damned sight better than the way both genders were being treated earlier.''

Percy cocked his head to one side as Merlin took another sip of coffee. "But, as human beings are wont to do, the knights wound up needing a new goal to stave off the oppression of boredom. So I gave them one. They were to search for, find, and recover the Holy Grail. The cup from which Jesus Christ drank at the Last Supper.''

"Why?"

Merlin shrugged. "I don't know. It was the first thing that popped into my mind. It was either that or the Holy Plate. It hardly mattered what I came up with, as long as it was something to keep what I laughingly refer to as the knights' 'minds' occupied.''

"Are you saying there wasn't ever a Holy Grail?"

"No," said Merlin. "There might have been. And there might be flying saucers and the Loch Ness monster and honest used-car dealers and whatever other fantasies the human mind is capable of conjuring. What I'm saying is that I made up the Holy Grail. Certainly. I would have said anything to delay the splintering of the Round Table. Yet for all I know I actually hit upon something that existed. I couldn't say. Whatever I made up, however, you were the most dedicated in attempting to find it. For that is what you are—dedication personified."

"Yeah, yeah, so you said."

"So I said," agreed Merlin cheerfully. "And you have lived many lives, for you have always existed and always will. And no matter who you were or where you were, you have always been dedicated."

"Oh, yeah?" said Percy. "Then why," and he leaned forward intently, "why, if I'm so damned dedicated, am I a stinking drunk?"

"Because in this lifetime you were dedicated to your own self-destruction. And you were very good at it. If it hadn't been for me, you might have achieved it." Merlin frowned then. "And since you are the embodiment of the human spirit, I got you just in time. It would not have boded well at all for humanity if you'd allowed your liver to turn into a colander."

"Oh, yeah?" said Percy. "You don't know what made me the way I am."

"In fact I do. I have quite a few ways of searching out what I wish to know. It wasn't difficult. Good accountant, you were. One of the best. Worked for a big firm and discovered irregularities—funds disappearing for which you could not account."

Percy turned away but Merlin continued, his voice oddly flat and even. "You discovered a higher up, a man you respected tremendously, had been jerking the company around. He fed you a sob story that wrenched your heart. Ever sympathetic to the human condition, you agreed to cover for him. And you did, until the auditors found it. But the higher up managed to pin the whole thing on you. Fired. Disgraced. No one would hire you. Your world in the toilet, you had no goal to achieve. So you sought escape in a bottle—"

Percy slammed his hand down on the table, rattling the ketchup and the salt and pepper shakers. Everyone in the coffee shop jumped except for Merlin. "All right! That's history, Merlin."

Merlin nodded once. "Fine. As long as we're both agreed on that."

"Agreed."

"Fine. For I have a new goal for you. The election of Arthur, your former king, to a position that will be his stepping-stone to creating a new order of peace and greatness for mankind. And you will serve as something very important, Percival.'' He stabbed a finger at him. ''You're going to set an example for Arthur. So he won't get distracted.''

''Distracted? By what?''

''There are,'' Merlin said with a sigh, ''other aspects of the human condition which are eternally recreated. One such is evil, although if its personification exists reincarnated in this time, I have yet to find it. That worries me. But another aspect has already manifested itself. And poses a threat.''

''What would that be?''

With barely a trace of bitterness, Merlin said, ''The eternal ability of the human race to make a muddle of the best laid plans. A shapely monkey wrench has entered the works, and Arthur has cheerfully put it into the toolbox.'' He shook his head in wonderment. ''Sometimes I think there's just no understanding that man, no matter how many centuries I know him.''

Chaptre the Tenth

Arthur was in tremendous spirits when he came into the office the next morning. "Good morning, Gladys!" he said cheerfully to the receptionist.

She looked up at him with less than a kindly expression. "I can't stand it."

"Gladys, my sweet, nothing is going to dampen my mood. Not even you." He leaned over her desk and whispered conspiratorially, "But exactly what is it that you can't stand, hmmm?"

"First you have those two drug-addicted freaks out beating the drums for you—"

"Are you referring to Groucho and Chico, two of my most dedicated helpmates?" he asked archly.

"Right, the freaks. And then you hire that shrinking violet to be your personal secretary—"

"I heard that!" shouted an enraged Gwen, storming out of the alcove where her desk was situated. Her breast was heaving furiously in righteous indignation as she spat out, "Look, Gladys, you've been on my case since Day One. And if you're going to talk about me behind my back, the least you could do is do it when I'm not right around the corner." She turned on Arthur and pointed an angry finger at the receptionist. "Why is she such a shrew anyway?"

Arthur tilted his head and regarded her with a questioning

stare. "I will answer your question, Gwen, if you will answer mine."

"What? What are you—"

"Gladys acts like a shrew because Gladys is a shrew," Arthur said reasonably. "We needed an immediate office worker, so Merlin transformed her. But the problem is that you can change a creature's basic appearance, but you can never change the basic nature of that creature. Once a shrew, always a shrew. Right, Gladys?"

Gladys glared at him and growled deep in her throat. Arthur smiled and turned back to Gwen. "Now my question—why are you wearing sunglasses?"

"What?" Gwen touched the shades that perched on her nose, obscuring her eyes. "Oh, right. I felt like it. It's sunny out."

"Now why," said Arthur slowly, "do I have trouble believing that?"

Gwen laughed unpleasantly. "What, I'm supposed to believe you, with that cock and bull story about changing rodents into people? Get real, Arthur."

She started to turn, but Arthur abruptly whirled her around by the shoulder and yanked off the glasses.

"Good lord," he said softly.

Gwen's eye was blackened and swollen. And it was clear that it was just beginning to swell—it would be much worse before it got much better.

"Who did this to you?"

"No one. I walked into a door."

She tried to pull away, but he gripped her firmly by both shoulders. His face was only inches away from hers, and his voice was low and intense. "Who," he repeated with forced calm, "did this to you?"

"I punched myself in the eye."

"You hit yourself?"

"Yes."

"In the eye?"

"That's right."

"Why in God's name would you do that?"

"I was aiming at my nose and I missed."

The door opened and Merlin marched in, Percy Vale in tow. "Arthur, we're back!"

Gwen took advantage of Arthur's momentary distraction to

pull away from him and dash over to her alcove. Arthur started to follow her but she came flying back, her purse in her hand. She snatched the sunglasses from Arthur's hand and tried to jam them quickly onto her face. She succeeded only in poking herself in her right eye, and she moaned in pain.

"Gwen, for pity's sake—"

"Leave me alone!" she sobbed. "Don't you understand? I thought you'd be out again today for signatures! I didn't want you to see me like this! Oh, God . . ." and she ran out of the office, wobbling on her high heels.

Sensing what the king was about to do, Merlin said sharply, "Arthur! Don't you go after her."

"But Merlin—"

"Wart! Don't do it!" And then he softened his voice. "Give her time. She's going to have to deal with it herself."

Arthur was still clearly uncertain, and Merlin cursed inwardly. Never had he known a man of a more decisive, unwielding nature than Arthur—except where it came to women. And this woman, in particular. Remembering how he had resolved to solve this problem, Merlin said quickly, "Arthur, I'd like you to meet Percy Vale. Percy's the new accountant we were discussing."

"Oh. Right." He shook Percy's hand firmly. Percy smiled hesitantly until he realized that Arthur was staring intently at his eyes. "Is, uh, is something wrong, Mr. Penn?" he asked.

"What? Oh, no, nothing's wrong except . . . well, I could just swear I know you from somewhere." He looked at Merlin uncertainly. "Percy Vale, Merlin? Are you sure that—"

"It's coincidence, Arthur. Trust me." He spread his hands innocently. "Have I ever lied to you?"

"Probably," said Arthur reasonably. "I've just never caught you at it, that's all. Welcome to our little group, Percy."

"It's a pleasure to be here, sir. I'm sorry if I came at a bad time."

"Well, one can never know when the inappropriate times are going to occur."

The phone rang and Gladys promptly picked it up. "Arthur Penn's office," she said brightly. She paused, nodded, then put the phone on hold. "There's a Mr. Dredd wanting to talk to you," she said.

Arthur frowned and turned to Merlin. "Dredd?"

"Yes," said Gladys. "Moe Dredd."

"Modred!" He pointed an accusatory finger at Merlin. "There is a pattern! There is reincarnation! And she is Guinevere, isn't she?"

"Now Arthur—"

With one quick movement he was standing before Merlin, and with another he was holding the startled wizard in the air by the scruff of the neck. *"It's her, isn't it!"*

"Yes! Yes, damn you!" Merlin screeched in a voice filled with fury and fear. "It's her! But you don't need her, Arthur! She's going to bugger the whole works, just like she did last time! She's the eternal screwup!"

"I don't care if she's the eternal bloody flame. We belong together!"

"You belong in an asylum!" Merlin's legs pumped furiously. "Put me down!"

Arthur drew back his arm and flung the boy wizard the length of the office. Merlin slammed into the large sofa and rebounded onto the floor. He lay there, moaning.

Without another word Arthur turned and stormed out of the office.

Percy moved toward Merlin, but the prone magician waved him off.

"Uh, Merlin . . . I know I just got here and everything, but if it's okay, I'd like to offer a piece of advice."

Slowly Merlin turned his head to Percy. "And what . . . might that be?"

"If Arthur convinces Gwen to come back with him, I wouldn't get in his way. If I'm not out of line here."

"Point . . . taken, Percy."

Gladys bounded to her feet. Her wig bobbed on her head. "You can't mean that! I can't stand her! Everything about her is 'just so.' Her hair is just so, her dress is just so, her makeup is—"

Merlin staggered to his feet. "I get the picture, Gladys."

"No you don't! If she comes back, I'm leaving." Her voice rose in indignation. "I don't have to put up with this! I have rights! I—"

With pure fury in his eyes Merlin said, "Gladys, you don't have to quit." He clenched his right fist and then extended his thumb, index finger, and little finger, and pointed at Gladys. He spoke quickly, in a tongue that humanity had not heard in fifteen centuries. Eldritch energy sparkled from his hand, bathing Gladys in its light, catching her in mid sentence. Within less than the blink of an eye, Gladys was gone.

Percy could not believe what he'd seen. And in the next second he couldn't believe what he heard—with an angry squeal a small, gray furry creature with a long nose darted from behind the desk, scampered across the floor and ran under the couch.

"You're fired," Merlin said to the rodent cowering under the couch. "I'm going down to the pet store right now and arranging for your replacement. You're going to love her."

Merlin smoothed out his brown hair and straightened his T-shirt. "Percy," he said, "mind things until I get back."

"O-okay, Merlin."

"I don't want any more bizarreness today."

At that moment Chico and Groucho burst in, stumbling over each other in their excitement. "We got it," crowed Chico. "We have got freakin' *it*!"

"What?" asked Merlin impatiently.

"Signatures, kiddo!" They waved sheaves of paper in their filthy hands. "We got enough! All you need and lots more. Arthur, the guy with the Day-Glo sword, is now officially a candidate for mayor of New York!"

They stood there, arms spread wide, as if accepting thunderous applause. There was dead silence.

"Well," grumbled Groucho, "don't thank us all at once, y'know."

She had managed to stop crying, but her face was still tear-streaked as Gwen fumbled for her apartment keys in her purse. She breathed silent invocations, thinking, Please, please, please don't let him be at home.

She fished out her keys, unlocked the door, and stepped inside the dimly lit apartment. She glanced around at the empty living room and sighed relief. She didn't know where he was and she didn't care. At least he wasn't at home.

Lance stepped out of the bedroom, his hands on his hips. "So. You came back, did you?"

Gwen moaned and moved away from the door. She pulled the sunglasses off and tossed them carelessly on the floor as she staggered over to a chair and sagged into it. Lance walked over to her, laughing loudly, and took her chin in his hand, turning her head this way and that.

"Quite a shiner you got."

"I know. It's the birthday present you forgot to give me last month, right?"

"Now, now," he said, and swaggered away. "There's no need to get bitter. After all, you brought it on yourself."

"Me!" She lurched to her feet, feeling the familiar sting of tears at her eyes and fighting them off. "You're the one who came home drunk last night. Boozing and . . . and sleeping with whores. God knows what germs you picked up."

"Whores!" His voice went up an octave. "How can you say that? How can you say I was getting laid by strange women?"

"You reeked of cheap perfume."

He snorted. "I can't help it if women cling all over me."

"Lance, your pants were on backward! Why did you come home to me with your pants on backward?"

"It was a joke, for chrissakes."

"No, Lance." She shook her head furiously. "This whole relationship is a joke. And I'm the punch line. Especially when you came home the way you did last night, and you wanted to make love to me all reeking and disgusting. And when I refused you did this to me." She pointed at her eye. "You did this. Not me. You!"

"Yeah?" He got louder, angrier, and he advanced on her, his fist clenching and unclenching. "And I can do it again. And again. I'm tired of your superiority attitude. I thought you understood me. But you're just ignorant, like all the rest. Ignorant! But I'm gonna teach you!"

He swung his fist back. Gwen shrieked, throwing up her hands to defend herself.

A hand closed around Lance's wrist from behind.

Lance moaned in surprise as he felt a bone bend under the sudden stress. Then he was spun around, and Arthur, shorter than Lance, glared up at him. "You've made your last mistake," said Arthur in a deadly calm voice.

Arthur pulled him forward quickly and rammed his knee up into the pit of Lance's stomach. Lance gasped as the side of Arthur's hand slammed into his temple. Stars exploded before his eyes as he dropped to the ground, arms wrapped around his gut.

Arthur's lip curled in a snarl. "You piece of dirt. You don't deserve to live."

Gwen's eyes widened in shock as Arthur, still nattily attired in a royal-blue, three-piece suit, reached to his left hip under his coat. For a moment she thought he was about to draw a gun. Instead there was the smooth sound of metal on metal as Excalibur was drawn from its sheath. In the dimness of the apartment the sword glowed with a life all its own.

Lance scuttled back, crablike, toward the wall, never taking his terrified eyes from the darkly furious face of the warrior king. Arthur knocked a lamp out of the way with a sweep of the sword, advancing on Lance until the frightened man could back up no farther. He pulled his knees up to his chin like a frightened fetus and tried to stammer something, but failed.

Arthur poised with Excalibur over his head and brought the sword whizzing down.

Gwen screamed.

The sword came to a halt with the cutting edge barely touching the top of Lance's head.

Arthur grinned wolfishly. "What's the matter, fellow? Can't you take a joke?"

He took two steps back and sheathed the sword. But there was no amusement in his voice as he said, "Consider yourself fortunate that you did not have a weapon. For although I would not slay an unarmed man, I would cheerfully have gutted you from sternum to crotch, given the slightest opportunity. If you ever come near this woman again, nothing will stop me from taking your life. Is that understood?"

Lance's mouth moved in the formation of the words "Yes, sir," but nothing came out.

"I'll take that as an acknowledgment of our understanding."

He turned and walked over to Gwen with a relaxed, easy step. "I—" she stammered.

"It's all right, Gwen."

"I thought you were going to kill Lance just then."

"Lance?" He turned slowly, with narrowed eyes. "Lance. Lance what? It wouldn't be Lance Lake, would it?"

"W-what?" said Lance from his place on the floor.

"Lake. Or something to that effect?"

"No. It's Lance Benson."

"Good. Lancelot du Lac deserved better than you. I'm glad you are not he."

He looked down at Gwen, who was sprawled on the couch. With infinite tenderness he leaned over and picked her up, cradling her in his arms. "Why?"

She couldn't look at him, but she wrapped her arms around his neck. "Why what?" she whispered.

"Why did you come back here?"

"I had nowhere else to go."

He basked in the warmth of her body, held close to him. "Now you do."

He walked with her to the door. He looked back at Lance, who still cowered in the corner, then smiled again and said, "Have a nice day," and left with Gwen in his arms.

They went down to the street, and Arthur called "Taxi!" to the first unoccupied cab he saw. The cab swung over to the curb and the cabbie, a middle-aged Jewish man, looked out the window at them and said, "I think you'll have to put her down to get in."

"I believe you're right," said Arthur.

He let Gwen down to the ground and they popped into the back. As Arthur pulled the door shut behind them, Gwen said, "I couldn't believe it. I just couldn't believe when you whipped out your sword—"

"Hey!" said the cabbie angrily. "It's pretty obvious that you two are on your honeymoon, but let's keep the filthy talk to a minimum, okay?"

"Yes, sir," said Arthur meekly. He glanced over at Gwen and winked, and she smiled. It was her first real smile in weeks.

"So you two lovebirds want to tell me where you're going?"

"Yes," said Arthur. "Central Park."

"Sounds good." The car eased its way into the busy lunch hour traffic.

"Central Park?" said Gwen. "What's there?"

"My home away from home."

"Oh." She paused. "Thank you. About not hurting Lance."

Arthur turned and looked at her. "But he hurt you."

"I suppose in a way he was right. I had only myself to blame. Because I let him get away with it. But never again."

"That's the way I like my queen to talk."

She looked up at him dreamily. "I'm really your queen? You're really—"

"Yes. I am."
"And I'm really—"
"I think so."
"How can we know for certain?"
Arthur smiled. "I'll know."

Chaptre the Eleventh

Bernard B. Bittberg was accustomed to coming out of City Council meetings and being surrounded by the press. He smiled now into the cameras as they crowded around him on the steps of the big marble building he'd just left. Bernard struck a dramatic pose, one hand jauntily on his ample hip, his head cocked to one side, a smile plastered across his face. Moe floated unobtrusively in the background.

Bernard waited for questions about his plans for his campaign, his opinions on the current hot issues, his plans for the city if elected. And it was a tribute to Bernard B. Bittberg's skill as a politician that when the first question out of a reporter's mouth was, "What do you think of Arthur Penn's chances in the upcoming mayoral race?" he did not turn and slug the questioner.

"He's made quite a splash with his soapbox speeches, Bernie," shouted the reporter from Channel 4 news. "And some of the proposals he's made are quite unorthodox. Do you have any comment on—"

Bernard waved off the question and managed to keep his smile glued on his mouth. "Now boys, I have all of Mr. Penn's proposals under consideration, and before I make further comment I'm getting the opinion of my advisors on the matter. That's all, that's all." And he brushed by the reporters with uncharactertistic abruptness.

Moe followed on his heels, not thrilled by the turn of events, and when Bernie hopped into his waiting limo, Moe was even less thrilled that Bernie waved for him to get in as well. Bernie slid over to accommodate Moe and tossed one last wave to the reporters as the limo pulled away.

Once they were under way his friendly facade melted away like butter on a skillet. "What the hell was that all about?" he demanded.

"I'm not sure what you mean exactly," said Moe slowly.

"Then I'll explain it, exactly." Bernie lit up one of his dread cigars, and opened the window a crack to allow the smoke to trail out behind them. "You were telling me a couple of weeks ago that there was barely any interest in this Arthur Penn guy, that he was going to go away."

"I never said that, Bernie," said Moe reasonably. "I said I hoped he'd go away. There's a big difference."

"Wonderful. So I come out of a City Council meeting, all set to announce that we've reallocated money to fill potholes, and all I get are questions about this Penn guy. Now what, I wonder, put the press on to this guy. Huh?"

"Well, uh," Moe tugged uncomfortably on his collar, "I suppose in a small way it's my fault."

"*Your* fault. How is it your fault?"

"I called one of my contacts with the *Daily News*. I asked him to check through Penn's background, to find what he could dig up, dirtwise. He owed me a big favor, and he's one of the best muckrakers in the business. Frankly, I'm surprised the *National Enquirer* hasn't snatched him up yet."

"The point, Moe. Get to the point."

"The point is that he did the investigation. Real deep. Real thorough." Moe turned a dead glance on Bernie. "Know what he found? Nothing."

"Oh, come on," Bernie said incredulously. "Your man just didn't do his job, is all. Everybody's got something in their past that can be used against them as a weapon."

"This guy is squeaky clean, I'm telling you. It's easy enough for my friend to check, because everything's on computers these days. He checked with everyone from the FBI and the IRS to the Department of Motor Vehicles. Not only does Arthur Penn not have any sort of negative record anywhere—not even so much as a parking ticket or late credit card payment—but he has a distinguished service record in the army.

Everything about this guy checks out perfectly."

Bernie took a long, thoughtful drag on his cigar. "Maybe too perfect, you think?"

"It has crossed my mind, yes."

"You gonna keep digging on him?"

"I'm not exactly sure where to dig at this point. It's back-fired the first time around, because my reporter friend became so fascinated by Penn that he wound up doing a big spread on him. A lot of people have started getting turned on to Penn. If I get more people looking into his background, with my luck *60 Minutes* will come in and canonize him."

"So what do we do now?"

Moe interlaced his fingers. "We start analyzing his pro-posals, and elaborate for the edification of all and sundry ex-actly why they are stupid and unworkable."

"Sounds good."

"And in the meantime we can pray that our luck holds out."

"Our luck?" Bernie shook his head. "I don't see—"

"Penn could be making a lot more hay of this attention than he is. Instead he's playing it close to the chest. He sur-faces for a few hours in random parts of the city, pontificates, then vanishes again. I tried calling him in his office several times to arrange a meeting with him, just to get some reading of how he handles a one-on-one. I heard some shouting in the background the first time I called, and since then the guy's never there." Moe frowned. "A kid has answered the phone a couple times. He recognizes my voice and hangs up on me."

"Not exactly the way to make friends and influence people."

"My feelings exactly. Let's hope that we keep it up. The main thing we have going for us is this Penn's utter lack of ex-perience."

"Yeah." Bernie laughed with a cheerfulness he did not feel. "Can you imagine a guy who makes speeches and then vanishes? Never accessible to the press? What's he trying to do, run a campaign through word of mouth?"

"So it would seem. There's one thing that bothers me though."

"Yeah? What's that?"

Moe paused thoughtfully. "What if it works?"

* * *

Arthur stood outside the door to his offices, wrestling with a crisis of conscience. There was a part of him that wanted to take Gwen and hop on the nearest bus out of town. Or plane. Or boat! That would be excellent. A nice long cruise over the ocean, far away from Merlin and his machinations.

He looked at his reflection in the opaque glass. Who was he? he wondered. What had he become? For as long as he could remember—and he could remember quite a ways back—every action in his life had been made because he'd had to do it. Not because he wanted to, but because he had to. His was the eternal sense of obligation, and it had begun to take a toll on him after all these years.

"Why me?" he said to no one in particular. "Why can't I have a normal life? Why must I always be a tool of some 'greater destiny'?"

"Because that's the way it is."

Arthur looked down. Merlin was standing at his side, looking straight ahead. No matter how many times Arthur saw him, he didn't think he would ever get used to seeing his mentor clad like a street urchin.

"You've been dressing down lately, Merlin," he observed.

The young wizard shrugged. "I've always worn what's most comfortable. In this age it's jeans, sneakers, and T-shirt. Where the devil have you been the past week?"

Arthur smiled. "What's wrong, Merlin? I always thought that you believed what was sauce for the goose was sauce for the gander."

"What, you mean because I spent a week out of sight trying to help a man put together the pieces of his life, you took that as an excuse to vanish for a week as well, to pursue God knows what?"

Arthur turned and looked down. "Did it ever occur to you that I might be pulling a life together too?"

"Really?" said Merlin with a raised eyebrow. "Whose?"

"Gwen's. And, to a large extent, mine."

Merlin winced. "I don't want to hear it."

"I wouldn't tell you. After all," and he smirked, "you're under age."

He turned away and opened the door, feeling for some reason that he had achieved a minor victory. What that victory was, he wasn't quite sure. But it was something.

He swung open the door and was slammed with a blast of

noise that was like a living thing.

Phones were ringing, people shouting to each other, type-writers clacking furiously. And as he stepped into the waiting area, he saw to his shock that the entire interior of the office had been redone. The partitions between the small offices had been torn down, and now all the square footage stretched out like a small football field. Desks were sticking out in every possible direction; there were about a dozen in all. Each one had a phone, and there was a young man or woman on each phone. Arthur's eyes widened as he recognized the girl from the crowd who had been wearing the NYU sweatshirt . . . his first speaking engagement, of sorts. She was the first to glance up and see him, and she immediately put her phone down, leaped to her feet, and started applauding. Others looked around to see the source of her enthusiasm, and when Arthur was spotted, everyone else in the crammed offices immediately followed suit.

Arthur was dumbfounded, astounded, and flattered by the abrupt and spontaneous show of affection. He nodded in acknowledgment, put up his hands and said, "Thank you! Thank you all. You're too kind, really." He leaned down to Merlin and whispered, "Merlin, who are all these people?"

"Volunteers, mostly," said Merlin pleasantly. "Some paid office workers. Word of you is getting around, Arthur. We're going to have to start putting together a solid itinerary for you. Perhaps even explore a series of commercials."

"The packaging of the candidate, Merlin?"

Merlin sighed. "Arthur, the sooner you manage to come to terms with the way things are, the happier a man you will be. Understand?"

"I suppose."

Arthur glanced toward the receptionist. To his surprise, a striking young woman was seated there. Her hair was long and black, her eyes almond-shaped and green. "Uh . . . hello."

"Hello, Mr. Penn," she purred. "I'm your new reception-ist, Selina."

"Hello, Selina. Might I ask where your predecessor went to?"

Merlin whistled an aimless tune, and Selina merely smiled. Arthur looked from one to the other suspiciously. "Merlin," he said suspiciously. "All these people here . . . did you—"

"Create them all from animals? Of course not. That would

be a bit of a strain even for me. Only Selina is . . . she was once," he said with pride, "the most stunning black cat you've ever seen."

"Oh, really?" He looked at Selina, who smiled and gave a little wave. "But Merlin, that still doesn't answer the question of what happened to . . . to . . ."

Selina ran her tongue across her lips and made a little smacking sound.

"Let's just say," deadpanned Merlin, "that Gladys won't be filing for unemployment anytime soon."

Arthur was in his office until eight o'clock that evening, going over plans and itineraries for the next several months. He noticed and appreciated the fact that Merlin was deliberately hanging in the background, letting him run the show without unasked-for advice. And he found his blood really pumping for the first time. The excitement was beginning to build as a plan was formulated. Arthur was fond of strategies, of form and substance. There was no time for the earlier, self-centered fears and frustrations of someone wishing that they were something they could never be.

Nevertheless he was glad when the day was over.

The cab dropped him off in Central Park and he made his way across, lost in thought. This night there were no interruptions from would-be muggers or helpful policemen. In the distance on one of the streets that cut through the park, Arthur heard the nostalgic sound of horse's hooves clip-clopping on the road. By the rattle of metal he could tell that it was a horse-drawn carriage. He drew a mental picture for himself, however, seated proudly on a great mount, his sword flashing, the sunlight glinting off the shield he held and the armor he wore.

It was an image to do him proud.

But it was just that—an image. A part of himself he could never recapture.

The castle loomed before him, and yet so lost in thought was he that he almost walked right into it.

Everyone knew the castle in the middle of Central Park. A complex weather station was situated inside. Whenever early-rising New Yorker's ears were tuned to their radios, the statement that it was such-and-such degrees in Central Park came from the readings taken here, at Belvedere Castle.

Yet a weather station was no longer the only thing occupying the castle.

Arthur walked slowly around the other side, looking for a certain portion of the wall that he knew he would find. And sure enough there it was, as it had been the other nights—a small cylindrical hole in the wall toward one stone corner.

Arthur drew Excalibur, reveling as always in the heady sound of steel being drawn from its sheath. Then he took Excalibur, and holding the hilt in one hand and letting the blade rest gently in the other, he slid the point into the hole.

With a low moan and the protest of creaking, the section of the wall swiveled back on invisible hinges. Before him was a stairway, the top of which was level with the ground in front of him, the bottom of which disappeared down into the blackness that was the castle—or at least an aspect of the castle.

Arthur was never thrilled about the prospect of going somewhere he could not see, but he knew he was going to have to live with it. He entered the doorway, and the moment he set foot on the second step, the door swung noiselessly shut behind him. He was surrounded by blackness, illuminated only by the glow from Excalibur, which accompanied him like a friendly sprite. "My old friend," he whispered.

He walked for a time, impressed as always by the total silence of the supernatural darkness. Then, several steps before the bottom, Excalibur cast its glow upon a heavy oaken door. He walked the remaining steps down to it and pushed. It yielded without protest, and he stepped into his castle.

He passed through the main entrance hall, with its suits of armor standing at attention like legions waiting for his orders. He entered his throne room and looked around in satisfaction. Everything was exactly as he'd left it, and yet he could sense, somehow hanging in the air beyond his eye but not beyond his heart, the presence of the Woman. He smiled, the mere image of Gwen in his mind's eye enough to bring an adrenaline rush that made him feel centuries younger.

There was an elaborate tapestry hanging behind his throne. In it was a representation of Arthur seated at the Round Table, and seated around it was an assortment of knights clearly engaged in some deeply intense discussion. None of them really looked like the knights Arthur remembered— the portrayal of himself was recognizable only because of the

larger chair. But that was all right, since the weavers of
the tapestry had doubtless created it centuries after the table,
and its members were part of the legends rather than living,
breathing men.

"It's very nice. I've been admiring it for some time now."

Arthur turned and a grin split his face. Gwen was standing
in one of the side entrances. She was wearing a simple blue
frock which served to accentuate the loveliness of her features.
She ran her fingers through her strawberry-blond hair and
said, "I saw all the nice dresses you had hanging in that ward-
robe in my room. I hope you don't mind that I felt like wearing this outfit. It's not very fancy. . . ."

Arthur stepped forward and put his hands on her shoulders.
"Gwen, what happened to the strong-willed resolve? Doing
what you feel comfortable with, without having to rely solely
on the approval of others?"

"I know, I know," she sighed. "It's a habit. Still, I suppose
I feel a little guilty."

"In heaven's name, why?"

"Because I haven't been much of a guest. Most of the time
I've just been sleeping and sleeping and sleeping."

He laughed and draped an arm around her shoulder as they
walked toward the dining room. "From what I've learned of
your life the past several years, my little Gwen, you probably
haven't had a good night's sleep in quite some time. You're
just making up for all those lost hours."

"The bed's been unbelievably comfortable. And it's so
quiet here, but not, you know, quiet in a spooky way. Quiet in
a friendly way. You can just lie back and listen to nothing, and
enjoy it."

She turned then, and faced him. Arthur was amused to
recall that once upon a time his Guinevere had had to almost
crane her neck to look at his eyes. Now they were practically
on eye-to-eye level. Arthur mused that if he disappeared into a
cavern for another millennium, he would be a midget when he
came out.

"Arthur, where are we?" she asked intently.

"Why, we're right outside the dining room." With a sweep
of his arm he indicated the table, which was already set. As
always there was enough food there to feed a regiment—where
it came from, Arthur never knew. It was just there when he
needed it. With the bounty available, sustenance for his "cas-

tlemate'' had been no problem at all.

She shook her head. "No, that's not what I'm saying. I once took a tour of Belvedere Castle, and I know for sure that there was nothing like this. Yet you say that we're in that castle. I find it so hard to believe, and yet—"

"Gwen," he said firmly. "I never lie. Not to you. Not to anyone. To lie is to diminish one's own feeling of self-worth."

"I know, but then . . . how?"

"You saw how when I first brought you down here a week ago."

"Oh, yes, I saw. I saw but I didn't understand. I mean," she stepped away and shook her head in puzzlement, "I saw what you did with the sword, and the door swing open and the darkness. But none of it really made all that much sense or registered. I think part of me believed that I was actually dreaming."

"In the middle of the day?"

"Why not?" she said reasonably. "After all, many of my daylight hours have been nightmares anyway. Arthur, I don't understand how any of this works."

Nodding slowly, Arthur crossed slowly to this throne, pulling at his beard as he searched for a way to explain it to Gwen. Which was going to be a slick trick, considering that he didn't fully understand it himself.

He went up the two steps to the throne and paused there a moment. Then he said, "Gwen, how do you turn on a light?"

"What, you mean like when you enter a room?" He nodded. She looked at him suspiciously. "Is this a trick question? Like 'How many Jewish American princesses does it take to screw in a lightbulb?' "

"What?" he asked in utter confusion.

"No, I guess not. Uh, okay." She leaned against the stone wall which, unlike every other castle she'd ever been in, was warm to the touch. "To turn on a light, you just flick the wall switch."

"Right. And what happens?"

"The light comes on."

"Yes, but why?"

Now Gwen was confused. "Because you turned on the light switch. Arthur, if this is your idea of an explanation, it really sucks."

"Gwen," he said patiently, "what is it that makes the light

go on when you turn on the switch?''

"Electricity, I guess. It makes the bulb come on."

"How?"

She stamped a shapely foot in irritation. "Who cares? I'm not an electrician, for heaven's sake. You turn the switch and it activates some doohickey and the doohickey feeds electricity into the whatchamacallit and the light comes on. It doesn't matter to me so long as it works."

"Precisely."

"Precisely what?"

Arthur sat in his throne, looking bizarrely incongruous in his three-piece suit. "This little home-away-from-home of mine is something that Merlin arranged for me. Someplace to which I can return at night and feel that I belong, after spending a day feeling like a living anachronism. Which is how I do feel, despite my best efforts to acclimate to this odd little civilization of yours. Merlin was quite pleased when he put this together. He even tried to explain it to me—something about transdimensional bridges and relative dimensions in space and other nonsense. And I said to him about New Camelot exactly what you say to me about electric lights—who cares as long as it works?''

"But Arthur, you don't understand!"

"Odd, that's just what Merlin said."

"Electricity and lights—that's all science. This is . . ." She waved her hands around helplessly. "This is magic!"

"Now, Gwen, magic is just another science. And if scientists acknowledged that magic existed and put their considerable talents to discovering what made it tick, a great deal more could be accomplished in this world. But scientists have decided that magic does not and cannot exist, so naturally they don't go out of their way to try and find the reasons for it." He shook his head. "Very shortsighted on their part."

Gwen put her hand to her head and sat down. "Arthur, you don't seem to realize that I'm a rational human being. I don't believe in magic. I don't believe in things just appearing because you need them."

"Oh no?"

"No."

"That chair you're sitting in? It wasn't there a moment ago."

She sprang from the chair as if propelled by springs. Her

hands fluttered to her mouth and her voice was a combination of surprise and hysterical laughter. "This is crazy!"

"Why?"

"Because I was always taught to be a very rational person!"

"Faugh! Rationality always gets in the way of common sense. Common sense tells you that no other explanation is possible for what you see. But when you try to rationalize the unexplainable, you run into problems."

She was delicately tapping the arms of the chair as Arthur said in a softer voice, "Like us."

She looked over to him and saw the way he was looking at her. She felt her cheeks color and looked down. She couldn't remember the last time she'd blushed.

"Arthur." She looked up at him tentatively. "Arthur . . . are you really him? I mean, the original King Arthur?"

"Yes."

"But . . . but it's so difficult to believe."

"Ah-ah," and he put up a finger. "You're rationalizing again. Didn't I tell you how that gets in the way?"

"But if I believe what you're saying," and she walked slowly around the perimeter of the room, "then I would also have to accept the part about my being a reincarnation of your Queen Guin . . ." Her voice trailed off and her eyes widened in surprise. "You know, Arthur, my name—Gwen DeVere—that sounds a lot like Guinevere, doesn't it?"

"By Jove, you're right!" He sagged back in the throne. "Fancy that."

They smiled at one another, and then Arthur stepped off his throne and walked slowly toward Gwen. She stood there, her arms hanging loosely at her sides. He came very close to her, then paused and ran his hand gently across her face. She closed her eyes and sighed, and a little tremble rushed through her.

"Arthur . . . we were married once, weren't we?"

He shook his head. "No. We were married always."

"But I hardly know you."

"You've always known me," he said softly. "We have always been. We shall always be. Not time, not distance, not lifetimes can do more than momentarily interrupt the coexistence we are meant to share."

He felt the softness of her hair, and she said, "Arthur?"

"Yes?"

"Have you really been locked in a cave for fifteen hundred years?"

"Thereabouts, yes."

She whistled. "You must be the horniest bastard on the face of the earth."

The expression on his face did not change, but he said, "Gwen, would you mind waiting here a moment?"

"Uh . . . sure."

Arthur stepped back and went into another room. She pricked up her ears and heard the sound of pages turning. She realized abruptly that he was consulting a dictionary, and stifled a desperate urge to giggle. There was a momentary pause in the page turning, and then she heard the book close. She fought to keep a straight face but felt the sides of her mouth turning up involuntarily.

Arthur came back into the room and faced her, looking deadly serious. "Gwen," he said with great solemnity.

"Yes, Arthur?"

"You're right."

They both dissolved into laughter.

Dinner was very quiet, but then, they felt no need to talk. There was the easy comfort in each other's presence that it takes most couples years to achieve, if they ever do.

When dinner was finished and the bones of the bird they had eaten were all that remained (and that would naturally be gone in the morning), there was a long pause. Then Gwen said softly, "Good night, Arthur."

He inclined his head. "Good night, Gwen."

She stood and left the table, leaving Arthur at the table, lost in thought.

Arthur lay in bed that night, alone, as he had been all the previous nights. He slid his hand slowly across the empty side of the bed and sighed deep in his chest, deep in his soul.

He heard a footfall at his door and sat bolt upright, his hand already reaching for Excalibur. The door swung open and Gwen was there. Candlelight from the hallway illuminated her from the back, showing the silhouette of her body through her white shift.

His breath caught as she said in a low voice, "I don't think you'll be needing a weapon, Arthur. I'm unarmed."

She glided across the floor to him and sat down slowly in the empty part of the bed. Arthur touched her arm and felt an inner trembling. "Gwen, you don't have to. Not if you're not ready."

She laughed lightly. "According to you, I've been waiting for you for centuries . . . lived many past lives, but you were always my Mister Right. When has any girl had to wait as long for her perfect man as me?" She stroked his beard and asked, "Arthur? Am I . . . do I look as pretty to you as when you first knew me? Back in . . . in your days?"

His voice choking with emotion, he said, "You are as I have always loved you."

He took her to him.

Merlin snapped off his TV set. "Well," he murmured, "I don't have to see this part. I know where it's going now." He sighed. "Kings. Can't live with them, can't live without them."

Chaptre the Twelfth

It had now been close to two months since Arthur had first clung batlike to the statue of Father Duffy and began espousing his views. In that time interest had mounted as word spread throughout the city. Jimmy Breslin picked up on it, the wire services picked up on it from Breslin, and soon it became quite a cachet to have been present at one of Arthur's speeches. However, campaigns cannot be won solely through word of mouth, and so it was that the press was cordially invited one day to the cramped, busy offices of Arthur Penn at the Camelot Building, to officially meet the Independent candidate for mayor of New York City.

Chairs and a podium were set up. Wine and cheese were served, and the reporters milled around, trying to pump the office workers for information. The office workers merely smiled, having been primed not to say a word until after Arthur had had an opportunity to address the press. Eventually the reporters started interviewing each other. One of them bumped into a small boy, nattily dressed in white ducks and a blue blazer with a little anchor on the pocket.

"Hi, kid," he said heartily. "You look a little young to be in politics."

"And you look a little old to be a fool," retorted Merlin, pushing his way past to the cheese balls.

There was a rapping up at the podium. Percy Vale was

standing up front, and in a strong, proud voice, he said, "Gentlemen and ladies of the press, I would appreciate it if you could take your seats. I thank you all for coming, and I assure you that it will be well worth your while."

There was shuffling of the chairs while the TV camera crews stood to the sides of the podium, checking the lighting and their range. Percy paused a moment and then said, "As you know, Mr. Arthur Penn has been creating quite a stir throughout the city over the past months. His style has been referred to in the press as guerrilla politics. The truth of the matter, gentlemen, is that Mr. Penn has been so busy meeting the people, it's kind of slipped his mind that he should really be getting to work on the business of being elected mayor of this great city." There was a small ripple of laughter, and Percy continued, "And make no mistake, my friends, I guarantee that you will be looking at the next mayor of New York when I say that I would like to introduce you to Mr. Arthur Penn."

Percy stepped back from the podium as the once and future king made his way from the back of the room.

The reporters had met many a politician in their collective lives. They had seen all the types—the charismatic ones, the old-boy ones, the intellectual ones, the forthright, the sneaky, the slick, the snake-oil salesmen, and every permutation of human being in between.

And they had all had one thing in common: They all regarded the press as a necessary evil. Something that had to be lived with, tolerated, used and maneuvered.

But this Arthur . . . what was the name, Penn? This Arthur Penn, as he walked forward shaking their hands, squeezing their shoulders affectionately, as if they were old buddies, smiling a totally disarming smile . . . this guy actually seemed happy to see them.

He made it up to the podium, slapped Percy affectionately on the shoulder, and faced the press. He blinked repeatedly as the flashbulbs went off, looked around at the crowd facing him, and then saw Gwen standing in the back. He smiled to her and she smiled back, almost schoolgirlishly, as he said, "Thank you for coming, gentlemen and ladies of the press. As you will be able to tell from the kits you should all have, I am Arthur Penn. We've paid outrageous sums for the production of my biography and to have a photographer take a black-and-white photo of me that makes me look as attractive to female voters as possible. So I would greatly appreciate any attention you might pay them."

There were appreciative laughs, and he continued, "I've taken this opportunity to meet with you because I value your function very highly. I am hoping that you will be able to pass my message on to the wide voting public, since I have researched the matter very carefully. For me to speak personally with all of my potential voters would take at least five years, and I'm afraid that I have not been allotted that much time."

He paused a moment and smiled. "My friends, quite simply, I wish to be the next mayor of New York City. I will now take questions."

There was a moment of surprise, and then hands were raised. Arthur picked one at random. "Mr. Penn—"

"Call me Arthur, please."

The reporter blinked. "All right . . . will we still call you Arthur if you're elected mayor?"

"I should think 'your highness' would suffice."

In the back Gwen stifled a giggle and turned away.

The reporter smiled and said, "Arthur . . . that was a very short opening statement."

"I was always taught to regard brevity as a virtue."

"Mister . . . Arthur, I'd be very interested in your background."

"So would I. Feel free to read through the papers before you to see what sort of records my staff has fabricated." He pointed to another reporter. "Yes?"

Gwen's face bore an expression of complete awe. Arthur was keeping to what he'd once told her—he would not lie. Every question was being answered, and if it was about a potentially touchy aspect, he deadpanned the absolute truth and usually got an amused reaction from his audience. Remarkable. She glanced over and saw that Merlin was standing over in a corner, arms folded, nodding slowly whenever Arthur spoke.

The next reporter stood. "Arthur, I'd like to know how you stand on certain issues."

"Let's find out together," said Arthur.

"Prayer in school, for example."

Arthur shrugged. "You mean before a difficult examination?"

"No," said the reporter, unsure whether Arthur was joking

or not—a state most reporters would find themselves in during the months to come. "I mean organized prayer. . . ."

"Oh, of course! Organized prayer in the morning, that sort of thing. Well, I've never been one to stand in the way of how someone wishes to worship. However, I recall reading something in the Declara—no, the Constitution, isn't it? About separation of church and state. It would seem to me that prayer and church are usually equated, aren't they?" The reporter nodded, and Arthur smiled. "Well, that's it then. No prayer in schools . . ."

"But it's not that simple," said the reporter.

"Then it should be. What else would you like to know about?"

"Your stand on abortion?"

Arthur shuddered. "Terrible mess. None of my bloody business, though, what a woman does with her body."

"Are you in favor, then, of state money and government money going to fund abortions?"

"I imagine it's better than feeding the poor little buggers, isn't it, once they're born into unwanted and miserable situations?"

The reporters looked around at each other. One of them whistled silently.

"Are you concerned, sir, that some pro-lifers may find your attitude, well . . . callous? That you're sentencing unborn children to death?"

Arthur regarded him oddly. "I have seen more death, son, than you could possibly imagine. Not to become maudlin, but I value life no less than anyone else. But life is difficult enough when you come into it wrapped in the arms of a mother who wants you. Coming into it unwanted is more than any helpless infant should have to bear." His eyes misted over. "I remember a time . . . unwanted children left exposed upon a hillside. Or women bleeding from their bellies, thanks to the tender mercies of charlatans pretending to be doctors. At a time such as that we prayed for the knowledge to prevent such monstrosities and outrages. Now we have it, and it would be equally as monstrous not to use it. Yes, money to help those unfortunate women. And money also to educate them so as not to let themselves become with child in the first place. And men, too, for God's sake. We don't have thousands of madonnas being impregnated immaculately out there, you know."

"You are aware," said one reporter with a half-smile, "that some of your attitudes may be regarded as controversial."

"Yes. I suppose so. Common sense usually is." He pointed to another reporter. "Yes?"

"Your stand on Westway, sir?"

Arthur looked at him blankly. "What way?"

"Westway."

"I haven't the foggiest. What the devil's that?"

"I'm surprised, sir," said the reporter insouciantly, "that you're not familiar with some of the more controversial aspects of New York politics."

"Don't be," said Arthur, ignoring his tone. "Why don't you apprise me?"

"Well, sir, the debate in a nutshell is whether to use certain monies for construction of a major traffic artery called Westway or whether to use that same money to improve the subways and mass transit. It was supposed to have all been settled a couple of years ago, but somehow the issue keeps coming up."

"Oh, anything that will improve the subways sounds smashing to me."

"Then you're against Westway?"

Arthur sighed. "Good God, you lot are slow, aren't you? Yes, I suppose I am."

"Are you aware of the other aspects—"

"Of course I'm not," said Arthur with no trace of impatience. "Is your basic summation of the situation accurate?"

The reporter looked around at his colleagues, in a total quandary. The others half shrugged or nodded.

"Um, yes, I believe it is."

"Well, that's it then. First thing you'll have to learn about me," said Arthur reasonably, leaning over the podium. "I never want to get bogged down with facts. Facts get in the way of decisions. Give me a basic summary of the situation and I will generally decide," and he tapped his chest, "based on what I feel here. I would wager that others will bog themselves down with umpteen reports and countless charts and the like, and it will all still boil down to the basic feeling of what's right and what's wrong." He smiled. "After all, it beats trial by combat."

Arthur, Gwen, Merlin, Percy, Chico, and Groucho sat

draped around various parts of the office. Merlin sat upright and cross-legged while the others were fairly at ease. Chico was stirring a Bloody Mary with his finger. The others were drinking soda or iced tea.

The reporters had left some time ago to file their stories, and everyone in the room seemed concerned about what would be said . . . everyone except Merlin and Arthur.

"I did my best," said Arthur reasonably. "If they don't like what I had to say, what am I supposed to do? Be sorry that I said it?" He shook his head. "No, they're going to have to warm to me or not, based on who I am."

Gwen smiled. "If they knew who you were, they'd vote for you in an instant."

"Would they?" asked Arthur. "Do you think so? My earlier endeavors hardly ended in glowing triumph, now did they?"

"Oh, people remember what they want to remember," said Gwen. She stood and walked over to Arthur's side, sitting on the arm of his chair. "After all is said and done, most people remember Camelot as a time of achievement and pride. I mean, the happiest times this country remembers were with Kennedy's whole Camelot thing."

"Ah!" declared Arthur. "Merlin said that to me once. Didn't you, Merlin? You see—the two of you do see eye to eye every now and again."

Merlin made a face. Then he said, "Arthur, I think it best that you spend the night—the next few nights, in fact—in that apartment you've got rented over in the Village."

"Oh, Merlin, is that really necessary?" said Arthur unhappily. "It's so bloody small. The castle is really so much better."

"Arthur, try to be reasonable. It wouldn't be good form for the press to discover that the Independent mayoral candidate makes his home in a pile of transdimensional rocks in Central Park."

Groucho perked up slightly and said, "Sounds okeedokee to me."

"Proof enough," said Merlin tartly. "Arthur, it's been set up for you, and I suggest that you try to make use of it. If all goes well, the press is going to become intensely interested in such minutiae as how you like to have your English muffins for breakfast. And if you have mysterious comings and goings, it could prompt digging in areas we'd much rather leave undug."

"All right, all right," sighed Arthur. "Gwen, let's go."

"He's going to have a roommate!" yelled Merlin. "That's just ruddy wonderful!"

Arthur's tone was warning. "Merlin . . ."

But a gentle touch rested on his arm. "No, Arthur, Merlin's right," said Gwen reasonably. "Your style is going to be somewhat . . . unorthodox for a number of voters. Perhaps we shouldn't try to drop too much on them right away. I'll find someplace."

"Merlin, could you find her someplace inexpensive? In Manhattan?"

"What?" Merlin laughed in disbelief. "Arthur, I'm a magician, not a god. Do you know what *your* place is running you?"

"She could bunk in with us," offered Chico.

Gwen looked at them. "Oh. How . . . nice," she said, with as much enthusiasm as she could muster.

"Yeah! You could have Harpo's piece of dirt. Who knows when he's coming back?"

"*I* certainly don't." She smiled. "Thanks all for your concern, but I have a friend I can stay with out in Queens until I find a place of my own." She shook her head in wonderment. "You know, I've never had that. When I went into college I went from living with my parents to living in a dorm. And from there I went to living with Lance."

"Lance?" Percy Vale looked up.

Arthur shook his head. "No relation."

"So I'll finally be out on my own. It's scary." She looked thoughtful. "Poor Lance."

"Why poor Lance?" asked Percy. Arthur leaned forward, curious to hear her response.

"Why, because the more I've thought about it, the more I've come to realize that he needed me a hell of a lot more than I needed him. He was just determined that I not know that. I think my being on my own is going to be a lot harder on Lance than it will be on me."

Arthur's mouth twitched. "My heart bleeds for him." He lifted his glass.

Lance leaned against the wall of the building to keep himself from toppling over. He felt the solid brick wall waver under his fingertips for a moment before righting itself, then he breathed a sigh of relief that it had sorted itself out before falling.

It was night, starless. The full moon was blood red—it would have tinted the clouds, had there been any clouds. Up on Eighth Avenue this late at night there were only a few cars heading uptown. Most people drove through that area with their car doors locked tight. Drivers would glance disdainfully at the human refuse that lined the streets. Lance was one of those receiving the disdainful glances.

He sank slowly to the ground and smiled, incredibly happy. Lance had certain images of himself that he felt constrained to live up to. Once that image had been of Suffering Writer. To that end he'd spent long hours churning out reams of garbage, comprehensible only to himself (oh, Gwen had pretended to like them, but he knew better). He had starved himself, refused to go out in the daylight if he could help it. When he did feel the need for sexual release, he'd found hookers with hearts of gold to whom he could vent his creative spleen, not to mention his pent-up urges. For naturally, as with any good tortured writer, he had a woman who did not understand him and wanted him to get a regular nine-to-five job. (Whether Lance's reality bore any resemblance to reality, is utterly irrelevant.)

When Gwen had walked out on him, it had permitted him to shift over to a new persona—Utterly Dejected Writer at the End of his Rope. He looked at his distorted reflection in a puddle of water and was overjoyed at what he saw. He was strung out. Dead-ended. Down and out. Ruined by the complete collapse of his one true love's confidence in him, he had now attained that point where he could die alone, unloved and misunderstood in the gutter of New York. Then some students or somesuch, cleaning out his papers, would discover the heretofore undiscovered brilliance of Lance Benson and make it public. He'd be published by some university press somewhere and become a runaway hit. He smirked. And he'd be dead. They'd want more of his brilliance, and he'd be dead as a doornail. That would sure show them!

The clack-clack of the heels had been sounding along the street for some time, but Lance had taken no notice of them. Now, though, he could not help it. The heels had stopped right in front of him. Stiletto heels supporting thigh-high black leather boots which were laced up the front.

Slowly Lance looked up. The woman before him was dressed entirely in black leather. Her clothes looked as if they'd been spray painted on. The only part of her body that was not covered were the fingers, projecting through five holes cut in each glove. She wore a black beret on her head, which blended perfectly with her black hair. (Once the hair had had streaks of gray in it. Now there was not the slightest trace.)

Her lipstick and mascara were black as well. They floated against the alabaster of her skin.

"Hi," she said. Her voice was low and sultry. "Nice night."

"If you like the night," he said indifferently, and looked down.

"Oh, yes. Yes indeed, I love the night." Her voice dropped to a whisper. "What's your name?"

"Lance."

"Lance." She rolled the name around on her tongue, making it sound like a three-syllable name. "Lance, you look very lonely. Would you like to have a good time?"

He laughed hoarsely. "Yeah, sure. But my idea of a good time and your idea of a good time probably don't jibe."

"Oh, really?"

"Yeah, really. My idea of a good time is sitting here and watching my life pass before my eyes as I prepare to die."

"Oh, you're right," said the woman. "You're very right." She shook her head. "That's not my idea of a good time at all. Tell you what—why don't I show you my idea of a good time? If that doesn't do it for you, then we'll bring you back here and you can continue your little headlong drive to self-destruction. How does that strike you?"

Lance shrugged. "Whatever makes you happy. I don't much care." He got to his feet, and the woman took his hand. He hobbled at first, since his right leg had fallen asleep. "So where are we going?"

"My place," she said. She wrapped her fingers in between his, and he shuddered. Her hand was cold, and he told her so. She nodded her head slightly in acknowledgment. "Yes, I know. My body temperature is perpetually ninety-one degrees. But don't worry," and she licked her lips slowly, "I can warm up quite nicely."

Abruptly Lance dug into his pocket. "I don't have any money, really," he said.

She waved a hand airily. "Don't worry about it. Think of it as a freebie, Lance. I'm sure you'll be able to do something for me."

His spirit brightened for the first time since Gwen had left him some time ago. "Gee, thanks. You know, I don't even have your name."

"Morgan," he was told.

He nodded. "Morgan? Isn't that a man's name?"

She smiled. "Only if you're a man. But I happen to be a woman, my dear Lance. More woman, I would suspect, than you would even believe you could possibly handle."

"Oh," said Lance uncertainly, and then smiled with grim determination. "Well, I guess I'll just have to do my best."

"Oh, yes, Lance," said Morgan. "I know you will, I just know it."

Chaptre the Thirteenth

It was well into spring when the first of the commercial spots was aired.

Percy Vale, hunched over his ledgers in the offices of Arthur Penn, the checkbook and bank balances spread out nearby, had the television set on in the background. Campaign workers sat around stuffing envelopes and sealing them, or canvassing telephone books and comparing names to lists provided by the League of Women Voters, to see if they could encourage those not already registered to do so.

The portable color Sony had Kermit the Frog on the screen, and that charming amphibian disappeared to be replaced by the smiling visage of Arthur Penn.

Someone called out, "Here it is! Here it is again."

Most people reacted only casually. They had, after all, seen it before. Still, Percy put down his work momentarily to watch. Arthur's commercial had been shot in an empty studio, the only prop on the set being a stool. Arthur was leaning against it, gazing out at the viewer with that easy familiarity of his.

"Hello," he said pleasantly. "I'm Arthur Penn. I want to be the next mayor of New York City. Vote for me. Thank you."

The screen then went to black, and Gwen's voice, sounding

very sultry, said "Paid for by the Arthur Penn for Mayor Committee."

Percy smiled and returned to his work. He remembered when Arthur had first presented the script for the commercial to all and sundry. There had been a long moment of skeptical silence, but Arthur had remained firm, despite the swell of subsequent protest and disbelief. As the primaries had approached, Arthur had studied the commercials of other candidates very carefully. His decision was to try and find a different angle. Once he had eliminated the Meet the People Approach, the Photographed in Front of a Recognizable Monument approach, the Meet My Family Aren't We Wholesome approach, the Hard Hitting Tough Talker approach, and the My Opponent is a Cheating Son-of-a-Bitch approach, that had left him with exactly one option.

"But Arthur," Percy remembered himself complaining. "All that's going to happen is that people will see your commercial and wonder, 'Yeah, but why should I vote for him?' "

"Precisely!" Arthur had said delightedly. "The beauty of this commercial is that it's only ten seconds long. So we can afford—what is it called? Saturation, that's it. And we'll get people curious. People like to be tested, to be challenged. Every politician sounds like every other politician. As far as I'm concerned, people are no different now than they were centuries ago. Before you can accomplish anything, you have to get their attention. And frequently the best way to get their attention is to hit them on the nose with a rolled-up newspaper." He grinned. "My entire campaign is directed toward hitting them with that newspaper. To a large extent what I say is irrelevant, as long as it's making people"—he tapped his temple with his forefinger,—"think! No one thinks anymore. Well, my friends, this campaign is not going to lay things out in nice easy packages."

That's for sure, Percy thought to himself. He shook his head. This whole campaign was hardly an easy package. As the treasurer of the Arthur Penn for Mayor Committee, he had his work cut out for him.

Merlin had certainly done his groundwork, paving the way for Arthur's return. That much was certain. An entire fictive history of Arthur being silent partner in a number of wealthy businesses had given credence to Arthur's personal fortune. The actual origin of the fortune was unknown to Percy,

although he had a suspicion that if someone happened to
stumble over the pot at the end of the rainbow, they might
now find it empty. Merlin had a knack for making things
happen. That same fictive history had supported Arthur's bid
for the mayoralty. Coming from outside of politics, he could
claim no prior party obligations. Coming (ostensibly) from a
background in business, he could claim that he had a businessman's sense of running things, and that was what New York
City needed. Someone who knew how to eliminate waste, to
maximize profits. In short, to run New York City like the
profit-making center it should and could be.

It all sounded great. Percy just hoped that Arthur could pull
it off. And he hoped that no one tumbled wise to the whole
setup. Percy wasn't sure, but he had a feeling you could go to
jail for being the treasurer of an organization backing a candidate for mayor who had supposedly died over a dozen centuries ago.

Moe Dredd, his middle swathed in a white towel, sat back in
the steam room of his favorite health club. He could feel his
pores opening, his skin breathing in the healthful mists around
him. Sweat beaded his forehead, slicked his back and upper
arms. His hands rested comfortably on his lap.

The door to the steam room opened. Moe looked over with
half-closed eyes and dimly made out a figure through the
steam. "Is that you, Cordoba?" he called out.

There was a pause, and then a voice called back, "No. It's
me, Arthur."

Moe shrunk back against the wall as Arthur stepped out of
the fog, smiling pleasantly. He wore a towel as well, except
that it was wrapped around him like a toga. And it was purple.

"You wouldn't by any chance be referring to Ronnie Cordoba, would you, Moe?" asked Arthur with what sounded
like only mild interest. "The old racquetball companion of
your leash holder, Bernie Bittberg? You might be interested to
know that, with the primary only a month away, old Ronnie
has joined my team. Seems he has a flair for public relations
and Bernie was attempting to funnel it into the standard chan-
nels. So Ronnie came over to us. We're a good deal more flexible."

He sat down next to Moe and patted him on the back. Moe
recoiled from his touch.

"So," said Arthur, "this is our first opportunity to really talk. So tell me—how are you doing, you little bastard?"

"Mister, um, Mr. Penn, I don't see—"

Arthur raised a preemptory hand. "Don't. Don't even try to lie to me. It's foolishness. I know who you really are. Honestly, with the perversity with which fate names the players in our little drama, it would be a minor miracle if I didn't know you." He sighed and shook his head. "I thought we'd seen the last of each other on the field of battle, Modred, those many centuries ago. And before you try to protest again, I must re-emphasize that I know who you are, and I know that you know who you are. I have every confidence that my half sister, your mother, discovered you reincarnated in this"—he glanced down,—"less than impressive form."

"Well, I like that," huffed Moe Dredd.

"Just as I," continued Arthur, as if Moe had not said anything, "rediscovered Jenny, and Merlin found Percival."

"Ah, yes," said Moe Dredd disdainfully. "Gwen DeVere, the president of your reelection committee—an appointment that came as no surprise to anyone, I assume."

"Not to anyone who knows Gwen and knows what she's capable of."

Moe wiped the sweat from his eyebrows as they began to drip into his eyes. "That's not half as funny as putting an alcoholic in as your treasurer."

"Percy is not an alcoholic anymore," said Arthur evenly.

"Once a drunk, always a drunk," said Moe. "Even a drunk will tell you that."

"Perhaps. But I'm willing to give people a chance, despite their character flaws. Just as I'm willing to give you a chance."

"What?"

"You may not recall, Modred, but on that last day, when I received the wound that nearly killed me—and indeed, the day you were killed—you claimed you were willing to make a peaceful settlement with me. Suddenly, at the last moment, a poison adder appeared from nowhere and laid me low. My men, not seeing the snake, thought you had betrayed me, so they attacked. And that was the finish of us all."

He leaned toward Moe. "The thing I've always puzzled over, and the thing to which I doubt I'll ever get an answer, is my question of whether you arranged for that poisoned snake yourself, or whether you were actually willing to negotiate for peace. On that basis, Modred, my reincarnated bastard son, I offer you a place within my organization. Because I want to be able to trust you.''

Modred stared at him. Then he stood, said, "I'm sorry, I can't. I just can't," and left quickly.

Arthur could have gone after him. If he had, things might have turned out differently. If he had, he might have actually become allies with Modred, instead of ending up facing his son in battle several months later. But he didn't. He let Modred go, electing to stare into the steam, and so the future was allowed to run its course, which was remarkably similar to the past.

Gwen stood in front of the door to her former apartment, listening carefully for some sound of movement. There was none.

It had been a rainy summer day, and Gwen pulled her raincoat more tightly around her. She tossed her head, smoothing out the damp strawberry-blond hair which she had permitted to grow to shoulder length because that was the way He liked it. She smiled mirthlessly to herself. Lance had always insisted that she keep it short. She wondered what he would say now.

She wondered for the umpteenth time if she should have told Arthur she was coming back to her former home to finally reclaim items she'd abandoned when he'd carried her away. How long had it been? she wondered. She couldn't quite recall, for the past months had been idyllic. Although Arthur had been residing in his more traditional-style apartment, he and Gwen had found many an evening to sneak off to the castle and have, as Arthur referred to it, a dalliance.

In addition her self-respect had shot up a hundredfold when she'd been voted president of Arthur's election committee. Merlin had pitched a holy fit on that score, but it had been fair and square. Everyone who worked with Arthur had come to genuinely like Gwen, and she'd blossomed under the appreciation to become a hard-working, quick thinking, aggressive woman—the woman she'd always had the potential to be, until Lance had smothered it. But he could only smother it for as long as he was an influence on her. And now that influence had been broken.

And yet . . . and yet . . .

She was back. Because she'd left behind books, clothing, and other personal possessions. But mostly because she had left behind a part of herself. And she wanted to reclaim it, clear up the "unfinished business" between herself and Lance. Last time she'd left, she had been swept up and saved by her shining knight (and what a warm feeling just thinking of that moment gave her). This time she wanted to walk out on her own, head held high. It was what she knew she needed.

So why, with all that, did she feel a mixture of disappointment and relief that Lance might not be home? That her big confrontation would not occur? She didn't know, but rather than stand in the hallway and procrastinate any longer, she reached into her purse and pulled out her keys.

It didn't occur to her until that moment that Lance might have changed the lock. Fortunately he hadn't. She opened the door and stepped into the apartment.

A woman was lying on the couch, waiting for her.

Gwen's breath caught in surprise, and she glanced at the door to make sure that she had the right apartment.

"Oh, yes," said the woman. "You have the right place. Come in, Gwen, come in."

Gwen walked in slowly, cautiously, the hair on the back of her neck prickling. The apartment was dark, illuminated only by the hazy glow of the television set which faced the couch. "Do I, um, know you?"

The glare from the television played odd light images off the woman's angular face,—flickering, giving her a look of non-substance. She was wearing a long black gown with a low-cut front which displayed a generous amount of cleavage. Again Gwen said slowly, "I don't know you . . . do I?"

"From another time," said the woman slowly. "Another life. However, I won't take it as a personal affront that you don't recall me. My name is Morgan."

Gwen blinked. "Morgan. Morgan . . . Le Fey?"

Morgan inclined her head graciously.

"Arthur's sister?"

"Half sister, if you please, my child."

"I . . . I thought you were dead. A long time ago." Gwen felt a weakening in her knees, and she rested one hand against the wall to support herself. She saw the look in Morgan's eye when Arthur was mentioned, and for the first time that she could ever recall, she actually feared for her life. She wanted to run screaming from the apartment, but some instinct warned her that backing down from Morgan now would most certainly mean her end.

Morgan shrugged. "That is what was believed. Of me. Of Arthur. Of Merlin. But it's difficult to extinguish pure good . . . or pure evil." She laughed. "Tell me, Gwen . . . do I look evil?"

"I'm not . . . no. That is . . . I'm not sure."

"Looks can be deceiving," said Morgan pleasantly. "I'll tell you a secret, my child—good, evil, it's all subjective. No one really knows what good and evil is, except that those in charge invariably judge themselves good, and those who are not are judged evil by those who have judged themselves good. Do you see? And if I were in charge, I would be able to label as evil the actions of those whom I did not like, and I would be considered good. And who would there be to say me nay?" She gestured for Gwen to come toward her. "I have something to show you."

But Gwen didn't move from the wall. "Why haven't you then? Tried to put yourself in charge, I mean?"

Morgan smiled. "Oh, my darling, if you could only have seen what I've seen all these centuries. When Arthur was first locked away in that cavern, after his near-fatal wound in battle, I could scarcely believe my good fortune. Arthur was gone. Merlin was already long gone. The world was easy pickings for me, or so I thought.

"The problem was, I had spent much of my life's work on Arthur's destruction. It had become such an obsession for me that, once he was out of the way, I found myself then facing the rest of the world. It was, to put it mildly, daunting."

She sat up, tucking her long legs under her. She patted the couch next to her, but Gwen still kept her distance. Morgan shrugged. "Oh, I had my followers. I had demons upon whom I could call for assistance. But many of these were susceptible to cold steel—very susceptible. In any sort of pitched battle my forces would have been slaughtered, and not all my magicks could have prevented it. So I appeared at courts, but my name and image were already well-known. Many kings and landowners would not even let me in to their homes, and those who did, did so only under feeling of obligation to their departed liege, Arthur. And they kept quite a close eye on me, I can assure you.

"So I became a wanderer, plotting as I wandered how I could possibly, as you said, assume the power that I sought. My wanderings led me to some incredible discoveries . . . the infinite prolongation of life, for one. Astral projection, a feat that had been beyond me during Arthur's lifetime. And the most depressing discovery of all—that time was against me. The world was growing, my pet. Beyond my meager ability to control it."

She got up from the sofa, then, with a little huff of impatience, and walked over to Gwen. She stroked Gwen's cheek gently, and Gwen shivered with horror at the coldness of the woman's touch.

"Oh, I kept my hand in, of course. At the time I was very embittered, you see. I had been given a world that was free of Arthur and Merlin, and yet that world had not become the easy pickings I thought it would be. I admit I had considered no further than what would happen once those two blights were gone. Once they were, I had nothing. So I vented my frustration. I like to think I cut my own swath through history. A plague here, a disaster there. A normal man who inexplicably begins slaughtering helpless innocents. A demon cult arising, performing ritual sacrifices. Fortunes lost, lives destroyed." She shook her head. "But one can only have random fun for so long before it begins to pall on you.

"And finally, after uncounted years, my anger began to turn to a sense of helplessness. Inflicting misery on others can only bring happiness for a time. And the unspeakable happened—I started to reminisce for the good old days. The days when my goals were clear-cut. Destroy Arthur. Destroy Merlin. Thwart their horrendously humanitarian intentions, bollix their plans at every turn. Bring about the downfall of everything my accursed half brother held dear. Those were pleasant times, and I wanted them back.

"So I waited. Oh, I could have set Merlin or Arthur free, I suppose. But that would have destroyed the spontaneity. Besides, knowing those two, they would have gone back into seclusion, contending that they would come out when they were damned ready."

"So I became a sentinel. Keeping vigil. Waiting for the time when they would leave or escape their imprisonment, and the battle for supremacy could begin anew. But century after century passed, and I began to despair of their ever returning.''

She turned away from Gwen and folded her arms. ''A year ago, my sweet, you could not have recognized me. I shudder when I think of what I became. But it's all behind me now.''

There was a long silence, and Gwen swallowed. ''Where's Lance?''

Morgan faced her, a wolfish smile on her face. My God, she looks like Arthur, thought Gwen.

''I was wondering when you would ask that. Come here, my sweet. Come and see.''

Slowly, haltingly, Gwen walked to the television set and looked on the screen. Her hands flew to her mouth to stifle a scream.

Lance was on the TV. He was naked, chained and spread-eagled against what appeared to be the wall of a dungeon. His head lolled against his chest.

The image was there for a moment only, before the screen abruptly went blank, but it had seared itself into Gwen's mind. She spun on Morgan, her fists clenched. ''Why?''

''Because,'' said Morgan easily, ''I want Excalibur.''

Gwen stepped back, aghast. ''I . . . I don't know what—''

Morgan raised a cautioning finger. ''Now, now, love—don't try lying to someone who is infinitely your superior when it comes to lying. You know Excalibur. Where does Arthur keep it?''

''With him. All the time.''

''*All* the time?''

Gwen blinked a moment, not understanding, and then she colored. ''You mean, like when we're—''

''That's right.''

''Oh, no. No, I couldn't.''

Morgan crossed to her quickly and grabbed her by the wrist. Her pleasant demeanor disappeared as she spat out, ''Then your precious Lance dies.''

Their gazes locked, and then Gwen said as levelly as she could, ''So kill him.''

Morgan released her in surprise. ''What?''

Gwen flounced across the room, her stomach churning as she said, ''Kill the bastard if you want. It doesn't matter to me.''

Morgan smiled then, that same wolfish smile. ''Very good.

Oh, that's very good. I wasn't expecting that." She started to walk toward the door. "Very well, my queen. As you wish. Lance is as good as dead."

She got to the door, opened it, and then Gwen came up behind her and slammed it shut before she could exit. Morgan turned, and the two women faced each other, glaring.

"You kill him," said Gwen slowly, "and Arthur will hunt you down and kill you."

"Are you sure?" said Morgan quietly. "There's no love lost between Arthur and your former beau. Are you willing to gamble Lance's life that that threat will keep me in line—particularly since I believe it to be without substance?"

They stood there for a long moment, neither moving, neither willing to bend an inch in will or spirit. Then Morgan said, "Lance has spoken of you recently. I must say he's taking being chained up very well." Morgan walked back into the room with a jaunty little bounce to her step. "When I told him I'd be seeing you, he asked me to ask you for forgiveness. If you must know, his exact words were, 'Tell her not to worry about me. Whatever happens, I deserve it.' "

Gwen's features crumbled momentarily, but she managed to quickly compose herself. "Look, Morgan," she said, trying to sound reasonable, "even if I waited until after Arthur and I had . . . you know . . . and tried to get away with his sword, it would never work. He's so attuned to it that the moment I lay a finger on Excalibur he'd snap awake and want to know what the hell I was doing."

Morgan regarded her, her eyebrows arched, and said, "You may be right, my love. Very well then. I believe we can hit upon a compromise, if you are amenable. Provide a minor distraction for me, and I in turn will release your precious Lance as soon as the deed is done."

"He's not my precious Lance," said Gwen tautly. "I have no feeling left for him. I—I can't allow an innocent to be injured as a result of all this. And I want you to know that what you're doing is despicable."

"Yes," agreed Morgan. "It's nice to know I haven't lost my touch. Now here, my darling, is what I want you to do. . . ."

Lance slowly raised his head as he sensed her nearness.

Morgan smiled at him, standing several feet away. Lance pulled against his chains, then, his hands flexing frantically as he said, "Morgan! Oh, please, no, not again!"

She nodded slowly, smiling. She reached behind her back as she said, "I just saw a friend of yours."

"Friend?"

"Yes. Barely an hour ago." Her hand made some motion and her black gown dropped to the floor. She stood naked before him. "Your friend was very concerned about you."

"Morgan, please! I'm telling you, I can't. . . ."

She pressed her body against his. The smell of her was intoxicating to him, and he trembled even as, much to his shock, he felt himself becoming aroused again.

"Didn't think you could again, eh?" said Morgan, nibbling at the base of his neck. "You might be interested to know, your friend wants me to let you go."

Lance moaned. "No! Please don't! Please don't let me go. Morgan, please . . ."

"Hush, my love." She placed a finger against his lips. "No need to worry. Morgan is going to take care of everything." She ran her fingers along the length of his body, and drifted toward his groin. "Everything . . ." she said languorously.

Chaptre the Fourteenth

The renovated storefront now had a huge banner draped across it, reading ARTHUR PENN FOR MAYOR HEADQUARTERS. Situated several blocks away from Arthur's main office in the Camelot Building, the move had been made due to space needs, not to mention higher visibility. Arthur and company now had 1200 square feet, and although at first that seemed like a staggeringly large amount of room, it had become filled up pretty quickly.

Arthur had laughed the first time he saw campaign posters with his picture plastered on them at bigger-than-life size. Below his picture was the tag line, *Arthur Penn—Common Sense.* Over the months Arthur's prevailing attitude of "Don't bother me with countless facts, they only get in the way of making decisions" had become fashionable. Arthur had rapidly become a candidate with broad appeal. His no-nonsense attitude was refreshing, and his self-possession came across superbly both in person and on camera.

It was eight A.M. now, and he sat hunched with Ronnie Cordoba, a list of meetings and appearances between them. Arthur was shaking his head in despair. "Are these all really necessary, Ronnie?" he was asking. "Why can't I just continue as I have been?"

"Because you need more concentrated media exposure," Ronnie was saying. He leaned back in the creaking wooden chair. "Your earlier tactics were fine, Arthur, in terms of basic introduction. But the Democratic and Republican primaries are just around the corner, and the election only two months after that. We're just kicking into high gear now."

"*Just* kicking into high gear? Ronnie, look at this schedule." He slapped the piece of paper. "Appearing in front of groups I've never heard of to discuss subjects I know nothing about."

"It would help if you had a speech writer and standardized talks," said Ronnie reasonably.

Arthur stood and hooked his thumbs into his vest. "Now we've been all through this. I don't want to hire somebody to write for me what I'm going to say."

"But everyone else does!" complained Ronnie.

"Yes, and they all sound homogenized—that's the word, isn't it? Gwen used it the other day."

"Where is Gwen anyway?" asked Ronnie.

Arthur shrugged. "She's had something on her mind the past few days. I've tried not to pressure her about it. I've generally discovered with women that it's not a good idea to try to make them talk when they don't want to. They'll generally come around."

Merlin walked in, dressed casually in jeans and a T-shirt. "Morning all," he said. "Percy's right behind me—he's stopping to get a bagel." He shook his head. "Fascinating thing, a bagel."

"Merlin, what do your folks think about your involvement in politics?" asked Ronnie. "I mean, are they going to make you cut back on your time when school starts?"

Merlin glanced at Ronnie, then back at Arthur. "Oh. That's right. We haven't told him, have we?"

Ronnie glanced around curiously. "Told me what?"

"About Merlin," said Arthur. "He's lived—"

"Alone," said Merlin quickly, shooting a poisonous look at Arthur. "Alone, for quite some time."

"Really? Merlin, do the authorities know?"

"Not if we don't tell them. Right, Ronnie?"

Ronnie looked at Arthur in confusion. "Arthur, are you sure we should have . . . well, a minor, as a part of this campaign?"

"I'd be lost without him," said Arthur simply.

"Besides, don't get yourself in an uproar, Ronnie," said

Merlin. "I'm living with someone now. Percy's moved in with me."

"What, there's room in your apartment?"

"Apartment? Oh, no. I have a house out on the Island. I commute."

"Oh," said Ronnie, nodding in understanding. "Long Island?"

"No. Bermuda."

Percy walked in carrying a small brown bag. "Morning, everyone." He cocked his head. "Ronnie, man, you okay? You look pale."

"Me? Naaah," said Ronnie. "Merlin, he was just kidding around with me, that's all."

"Oh, I see. You know, Ronnie, you've been workin' real hard. You should come out to Bermuda. Get some rest."

Ronnie nodded slowly, then leaned over the agenda for the day. "Ooookay. Arthur, most of this stuff is routine. You've got a women's group in the morning, senior citizens lunch, a citizen's watch group in the early afternoon, and then you're meeting with a group of Jewish community leaders in late afternoon. Then we've got the fund-raiser tonight—"

"Oh, right! I'm very upset about that, and I'm not going."

Merlin turned in surprise. "What are you talking about? Our money is starting to run low . . . you have to get more for your campaign fund. I can't continue to be the main funder for this race. . . ."

"There he goes again," said Ronnie. "Where did you get the money to back Arthur, eh, Merlin?"

"Stock market investments. I bought into IBM and Xerox back when they were still using abacuses and carbon paper, respectively. But Arthur, I don't understand. Why—"

"There are limits as to what I will do, Merlin. Gwen told me about this dinner tonight. She said I'd have to wear a monkey suit. Now if you think for one minute I'm going to dress like an ape simply to get votes, then, my little wizard, you have quite another think coming."

He sat there, arms folded resolutely, eyes smoldering. Ronnie and Percy looked at each other, trying not to snicker. Merlin rubbed the bridge of his nose with his fingers.

"Someone is going to have to talk to you, long and hard, about slang," he said.

*   *   *

The banquet hall was filled with men and women dressed formally, seated at large round tables, finishing their Chicken Kiev and assorted vegetables. And although the conversation at the tables was lively, attention kept returning to the long dais at the front of the room. There were seated Arthur, Gwen, Percy, and several known and respected celebrities in New York. For all of them it was their first lengthy meeting, and they found themselves, as always, charmed by Arthur's openness and frank manner of discussing issues.

Merlin was seated at a table close to the front. Arthur had wanted him to be at the dais but Merlin had deferred, observing that they didn't want or need endless speculation as to who the young boy seated with all the dignitaries was.

Seated in the middle was a former head of the United Nations General Assembly—a distinguished looking man who now stood and rapped his fork briskly on the side of his glass. Slowly, conversation throughout the room quieted. In the back of the room TV news cameras focussed.

"Ladies and gentlemen, I thank you all for coming this evening," he said. "I hope that you all enjoyed your dinners—usually these things seem to have meals made from Styrofoam." There was agreeing laughter. "However, trust to our host to be more concerned about the welfare of his patrons than that. As have many of you, I have been fascinated by Mr. Penn's rapid rise to the public awareness in the past months. As have you, I have found myself impressed by his straightforward thinking, his unflinching addressing of any problem. While other politicians seem to delight in straddling both sides of the fence, Arthur Penn is unafraid to speak his mind. To those people who agree with him, he is a sound ally. To those who disagree with him—well they respect him nevertheless and know, at least, that if Arthur Penn tells them something, it comes from the heart, and it's not going to be changed to cater to whims or political expediencies.

"Let me give you a little background on the Independent candidate for mayor of New York City . . ."

As he spoke, the waiters in the room, who had been scattered at random points throughout, slowly began to work their way forward. No one noticed it. Who pays attention to the movements of waiters?

Merlin felt a faint warning. He wasn't sure what it was— some bothersome feeling in the back of his head, like an angry gnat, letting him know that something was not quite right.

He looked around his table. The eleven other people seated with him seemed harmless enough, attentive enough. He looked at the other tables, but saw no cause there for alarm. So what was it? Where was it?

I have not, thought Merlin, lived this long without learning to trust to my instincts.

A movement caught the corner of his eye. One of the waiters had an odd look on his face, a look of great intentness. Merlin pursed his lips. He looked around and saw a half dozen other waiters, all with the same determined expression. No, something was definitely not right.

Merlin quietly slid the ashtray off the table. Miraculously, no one had smoked at his table—the glass of the ashtray was clear. Merlin reached into the pocket of his black jacket—his monkey-suit jacket, he thought grimly—and pulled out a small flask with blue liquid inside. With one small hand he uncorked it and poured the liquid into the ashtray. It spread rapidly, like a thing alive, coating the surface with blue. Moments later he held the ashtray up to his eye, peering through the blue filter of the liquid.

He gasped as he looked at the waiter nearby.

"And so, ladies and gentlemen, I give to you, Arthur Penn!"

Merlin's head snapped around. Arthur had risen behind the dais and was smiling out at this supporters. Merlin started to stand, to jump and shout to Arthur exactly what was surrounding them. Then he slowly sat again, unsure of how to warn Arthur without setting off a general panic. Or how not to sound insane.

Arthur leaned forward and said, "My friends . . ."

There was a low moan from his left. He looked around just in time to see Gwen, hand on forehead, eyes closed in a swoon, topple over backward.

"Gwen!" he shouted, and immediately moved to her. At the end of the table a noted attorney asked loudly, *"Is there a doctor here?"*

Eighteen doctors glanced at their watches and wondered if this might be a good time to leave.

Arthur knelt at Gwen's side, having already dabbed a napkin into a glass of ice water. He dabbed it across her face, saying urgently, "Gwen? Gwen, what's wrong?"

She opened her eyes. He saw no illness in them. Only fear.
"Gwen, what—"

There was a sudden tug at his hip.

He looked around to see a waiter behind him. The man's
face was narrow, almost satanic, as with a fierce certainty he
grabbed the invisible scabbard that hung at Arthur's side and
yanked. There was a rip as the scabbard came free and the
waiter leaped back, the invisible prize in his hands.

Arthur completely forgot about Gwen as he leaped toward
the waiter, who backpedaled furiously. The entire room was
now in an uproar. Everyone was demanding from each other
what the hell was going on, and no one knew. Men grabbed
for their wives, wives grabbed for their pocketbooks.

The waiter who'd grabbed Excalibur jumped down from the
dais and darted past Merlin's table. Hard on his heels came the
former King of the Britons.

"Arthur!" shouted Merlin, and he tossed the blue-stained
ashtray. Arthur caught it without breaking stride and shoved
it in his pocket, not having the faintest idea why Merlin had
blessed him with such an odd gift at this particular moment.
Just before he was out of earshot, Merlin shouted, *"Look
through it!"*

The half-dozen waiters had regrouped, and as one they ran
out the back of the room, through the swinging doors. Arthur
was right after them, and right behind them came the TV
camera crews, excited by the thought that what had seemed a
standard money-raising dinner had suddenly blossomed into a
potential lead item for the eleven o'clock news.

The waiters smashed through the kitchen, the holder of Excalibur in the lead. Cooks were pushed roughly out of the way
and kitchen utensils clattered onto the floor. Arthur did not
even take the time to mutter "Excuse me" as he shoved past.

There was a rolling cart of dishes off to the right. One of the
waiters paused momentarily, grabbed it, and toppled it. A resounding crash rang through the kitchen as miles of dishes
spilled out and shattered in Arthur's path. He vaulted, skid-
ding slightly when he alighted but recovering and continuing
the pursuit. The camera crews, on the other hand, were not so
lucky. They slid headlong into the mess of dirty dishes and
leftover food on the previously spotless floor and with a yell
went down, one atop the other.

Arthur burst out into the open air of the back alley. It took a moment for his eyes to readjust to the gloom of the night, and then he saw the bright red jackets of the waiters only yards away, dashing down the alley toward the street. Arthur gave chase, shucking his four-hundred-dollar dinner jacket and tossing it aside.

The waiters made it to the sidewalk and then did exactly what Arthur feared they would do—split up. Arthur felt a surge of panic. How was he supposed to follow the one with the invisible sword? Which one had it?

He felt a bulge in his pants pocket and remembered the ashtray. What had Merlin said? Look through it. He pulled out the ashtray and peered through the blueness.

He made an awful sound deep in his throat. He had spotted the waiter bearing Excalibur immediately—through the blue lens the sword became visible, even though it had not been drawn from its scabbard. But what horrified Arthur was the thing holding it.

It was covered completely with brown scales, its torso elongated so that it was hunched over. Its hands ended in three long, tapering claws. Its head was similar to an alligator's, except the snout was not quite as long. It turned its malevolent green eyes on Arthur and snarled a guttural warning through a double row of pointed teeth. However, it did look snappy in its red waiter's jacket and pressed black slacks.

It turned and faced Arthur, drawing Excalibur from the sheath. Arthur saw his sword glowing dimly in the evening light, and rather than fear, he felt rage that this . . . this thing was soiling his beloved sword with its foul hands.

Passersby who saw only an angry waiter, incensed perhaps because he'd been stiffed on a tip, nevertheless drew back in fright when they saw the immense sword he wielded.

Arthur approached cautiously, arms spread out, legs flexed, never taking his eyes from his opponent. He growled low in his throat as he inched closer and closer to the demon. Cars slammed to a halt on nearby Forty-seventh. Two small children, who lived in an apartment above a deli that had closed for the night, leaned out their window and watched in fascination.

The demon swung Excalibur in an arc and hissed, "Morgan Le Fey sends her regards, King of Nothing!" The demon slashed Excalibur down and Arthur dove to one side, rolling and quickly getting to his feet. The demon closed on him, swinging the blade back and forth. It whizzed through the air like an angry hornet, and Arthur could do nothing except stay the hell out of the way. He stumbled once and the demon almost caught him flatfooted. The demon swung Excalibur around, and Arthur leaped out of its path. The blade sliced through a parking meter, cutting it neatly in half at the middle of the pole.

Arthur backed up, looking around desperately for something to intervene. He heard a police car's siren, but it was a long way off, and besides, there was a chance that police would not be able to aid him against this nightmare creature.

"Afraid, Arthur?" crowed the demon. "You have a good head on your shoulders. Let's see if you can keep it there."

Arthur retreated farther, thankful at least that the bystanders had had the good sense to get away. Then his retreat was momentarily halted as he bumped into a large iron object behind him. His questing fingers immediately informed him he'd run up against a fire hydrant.

The demon was barely a yard away, and this time Arthur didn't flinch. "All right, you bastard," he snarled. "Give it your best shot."

With unearthly glee the demon brought Excalibur back over its head and then brought the blade swinging downward.

Arthur waited until the last possible instant, waited until the weight of Excalibur would make the sword's trajectory unalterable. And when it was bare inches from the top of his head, Arthur sprang catlike to one side. Excalibur sliced deep into the fire hydrant.

In a rage the demon yanked Excalibur to one side. The blade effortlessly cut through the rest of the hydrant, and with a sudden gush water blew forth from the broken hydrant. It sprayed upward and sideways. The demon was caught in the face and chest by the full impact of the water. With a howl it went down, clawing at the clean water that to the demon was like acid. Excalibur flew from its grasp and clattered to the ground.

Arthur was on the sword in an instant, and within the next was upon the demon. He held the sword at the creature's neck and snarled, "Give Morgan my thanks . . . should you see her on the way to hell."

Then he drew Excalibur back and rammed the point through the inhuman thing's throat. Its angry howl of anguish was cut short, and it clawed at the blade even as the life fled from it.

A hole appeared in the demon's chest. Arthur looked down in surprise as a small creature darted forth from the already disintegrating body of the demon. It flittered this way and that, leaving a trail of flame behind it. Arthur stared at it in wonder and muttered, "A fire elemental. Upon my sword, I thought I'd seen the last of—"

The elemental gingerly danced around the water droplets which sprayed from the fountain. Then it caught sight of Arthur, and it flared in alarm and anger. Arthur frowned, suddenly aware that this small creature intended no good at all. He yanked Excalibur from the demon's throat and in one smooth movement sliced upward at the fire creature. The little ball of flame avoided him, spun around his head so close that it singed his eyebrows, then headed straight for the building that housed the closed deli.

"No!" shouted Arthur, but it was too late. The elemental hit the building at full steam. There was a loud *fwoosh*, and it was as if the two-story building had been firebombed. The downstairs windows exploded as fire leaped out from them, illuminating the street in a nightmarish glow of orange. Smoke poured out from the shattered windows, both downstairs and upstairs.

And as Arthur's gaze took in the second floor, he was horrified to see two children in one of the windows. Moments ago they had been witnesses to Arthur's struggle with the demon. Now their eyes were riveted elsewhere—behind them, as they saw the room they were in engulfed in flame. The air crackled, became acrid with the biting sting of the smoke. The children screamed.

The police car was pulling up, but how long now before a fire truck could be summoned? And, Arthur looked around the area in horror, what would they hook up to? The hydrant had been slashed in half, thanks to his brilliant tactic.

Without hesitation Arthur stepped into the stream of water that gushed from the hydrant. The water soaked his clothes, his body, his hair. He glanced over to where the demon lay, and was pleased to see nothing but a small pile of soot where the creature had once been. That was convenient—he hadn't relished the thought of explaining the presence of a recently slain corpse to the authorities. Arthur stepped out of the water, then, grabbed up Excalibur's scabbard, and slid the weapon back into his sheath, buckling the now-unseeable blade back onto his belt even as he raced toward the burning building.

The TV crews arrived just as the police cars did. Seeing the fire, the newsmen automatically trained their minicams on the blaze. It took them a few seconds to realize that there were children trapped inside, and even a few seconds more before they saw that the would-be next mayor of New York was risking his life in a mad dash into the inferno.

Arthur took one glance upward, saw that the children were hysterical, saw that there was no way he was going to be able to talk them into trying to jump down. However, he did not relish the idea of entering the building—the intensity of the heat was almost overwhelming.

Then, as he studied the wall, he had an idea. He removed his shoes and began to scale the side of the building.

It was easier than he'd dared hope. The building front was brick, and the windows and doors had been built with so many outcroppings that it had been practically designed for handholds. From the corner of his eye Arthur saw that residents of the buildings to either side were clearing out, and he was thankful for that.

He went higher, higher. Flame flared out from the window beneath him, licking at his pants cuff, and he had to reach down to pat it out. The wall was heating up under his touch. In moments it would be too hot for him to hold on. Bracing himself, he thrust himself higher, and his desperate reach grabbed the outcropping of a narrow ledge. It was all that he needed to pull himself up and away from the window. He scrabbled apelike (and he thought for a moment of Gwen's reference to a monkey suit—how right she had been) with his hands holding the ledge and his feet braced on the wall directly below.

He heard the sound of the children before he saw them. Hundreds of sparks flew at him and dissipated on the fabric of his wet clothing. He thanked his common sense for the move he'd made earlier for protection, or otherwise he'd have had a lot more to worry about than that one singed pants cuff.

He looked up through the smoke at the crying children.

"Hold on," he called. "I'll be right there!" His heart pumping furiously, Arthur pulled himself up so that his face was right even with the bottom of the window. He saw the frightened, smoke-smeared faces of the children, and it was all the incentive he needed to hoist himself upward and into the room with them.

The features of both of them were obscured by soot, but they clutched at his legs and cried hysterically for their parents.

Arthur scooped up the two children, one in each arm. The little boy, despite his fright, still took the opportunity to stroke Arthur's beard in wonderment. "Are you Santa Claus?" he sniffled out.

Arthur climbed up into the frame of the window, balanced there for a moment, and reviewed his options. The review came to an abrupt end when the ceiling behind him started to collapse and flames leaped at the three people. Breathing a silent prayer, Arthur Pendragon hurled himself and the children to the ground below.

The children shrieked into his ears, almost shattering his concentration. The ground arrived with dizzying speed as Arthur landed on his feet. Pain stabbed up through his legs, and he rolled, bringing the children in close to his chest and taking the impact on his shoulder. In the window where he'd just been, a ball of flame roared out, as if the fire were angry that he'd escaped and was venting its fury.

Arthur rolled off the curbside and into the street, even as police officers pushed through the crowds of people starting to ring them. Now there were more sirens coming—fire engines and ambulances. Two policemen wrestled momentarily with the TV cameras, who also wanted to push through the crowd to get close-ups. "Move it or lose it!" snapped one of the cops, and the cameramen chose to move it.

Arthur lay in the center of the circle, moaning softly but sitting up, massaging his bruised shoulders. The children stood on either side, no longer crying, almost forgetting Arthur completely as they watched their home burn.

"Wow," murmured the little girl, "when Mommy and Daddy come back from the movie, they're gonna be mad."

"Would you tell them we didn't start it, mister?" said the boy.

Arthur forced a smile. "Certainly. Right after I give them a long talk about leaving children without baby-sitters.''

"If we'd have had a baby-sitter, you'd have had to rescue her too."

Arthur stared at the boy. "You have a point," he admitted.

The cops broke through to the center. "Okay, no one move. You're all gonna be all right, an ambulance is on its way!"

"Ambulance?" said Arthur.

"To take you to the hospital. Geez, mister, you shouldn't try stunts like that," said the cop, a young blond-haired rookie. "You should wait for the fire trucks to show up."

And as the fire trucks rounded the corner, the roof of the building collapsed in on itself with a heart-rending crash. Arthur looked up at the officer and said, with as little sarcasm as he could manage, "I'll remember that next time. I can't go to the hospital—I have a speech to make. People will be disappointed. . . ."

He started to get to his feet, and immediately pain shot through his right leg. He crumbled, cursing, and muttered under his breath, "I'm getting a few centuries too old for this sort of thing."

"Arthur!"

He turned and saw Gwen shoving her way through the crowd. "Oh, thank the Lord, Gwen. It's good to see you." He winced as he touched his leg. "Help me get back to the hall. People paid good money to hear me babble about some nonsense or other. . . ."

An ambulance had pulled up, and paramedics were already leaping out of the back. "Arthur, don't be crazy!" Gwen was saying. She shouted to the paramedics, "Over here!"

The paramedics turned in their direction, but Arthur gestured toward the two frightened children. The paramedics nodded their understanding and headed over to the youngsters.

Arthur lay his head back in Gwen's lap. "I'll wait for the next one. Gwen, where's Merlin?"

There was a pause, and Arthur looked up into Gwen's eyes. "Gwen?"

She turned away. Arthur sat upright and his voice was harsh. "Gwen! Where the hell is Merlin?"

It had happened with incredible swiftness. Merlin watched, uncertain of what he should do, as Arthur dashed out the door after the creatures who had stolen Excalibur. He looked back at the dais, saw that Gwen was on her feet, and frowned. That was damned quick recovery for someone who had fainted dead away. And the expression on her face—it looked like the expression of a woman who had just done something frightful beyond imagining.

Merlin started toward her, questions forming on his lips, when someone blocked the way. The young wizard glanced up. It was another waiter, with a very unpleasant look. Merlin stepped back, but the waiter drew back his fist and sent a roundhouse punch sailing toward Merlin's chin. Merlin went down as if he'd been poleaxed, the floor spinning around him. He tried to stagger to his feet even as the waiter/demon grabbed up a chair and brought it slamming down on the magician's head. Stars exploded in Merlin's skull and he fell to the ground, unconscious.

Everyone from Merlin's table had already moved away, and so did not see the incident. But Percy saw, and he leaped over the head table, shouting, "Hey! What the hell do you think you're doing? Put him down, right now!"

He closed in on the demon, but the monster swept its arm around, knocking Percy back like a rag doll. Percy fell over the table, knocking over the centerpiece and catching up the tablecloth. He hit the ground and lay still.

"What are you doing?" shrieked Gwen. "You only wanted the sword! Morgan said all you wanted was the sword!"

The waiter grinned at her in an unearthly way. "Morgan lied," it hissed. "She does that sometimes."

"Merlin's gone?"

She tried to restrain him. "Now Arthur, try to stay calm."

He lurched to his feet, staggering desperately toward the convention hall. But Gwen's plaintive cry of "Arthur, it's too late!" brought him up short.

He turned and demanded, "How could you stand there while someone dragged Merlin off? How—"

"What was I supposed to do?" wailed Gwen. "I couldn't fight a demon. I've never fought anyone in my life, much less some creature."

"Yes. Yes, I suppose you're right." He smiled sadly and shook his head. Encouraged, Gwen came to him and supported him.

The camera crews were closing on him rapidly. They all had tape of Arthur's rescuing the children and now wanted some footage of the Hero. Arthur grinned wanly at them, and then a thought sliced through him like a dagger. Gwen yelped in startled pain as Arthur's grip tightened convulsively on her shoulder.

"Arthur, not so hard. You'll hurt me. That's no way to treat your crutch."

His voice was a sick whisper. "How did you know?"

"W-what? What do you—"

He turned to confront her, and Gwen's body shook with fear from the look in his eyes. "How did you know they were creatures from hell and not human beings?"

"You told me."

"No."

"Yes. Just now. You—"

"Don't make it worse!" he shouted at her. "Don't lie to me!"

Tears streamed down her face as she tried to shrink from him. "Arthur, please don't—"

"How did you know?"

"Morgan told me!" she screamed. "She told me they would be. She arranged for everything." She was speaking desperately, words tumbling one over the other. "But she just told me she wanted the sword. That's all. She swore no one would be hurt. I thought—"

"And you provided the distraction." His words were cold, burning with an icy flame that blazed in his eyes.

"Yes. But—"

He shoved her away roughly and stood there, fists clenched as he trembled with repressed fury. *"Damn you!* How could you betray me *again!"*

She staggered toward him, her body racked with sobs. "Arthur, please. I had no choice. Lance—"

"Don't talk to me. Don't even look at me." His voice was pure venom. "You're not fit for human company!"

He staggered away from her as the cameramen descended. "Mr. Penn, what does it feel like being the man of the hour?" the newsmen were shouting. "What were you thinking when you were hanging from the side of that burning building? Did you think you were going to die? How did you feel about—"

Arthur grabbed the first newsman who came within arm's

length and shoved him roughly out of the way. He spun and shouted, "Get away from me! Just . . . leave me . . ." His voice caught as he looked at Gwen's tear-stained face. "Leave me alone."

He limped away into the darkness, illuminated briefly in the flickering of the rapidly dying fire.

It was late at night in Central Park. The moon was obscured by clouds, and there were no sounds other than a young woman pounding on the uncaring stones of Belvedere Castle.

The sides of her hands were abraded from the stone as she continued to smash her hands against the wall in supplication. "Arthur, please let me in," sobbed Gwen. "You've got to let me explain!"

There was a tap on her shoulder and she whirled around. "Oh, Arthur, I—"

"No, my sweet," said Morgan quietly. "It's not Arthur."

"You! You . . . *bitch!*" She leaped at Morgan, fingernails bared like claws. Morgan caught her flailing wrists and tossed her roughly to the ground. She stood over Gwen and laughed harshly. "What a pathetic little fool you are." She nodded toward the castle. "Arthur's not in there."

"How do you—"

"I know a great deal about a great deal. Arthur's wandering the streets right now," said Morgan easily. "Angry. Confused. Hurt. I could attack him now, and probably defeat him utterly. But I've waited far too long to dispose of him so quickly. No, we'll let him stew. You, on the other hand, little queen," and she smiled menacingly, "you have served your purpose."

In a pure, white-hot fury, Gwen hiked up the hem of her evening dress and swept out with her legs. She knocked Morgan's legs out from under her, sending the sorceress toppling to the ground with her. Within moments she was upon Morgan, tearing at her hair, her eyes, her face. Morgan shrieked in anger and indignation.

Gwen felt herself abruptly being hauled off of Morgan's writhing body. She flailed at the men who stood on either side of them.

"Whoa! Hey! C'mon, slugger," said Chico, struggling to hold onto the infuriated Gwen. "This is, whattaya call, undignified."

Gwen stopped, looking from Chico to Groucho and back again. "What are you guys doing here?" she demanded.

"We live here," said Chico simply. "That's how we first met the king. And now we see you and this nice lady who you were tryin' to kill. I tell ya, y'meet the best people in the park."

Morgan staggered to her feet. "You'll regret that," she said, gingerly touching the scratches where Gwen had raked her face. "You'll regret that most dearly."

"What are you going to do?" demanded Gwen. "Kill me? I feel dead already. You couldn't hurt me any more than I've already hurt myself. Damn you! I should have gone straight to Arthur—"

"Yes. You should have," said Morgan with a twisted smile. "Are you wondering where your precious Lance is? I still have him. And you know why? Because he doesn't want to leave. It seems he's developed a fondness for bondage. Isn't that interesting?"

Chico raised an eyebrow. "Well, it's certainly got *my* interest."

"You're lying," snarled Gwen. "You lie about everything."

"Not about this," said Morgan. "I don't need to lie about this. Tell me—does Arthur ask you to talk dirty, the way Lance does with me?"

Gwen stared at her in shock. "My God. It was all for nothing."

"Yes." Morgan laughed. "All for nothing. That's all it ever was. That's all it ever will be."

Groucho took a step forward. There was a switchblade in his hand and a distracted tone in his voice. "You know, I don't like you."

Morgan stared at him for a time, and then she turned in an abrupt swirl of her long black cape. She strode off into the darkness and merged with the shadows.

Chico shook his head. "She must be zero fun at parties." He turned to Gwen and shook his shaggy head. "You look so sad."

"I had it," said Gwen. "I had it all. And I lost it. And I can blame Morgan, or Lance, or anybody I want."

Groucho stepped forward. "You can blame me if you'd like."

She smiled unevenly and patted his thick beard. She then unconsciously wiped her hand on her dress as she said, "That's sweet. But what I'm trying to say is that there's really nobody to blame but myself. That's the part that's tough to take."

Chico nodded, not understanding in the least, but determined to be helpful. "Gwen, if you'd like, you can stay with us tonight."

"What, under a tree? Gee, that's nice, but"—she wiped her nose—"I don't think that would be, well, right."

"Oh. You wanna, y'know, get married first?"

Gwen stared at him, and then, to her surprise, laughed. "You know, Groucho—"

"I'm Chico."

"I'm sorry. Chico. That's the first marriage proposal I've ever had in my life."

"You gonna turn it down?"

She nodded. "I'm afraid so."

"Don't worry. You'll get lots of others."

"I hope so. God, I hope so." She patted him on the shoulder. "Thanks anyway. I hope you're not too broken up."

"I'll live," said Chico.

"Okay," smiled Gwen. "Good night, then, boys." She turned and walked off into the night.

Groucho slammed Chico in the shoulder. "That was close! Idiot! What if she'd taken you up on it?"

Chico shrugged, massaging his hurt shoulder. "She never would have. I'm Jewish. She's not." He sighed. "It'd never have worked."

Chaptre the Fifteenth

Bernie Bittberg had been made the official Democratic candidate for mayor of New York City. The decision from the primary voting had been overwhelmingly in his favor, due to endorsements from the two New York newspapers, namely the *Times* and the *Daily News*—no one counted the *Post*—and from a concentrated media blitz that had effectively destroyed the credibility of his opponents' records.

So now, several weeks after that primary, and several weeks before the election, Bernie should have been happy. He was, in fact, anything but.

It was past midnight as he huddled with his staff in a classic smoke-filled room. Bernie sat forward, rubbing his eyes, his still-knotted necktie draped over the back of his chair, his vest open to allow for his considerable girth. Moe Dredd sat to his immediate right. The various officials who ran his campaign were also there, in varying degrees of wakefulness.

Bernie looked around and slammed his open hand on the table, effectively rousing everyone. "What the hell are we going to do about this Arthur Penn character?" he demanded.

Effecting a gangland tone, his treasurer said, "You want we should rub him out, boss? I'll go round up Rico and the boys and—"

"Shut up, Charlie," said Bernie tiredly. "Now dammit, I'm serious. You know my philosophy about political opponents." He paused expectantly.

Moe filled the void, reluctantly. "Stick it to 'em."

"Stick it to 'em. That's right. Except what the hell are we supposed to do about this Penn guy? He's got no political record to speak of. For most people that would be a detriment, but he makes it work to his advantage. The voters see him as a fresh face in a jaded political arena, and it gives us absolutely zilch to work with. His business practices? Squeaky clean. Hell, the man's never been investigated. All of his investments are sound and aboveboard. He's hardly been involved in running the day-to-day business of anything, so although there's virtually no one to vouch for him, there's no one to say anything bad against him either.

"And if that's not enough for you," said Bernie with genuine indignation, "the guy has to go and save kids from a flaming building. Kids! Isn't that just friggin' fabulous! With TV news crews there to tape him." A sudden thought struck him. "Hey, maybe he started it. Stan, you're the press liaison. You have the contacts. Anyone looking into that possibility?"

Stan shook his head. "Police looked into it for weeks and still aren't sure what caused it. It seems like some sort of spontaneous combustion. Either way, certainly no sign of any incendiary device."

The head of clerical, Marcia, put in, "That whole thing gets bigger with every retelling. The children were telling reporters that our Mr. Penn, before the fire started, was fighting a man with a sword, and the man supposedly turned into some sort of creature and then crumbled away once Penn defeated him."

Bernie moaned. "Just what we need. Folk legends arising from this clown. So where does this leave us?"

Moe shook his head. "In a couple of days there's that televised debate. It's going to be you, the Republican candidate, and Arthur Penn. Now—"

Bernie hauled his carcass to his feet. "Penn's in the debate? Since when?"

"Since the TV stations became interested in ratings," said Moe sourly. "Since Penn won that citation from the Fire Department for gallantry. Since *New York* magazine put him on their Most Eligible Bachelor Politician List. Penn was amassing a following before, but that whole fire business made him really hot, so to speak. They decided that a debate would not really reflect the voters' interest in the candidates unless Penn was present. Frankly I can't blame them.''

"Well, that's just wonderful, Moe," retorted Bernie. "And you won't blame the voters when they elect Arthur Penn instead of me or even the Republican candidate . . . uh, what's his name anyway?"

Everyone at the table looked at each other. Stan shrugged. "Who cares?"

"Yeah, you're right. Look, what it boils down to is this—I don't want to lose this race. I really don't. But the key to this is, I suspect, bringing down Arthur Penn."

"For what it's worth," said Marcia, "I think Penn's worst enemy right now is himself."

"Come again?"

"He was on a local news interview program the other day. He was snappish, irritable. Short with the interviewer. It's as if his mind is a million miles away."

"You know," said Stan, "come to think of it, he's been like that ever since the whole fire thing. Maybe it shook him more than he lets on. He could hurt his image if he keeps it up. Because it's starting to look as if he can't stand pressure."

"Yeah, well, it's looking that way to us, but not to the general public. Not yet at any rate. So we're going to have to bring it to their attention."

He looked around the table. "We're going to have to start playing hardball, ladies and gentlemen. I hope that we have a clear understanding of this. Because if we don't win . . ." his voice rose dramatically, and then he paused.

"Then we lose?" suggested Marcia helpfully.

Bernie covered his face and said quietly, "Meeting adjourned. Go home. Get some sleep. See you all tomorrow." He glanced at his watch. "Sorry, make that later this morning.''

Bernie himself started to rise, but he felt the gentle pressure of Moe's hand on his arm. He looked at Moe Dredd with curiosity, but Moe said nothing, didn't even look his way. Bernie lowered himself back into his seat, and they waited until the rest of the room had cleared out amidst tired choruses of "Good-byes" and "See you later."

"Nu?" said Bernie, once the room was empty. "What is

it?" His voice dropped to a confidential level. "You got something on Penn? Please, say you've got something on him."

"Oh, I've got something on him, all right," said Moe slowly. "But you're not going to like it."

"How can I not like it?" He frowned. "Is he a fag? Don't tell me he's a fag. Not that I wouldn't use it," he added quickly, "it's just that I find that whole thing so, I don't know . . . yuucchh."

"No. It's nothing like that." Moe took a deep breath. "You're going to have to be prepared to do something a little unorthodox. At the debate this Friday I want you to ask Mr. Penn something—"

"But we're not supposed to be talking directly to each other. Questions are being posed by moderators, and we're supposed to answer them."

Moe laughed curtly. He leaned back in his chair and said, "You telling me you're reluctant to start breaking rules?"

"Only if it's going to net me something big."

"It should."

"Only should?"

"All right, will, then. I want you to ask Arthur Penn who he is."

Bernie looked at him blankly. "What?"

Moe repeated it, and Bernie paused a moment, stroking his chin. "Moe, you know what the first rule is that a lawyer learns in the study of cross-examination? Never ask a question to which you do not already know the answer. So am I correct in assuming that the answer is going to be something other than the obvious?"

"Arthur Penn," said Moe, "is not his real name. At least, so he believes."

"What, he changed his name? Look, they made a big deal of that with Gary Hart, but I never thought much of it." He shook his head. "I'm not following you, Moe."

"Arthur Penn," said Moe, "is short for Arthur Pendragon."

"Pendragon? What the hell kind of name is that?"

"Medieval. Bernie, your opponent believes himself to be the original King Arthur."

The portly man stared at Moe. "Moe, let's cut the crap, okay?"

"I'm not kidding, Bernie. The man believes that he is King Arthur, Lord of the Round Table, ruler of Camelot, King of all the Britons. . . ."

Bernie heaved himself to his feet, knocking his chair back. "Moe, this is just too ridiculous! You're telling me that my main obstacle to being mayor of this city is as mad as a hatter?"

"I'm saying that the man thinks he's the original Arthur, son of Uther, Lord of—"

Bernie put up a beefy hand. "Please, spare me the litany, okay? You got any proof of this?"

"I've got one Lance Benson. He's ready to swear that Arthur attacked him with a sword in 'rescuing' Benson's girl friend from the supposedly vile clutches of Benson himself."

Bittberg's mouth dropped open. "Are you serious?" he whispered. "I want to meet this Benson guy."

"He's tied up at the moment," said Moe dryly. "But I'm sure he'd be happy to come forward when you needed him."

Bernie was silent for a long moment, trying to assimilate this new information. "He really, honest to God thinks he's King Arthur?"

"That's right."

"This is too much. But wait—" He turned on Moe. "How do I know that, if I ask him point-blank, he won't just lie about it?"

"Not Arthur," said Moe with absolute certainty. "He prides himself on telling the truth. It would be totally against his dementia to lie about who he thinks he is."

"Too much. Just too much." He stabbed a finger at Moe. "But I better not come out looking like an idiot on this."

"You can't possibly. You ask him point-blank what his real name is. Even if he maintains that it's Arthur Penn—which he won't—then you just cover yourself by saying that you'd heard he'd changed it, and you just wanted to make sure the record was straight. At worst it'll get you a raised eyebrow or two that will be quickly forgotten. At best," and he smiled unpleasantly, "it will get you the election in your hip pocket."

Moe stepped outside of the tall gray building that housed Bernard Bittberg's office. He glanced up at the moon and pulled his coat tightly around him against the stiff breeze. You could tell that winter was on its way.

He started walking, scanning the streets for a passing cab, when he suddenly felt an arm around his throat in a choke-hold. Moe tried to scream for help but his wind had been effectively and precisely cut off. His assailant dragged him into a nearby alleyway, pulling Moe as if his weight were nothing. Moe clawed at the arm around him, pounded on it, to no avail.

Once in the alley Moe was swung around and hurled against a wall. He slammed into it with bone-jarring impact, and with a moan sank to the ground. Distantly he heard the *shikt* of a bladed weapon being drawn from its sheath, and he tried to draw air into his lungs to shout for help.

The tip of a glowing sword hovered at his chest.

"I wouldn't, Modred," said Arthur quietly.

"You . . ." He swallowed. "You wouldn't kill an unarmed man."

"Perhaps," said Arthur. "Perhaps not. Are you willing to bet your life on it?"

He prodded Moe gently in the ribs with Excalibur. Moe shook his head frantically.

"Now then," continued the king, "where is your god-cursed mother? Because wherever she is, it's certain that's where Merlin is. So all you have to do is tell me where I can find them and I'll be on my way. And you'll have your skin intact."

Moe's mouth moved several times but nothing came out. Arthur sighed and said, "Oh, do try to get on with it, won't you?"

"I . . . I don't know where she is."

"You're lying," said Arthur tightly.

"I'm not! As God is my witness, I'm not! She said . . ." He swallowed. "She said she thought you might try something like this. So she deliberately didn't tell me where she was going to be hiding. Because she was afraid that I'd crack and bring you to her."

Arthur shook his head. "Ah, Morgan. Always the judge of character. All right, puppy, get up. Up, I said." He waved with his sword, and Moe staggered to his feet. But Arthur kept the point of Excalibur only an inch from Moe's chest.

"Tell her," said Arthur, "that when next we meet—no mercy from me. Is that understood? No mercy."

"Yes. Absolutely, no mercy. I'll tell her."

"You do that." Arthur stepped back and loudly sheathed Excalibur. Moe winced at the finality of the sound.

The sword and scabbard vanished from Arthur's hip and he stood there nattily attired in a gray Brooks Brothers suit and overcoat. He backed out of the alley, a sardonic look on his face, and Moe realized that Arthur wasn't turning his back on him for a moment. Moe took a degree of satisfaction from that.

Arthur didn't come in to his campaign headquarters until ten A.M. the next day, startlingly late. The moment he walked in, Ronnie was all over him. "Arthur, where the hell have you been? We're already late for—"

"Have you heard from him?" Arthur said urgently, just as he had every day for the past month and a half.

Ronnie shook his head and looked down. "Arthur, this is insane. You at least have to file a missing persons report or something."

He put a hand on Ronnie's shoulder. "Trust me, my friend. It would do no good at all." He looked around and frowned. "I assume Gwen isn't here yet."

"She called in, said she would be a little late. Said she had an errand to run. Arthur, look, it's none of my business but—"

"You're right, it's none of your business. Where's Percy?"

"He's floating around. He's been holding up pretty well— finding that furnished apartment for rent certainly helped. Was that really all on the level, that he and Merlin were commuting from Bermuda?"

Percy seemed to materialize behind them. "Hard to believe, isn't it?" he said cheerily. Then he turned serious as he said, "Arthur, we have to talk about you and Gwen."

"No, we don't," said Arthur, "and I wish that all of you would feel less constrained to meddle in my private affairs."

"Private affairs!" said Percy. "Arthur, the woman is the head of your campaign, and it's obvious that she is number one on your personal hit list. And none of us understands why. But it's starting to get on everyone's nerves, and frankly, it's hurting morale."

Arthur looked at the two men grimly and said, "Gentlemen, what has gone on between myself and Ms. DeVere is between the two of us. I do not consider her trustworthy—however, she seems to be doing a competent job as campaign head, and the staff likes her. So she is still here, but I do not have to be pleased by it. And that is all I have to say on the matter. Ronnie, kindly cancel the rest of my plans for today."

"What?"

"I want to discuss the debate this Friday. It's important that I have all the facts at my fingertips. I'm quite concerned about the entire affair, and the more prepared I am, the better I'll feel."

He stalked through the headquarters toward his office in the back. Workers greeted him, and were surprised when he did not do much more than grunt, if that. Percy shook his head. "It's nerves. That's all."

"Well, it wasn't a problem when Merlin was here," said Ronnie. "I never understood the relation between those two, but I never questioned it. And now he doesn't have Merlin, and it looks like he doesn't have Gwen. Still, he's got himself, and that should be enough."

"Uh-huh, except that I know what he's thinking. The last time he had only himself to depend on, everything fell apart."

"Really?" asked Ronnie. "When was that?"

Percy Vale sighed. "Long time ago," he said. "Before your time. Before my time, in a way. But for Arthur, it might as well have been yesterday."

The owner of the occult-supplies store down on MacDougal Street opened his doors and was surprised to find a young woman standing there, waiting for him. The owner was a big man. His head was shaven, but he sported a large handlebar moustache. "Yes?" he rumbled. "Can I help you?"

"Yes," said Gwen, walking past him into the cool darkness of the store. Once she would have been frightened to set foot in such a place. But that was a lifetime ago. Her eyes scanned the various accoutrements, the horoscopes, the tarot cards, the small bottled and carefully labeled ingredients for witches brews, and then she saw what she was looking for. She stepped over to a rack of ornate daggers and pulled one down from the display. It was small, in a black leather sheath. The thing that attracted her was on the pommel—a carved skull with red eyes, as large as her thumbnail.

"The lady would like a knife?"

"The lady would like this knife," said Gwen. She slid it out of the sheath and admired the sharpness of the edge.

"Are you purchasing this knife, may I ask, for protection?" asked the proprietor. "Or perhaps you had a certain ritual in mind?" He smiled. "If a sacrifice is intended, that knife might not be appropriate." He pointed to a large curved dagger on the wall. "Now that, on the other hand—"

"No," said Gwen, sliding the dagger back into its sheath. "This is just what I'll need. Small enough for easy concealment, yet large enough to effect damage."

"I would say kill, if at close quarters," said the owner. "I think I can thank my lucky stars that I am not the one who the lady is after."

"Yes," said Gwen pleasantly. "You can." She tucked the knife in her handbag. "How much do I owe you?"

Chaptre the Sixteenth

They had cleared out the Reeves Teletape theater for the event. The television facility, situated on Eighty-sixth Street and usually home to sitcoms and the like, was now decorated inside with three podiums at which the three principal candidates would stand, a center podium where the moderator would be stationed, and on one side of this trianglular arrangement, a table where three local journalists would be seated.

Arthur's earlier nervousness had been replaced by quiet calculation as he surveyed the setup the same way he would have looked over a battlefield before engaging the enemy. He stared at the TV cameras in awe; despite all his assimilation, there were certain aspects of modern-day society that continued to boggle his mind, and instantaneous communication was definitely one of those aspects.

There was a tug at his shoulder and he glanced around. Percy smiled encouragingly at him. "Turn around. Let's see you."

Arthur turned around obediently, and Percy straightened the collar of his suit jacket. He looked down and said, "Unbutton the bottom vest button."

"Why?" asked Arthur.

"I dunno, man. Because you're supposed to." He held out his hand and pointed proudly at the steadiness of it. "Congratulate me, Arthur. Ten months of sobriety. Haven't touched a drop.''

"Not even raised a flagon of mead?"

"Not a one."

Arthur smiled broadly. "Good for you. Um . . ." He looked around. "Gwen isn't here, is she?"

Percy stroked his chin. "For someone who doesn't care whether he ever sees a certain person again or not, you're awful interested in her whereabouts."

"Morbid curiosity. Nothing more."

"Uh-huh."

Ronnie came trotting over, a clipboard in his hands. "Arthur, you're here! Good. I was getting worried."

"Heavy traffic daunts even the best of us, Ronnie," said Arthur stridently. "Where am I supposed to be?"

"We've got an hour before the debate starts. They want to get you into makeup first."

Arthur took a step back. "Makeup?" he said cautiously.

"Yeah. Sure."

"Women wear makeup. I have put up with a great deal, but I will not look like a woman."

Ronnie stuttered, "B-but Arthur, you have to! You'll look washed out without it. I don't understand. You must have worn makeup when you did your commercials."

Arthur frowned. "Wait. They put something on my face—"

"That was it!"

"Oh. Merlin told me that was protectant salve, to prevent my being severely burned by the intense lights of the cameras."

Percy nodded, amused. "That Merlin was a smart little bugger."

Arthur turned on him with unexpected fierceness. "Don't talk about Merlin that way. In the past tense, as if he's dead."

Percy stepped back involuntarily. "Arthur," he whispered harshly, glancing around to see if anyone had noticed Arthur's sudden flare of temper, "I didn't mean anything by it."

"He's all right." Arthur paused, and then added fiercely, "He has to be." He turned to Percy. "Come, let's get this 'makeup' done. I have an urge to be quit of this whole debate. It's . . . unseemly."

From the opposite corner of the studio Bernard Bittberg

and Moe Dredd watched Arthur, Percy, and Ronnie stride toward makeup. "He's distracted," muttered Bernie. "Distracted real bad. That's gonna cost him." He turned to Moe and waved a finger in his face. "You better be right about this fantasy of his. I don't want to come across looking like some kind of schmuck."

Moe patted him on the arm. "Trust me . . . Mr. Mayor."

Bernie grinned, and looked up at the monitor overhead, with the podiums for the candidates on its screen. "Mr. Mayor. I like the sound of that. I could get used to that real easy."

"I knew that you could," said Moe.

If there were the equivalent of hell on earth, then it was in New Jersey. Verona, New Jersey, to be specific—named after the town in Italy where the star-crossed lovers of *Romeo and Juliet* had met their end. A small, unassuming jock town where, interestingly enough, creatures of evil were residing. But only in the not-so-nice sections.

It was a run-down two-story house, whose elderly owner had died ages ago, and it had sat vacant for years as courts tried to figure out who owned it. It finally reverted to distant family, who didn't even care enough to sell it themselves and so left it to a real estate agent, who went out of business a month later. Since then the house had fallen between the cracks in the attentions of all concerned. Ivy ran wild over the sides, and grass was supplanted by weeds stretching several feet high.

It was a dump, but Morgan called it home.

The insides had been done up superbly—exotic drapes and tapestries hung everywhere, illuminated entirely by candles.

Morgan strode through the house, her long black gown swirling around her bare feet. Trailing behind her was Lance, dressed in black leather and grinning like an imbecile. "Where are we going, Morgan? What's up? I adore you, Morgan—"

"Shut up," she said tiredly.

"Yes, Morgan."

She turned and stroked his chin fondly. "I don't need you, you know."

"Yes, Morgan. I know."

"You're a pathetic creature."

"Yes. But I'm your pathetic creature."

"Come. We're going to watch television."

"Wonderful! *Uncle Floyd*?"

"No, not *Uncle Floyd*," she grated. "There's going to be a debate starting in a few minutes. And I think it's going to be quite, quite interesting."

She walked into her inner sanctum. Pillows were scattered about for easy lounging. A television, the modern-day crystal ball, was set up on a small pedestal at one end of the room. Tonight, however, it would be used for something less arcane than spying on the movements of others. Tonight it would be used for something as pedestrian as watching a television program, broadcast live on WNYW, Channel 5, with the other local stations in attendance for taped highlights to be played later on their news broadcasts.

At the other end of the room was a life-size cylinder made of solid crystal. Encased inside the crystal, like a butterfly in amber, was Merlin. His eyes were open, burning with fury even after all this time. Morgan went to him and stroked the crystal lovingly. "Ah, Merlin. Your incarceration hasn't dimmed your anger, I see. But then, I suppose lengthy prisons are nothing new to you." She smiled, showing white, slightly pointed teeth. "You're in luck, however. Tonight I've arranged some special entertainment for you."

"It's *Uncle Floyd*!" said Lance cheerfully.

Despair welled in Merlin's eyes. If he could have moved any other part of his body, he would have screamed and beat his breast in fury.

"No it's not *Uncle Floyd*!" Morgan fairly shrieked. "Will you be quiet with your moronic *Uncle Floyd*." Her voice recaptured its sultry purr. "I know you have quite an interest in politics, Merlin. We're going to watch a debate. It's going to feature someone who's a friend of yours. You remember Arthur, don't you?"

Then she laughed at the look of hope in his eyes. "You still hope for my fool of a half brother to rescue you! Never! Never, little magician. You're mine, do you hear? Mine, body and soul, forever." She continued in a singsong voice as she went to turn on the television. "Forever and ever and ever and ever . . ."

Merlin closed his eyes. Encased, helpless, immobile in

crystal. Unable to send for help. Astral projection not even possible. Unable to help his king cope with a world that could be confusing and terrifying.

It could be worse, he mused. They could be making him watch *Uncle Floyd* again.

The floor director, earphones solidly in place, was calling, "Five minutes, everyone." He turned to the audience and said, "People, please. On air in five minutes. Please refrain from talking from this point on. If cameras are blocking your way, feel free to watch the proceedings in the overhead monitors. I appreciate your cooperation. Thank you."

Gwen sat in the front row, looking demure in a simple white blouse and denim skirt. Her purse was on her lap. The dagger she had purchased several days ago was still in it.

Arthur, stepping up to his station, looked out at the audience, and his gaze locked with Gwen's. She smiled encouragingly at him. He did not smile back. She bit her lower lip, but that was all, and then she looked up at the monitor, not being able to bear looking directly at him.

"Mr. Penn."

Arthur turned and saw the blond-haired, corpulent man standing next to him. There was a smile on his lips that went nowhere near his eyes. Nevertheless he stuck out a hand and said, "Bernard Bittberg. Your worthy opponent. I've heard a great deal about you, sir. It's a pleasure to meet at last."

Arthur nodded graciously, taking Bernie's hand and shaking it once firmly. "I've watched your campaign with great interest."

"Same here, Mr. Penn. Same here." He studied Arthur's handsome face carefully, trying to see some evidence of self-delusion there. What was he looking for? He wasn't altogether sure.

"Is something wrong, Mr. Bittberg?"

"What?"

"The way you're staring at me . . ."

"Oh, nothing. Nothing at all."

Arthur's podium was at the far right when facing the audience. Bernie was dead center. Arthur glanced down at the end. "There's another candidate, isn't there?"

"Yes, certainly. The Republican candidate."

"And what's his name?"

Bernie opened his mouth and then closed it again. "You know, I don't recall."

The three reporters came over and introduced themselves, greeting the candidates and wishing them luck. Arthur smiled wanly and cast his gaze toward the audience once more. He was able to pick out Percy and Ronnie, who both raised clenched fists in encouragement. Arthur blinked, at first thinking they were signaling that he should punch his opponent. But their expressions didn't seem to jibe with that intent. So he chanced it and raised a clenched fist back. They seemed pleased, so Arthur presumed he had given the right response.

He did not see Gwen. He did not look for her.

There was an expectant hush as the reporters went to their side of the room and as the floor director counted down. "And five . . . four . . . three . . . two . . . one . . ."

An announcer intoned, "Mayoral debate, live, from the Reeves Teletape Studio." Arthur glanced up at the monitor and blinked in surprise as the words *Mayoral Debate* appeared on the screen, superimposed over the image of the candidates. He looked around, trying to figure out where the words had come from, for they certainly weren't visible to him. He shook his head. And he had thought the things that Merlin had done were magic.

Merlin . . .

Arthur looked down toward the end of the row and saw that the Republican candidate had arrived. He was a sturdy-looking fellow, with thinning hair, thick glasses, and a determined, albeit slightly confused, air—confused because he didn't quite know where he was supposed to look.

"Good evening," said the moderator. "Thank you for tuning in. I'm your moderator, Edward Shukin. Debates are not always possible in every campaign, so I feel we should be appreciative that the three major candidates have seen fit to engage in this evening's forum. I'd like to introduce them to you now. On the far right, running as an Independent, Mr. Arthur Penn. In the center, the Democratic candidate and City Council head, Mr. Bernard Bittberg. And on the extreme left, the Republican candidate . . ." Shukin hesitated a moment, then glanced down at his notes. "Former Staten Island Borough President, Mr. Archibald Goodwin."

Goodwin bobbed his head slightly.

Shukin then turned to face the three journalists. "At the far left I have the first of the three journalists who will be posing questions to the candidates tonight. From the *Amsterdam News*, Mr. James Owsley—"

Owsley, black and proud of it, raised a fist midway in the air. Arthur immediately returned the gesture. Percy, in the audience, covered his eyes.

Shukin rolled merrily on, oblivious. "Next, from WNBC News, Ms. Sandra Schechter. . . ." Schechter, a no-nonsense redhead, allowed a quick smile. "And, from the *Village Voice*, Mr. Fred Baumann." Baumann tossed a wave at the audience and smiled lopsidedly.

"The rules for this debate have been agreed upon as follows," Shukin continued. "Our panelists will pose a question to a candidate on a rotating basis. The candidate will be given three minutes to answer. The reporter will be permitted one follow-up question, to which the candidate will have one minute to reply. The other two candidates will then each be permitted two minutes to respond to or rebut the candidate's response. With that understood, Mr. Owsley, I believe you won the coin toss backstage."

"Damned straight. Used my coin," muttered Owsley, provoking mild laughter. "Mr. Bittberg," he said, glancing down at his notes, "incidents of police violence, particularly in the course of arrests, seem to be on the rise. These incidents occur particularly in the apprehension of blacks, I have noticed. Yet in the overwhelming number of instances, subsequent investigations by the police have exonerated the officers who have committed the violence. Are you satisfied with the manner in which these internal investigations are being performed, or do you intend to try and have stricter procedures implemented?"

Bernie paused a moment. His eye caught Moe in the corner, who gave him a thumbs-up and a slow nod. Taking a deep breath, Bernie turned slowly to face Arthur and said, "Before we go any further, I'd like to clear up something, Mr. Penn."

Quick off the mark, Shukin jumped in and said, "Mr. Bittberg, you are supposed to be addressing the questioners, not the other candidates."

"Oh, this is just something very minor. Mr. Penn, who are you, really?"

There was a confused silence as the three reporters looked at each other. Shukin cleared his throat loudly. "Mr. Bittberg, I don't understand. Are you claiming this is not Arthur Penn?"

"No no no," said Bernie quickly. "I am asking him to answer a simple question . . . is your name Arthur Penn?"

Arthur smiled ingratiatingly. "Don't you like my name, Mr. Bittberg?"

But Bernie would not be dissuaded. "No, that's not the question. Is your name really Arthur Penn?"

Percy and Gwen were sitting riveted in their seats, Gwen chewing on her fist. Percy felt a cold sweat breaking on his forehead.

And Arthur did not flinch. "Is that really of interest?"

And now Shukin, an anchor for WNYW for twelve years, sensed that there was something brewing. "Mr. Penn," he said carefully, "you're not required to answer that. You're certainly not on any sort of trial here. But if it will," he chuckled pleasantly, "keep peace in the family . . ."

"Oh, very well. If you must uncover my deep, dark secret," said Arthur, "No. That is not my real name. It's shortened. My full name is Arthur Pendragon."

There was a mild laugh from the audience as Arthur said easily, "There, Mr. Bittburg. Are you quite satisfied?"

Baumann from the *Voice*, who had majored in English Literature, said, "Whoa! Great name! Any relation to *the* Arthur Pendragon?" When he received blank stares from all around, he said helpfully, "You know. King Arthur. Camelot. That stuff."

Trying to avoid having his debate degenerate into a friendly chat, Shukin said, "If we could get back to the issue at hand—"

But Bernie's voice rang out. "Why don't you answer him, Arthur? Why don't you tell him? You are King Arthur, aren't you? You believe yourself to be the original Arthur Pendragon, King of the Britons, son of Luther—"

"Uther," corrected Arthur.

"Thank you. Uther. You are him, aren't you? Aren't you?"

Shukin rapped with his knuckles on the podium and wished that he had brought a gavel. "Mr. Bittberg, you can't be serious—"

But Bernie, sensing victory, wouldn't ease up. He took a step forward, his voice lowering in intensity, and said, "He's the one who's serious. Go ahead. Look me straight in the eye and deny that you are the one, the only, the original King Arthur of Camelot. That you're fifteen centuries old. That you've been in a cave all this time and that you've returned to us because 'you're needed.' Deny it!''

There was a long silence. Arthur and Bernie stared at each other, each refusing to lower their gaze. Each trying to stare down the other. And Bernard Bittberg felt the full intensity of the man who was King Arthur Pendragon, felt the strength of his anger, the power of his spirit and grim determination. And he lowered his gaze.

And slowly Arthur looked straight into the camera, and in a tone as reasonable as if he were announcing the weather, he said, "It's true."

Gwen gave a small gasp. Percy closed his eyes, and Ronnie muttered to himself, "It figures."

"Yes," said Arthur. "I am everything Mr. Bittberg says. I was trying to keep it quiet because, frankly, I didn't want to use unfair advantage." He stepped to the side of the podium, interlaced his fingers and leaned on one elbow as if he were standing next to a fireplace mantle in his study. "I mean, after all . . . a cheap politician is a cheap politician. But a king . . . good Lord! How could anyone possibly fight competition like that? And a legendary king to boot! No, my friends. I felt it best to keep my true identity a low profile, so as to give Messrs. Bittberg and Goodwin a sporting chance."

The audience members looked at each other, unsure yet of exactly how they were supposed to react. A generation raised on canned laughter and applause signs occasionally has difficulty when it comes to spontaneity.

"But the word is out," said Arthur morosely. "Mr. Bittberg, for whatever reason, has decided to slit his own throat at this late date by guaranteeing the election for me. Ladies and gentlemen, it is I, King Arthur who stand before you." His mood shifted and he smiled broadly. "But perhaps it's better this way, for now I do not have to make pretense of being a man from this day and age. I can speak to you as a man from the past. A man who has seen what the world was, and who has watched what the world has grown into." There was genuine wonderment in his voice. "Good Lord, when I think what life was like in the old days. Only a few piddling centuries ago, my friends! A mere droplet in the great flood that is time, and yet look how far that droplet called humanity has gone! It's incredible. Look at yourselves! By and large you're better fed than my people were. Better dressed. Healthier. Longer lived. Smarter. Taller," he said, with some regret.

"Yes. I have returned. Some of you, such as Mr. Baumann here, might be familiar with the legends. That I would return when the world needed me. But you've taken that to mean that it would be in your world's darkest hours. Well I'm here, my friends, to tell you that is not the case. I am here to tell you that you stand on the brink of a golden age. A time of potential learning and growth that could make all your previous achievements look like mud on an anthill by comparison. And I think that perhaps you're all afraid of what you can accomplish. It's more than you can believe. And so you toy with the concept of self-destruction on a global scale. But I am here to lead you away from that. You have all the answers you need, right within your grasp. And I'm here to bring a fresh perspective, and a fresh understanding, and the knowledge to help you pick and choose the right way to go. And together, my friends, together . . . we can make it work. No, I recant that. Because I've seen what was, and I've seen what is, and I tell you that it is working. We can make it work *better*."

The words had not been delivered in a bible-thumping style. Instead they had been said with the quiet conviction of a man who sincerely believed every syllable of what he was saying.

Someone started to clap. Arthur didn't see who, but within seconds the entire studio was filled with the thunderous sound of applause. It lasted for a solid minute, and Arthur smiled through it. He didn't look at Bernie, or Archibald, or anyone at all in particular. He was looking at his mind's eye image of Merlin and thinking, Bloody hell, I should have done this months ago, eh, Merlin?

The director cut from the camera on Arthur to the camera on the audience, taking in the rousing and solid response.

Miles away, in New Jersey, Morgan Le Fey fumed as she stared at the TV screen. "I don't understand. It was perfect. My ploy of stealing Excalibur, that useless hunk of steel, succeeded in netting me my true goal, Merlin. Then with Merlin gone, Arthur should have become dispirited, demoralized. There was even my glorious fantasy that he would simply throw himself on his thrice-damned sword and end it all. Then the truth of his identity would be revealed on television before his precious voters, and he would be laughed out of politics as a total lunatic.'' She screamed at the television, ''Stop your damned clapping! You're supposed to think he's crackers!''

Unsurprisingly, they paid no attention to Morgan. And then her eyes narrowed as she spied Gwen sitting there, her hands tight on her purse.

''All right, Arthur,'' she said in a low, angry voice. ''If I can't take your ambition from you, I'll take your beloved Guinevere from you. Oh, you can't fool me. You may be angry with her now, but sooner or later you'll forgive her, like the moronic fool that you are. But I will take her from you, Arthur. On the eve of your would-be triumph, I will take her from you. And then I will use every sorcerous means at my disposal to bring your world crashing down!''

Sitting amidst the audience that applauded around her, Gwen watched Arthur and held her purse tightly to her. Concerned about what she was afraid would happen. Concerned about what she had to do.

Chaptre the Seventeenth

Rabbi Robert Kasman opened his door and saw an extremely scruffy-looking individual standing there.

"Yes?" he said cautiously, keeping care to have the chain lock in place on the door.

"Hi," said Chico. "I'm here to make sure you're registered to vote tomorrow. I'm with Arthur Penn, and—"

"Oh, the king!" said the Rabbi. "Yes, yes, I saw your fellow. Oh, not on the actual day, because they had the poor judgment to have the debate on shabbos. But it was rerun enough, you can be sure."

"I can be sure," Chico said agreeably.

"I don't know what that crazy Bittberg fellow hoped to accomplish by trying to embarrass that nice man, particularly after he saved those two children. Imagine, trying to convince everyone that your man actually thought he was King Arthur. Imagine!"

"Imagine," echoed Chico.

"Of course, just between you, me, and the hole in the wall," said the rabbi, "it wouldn't matter to me if he really did think he were King Arthur."

Chico blinked. "You know, that's what lots of people have said to me."

"Well, I'm not surprised," said the rabbi. "I mean, we all

have our own *mishugas*, right? New York has certainly had some genuine nuts for mayor. It would only be appropriate if we had a sincere nut for once. You know what I mean?"

"I know what you mean."

"So." The rabbi leaned against the inside of the door frame. "What did you want to know again?"

Chico stared at him, then scratched his head. "I can't remember."

"Oh. Well, I'm sure when you remember you'll come by again."

"You bet."

The rabbi closed his door and went on about his business. Five minutes later there was another knock at his door. He peered through the peephole, frowned, and opened the door.

"Hi," said Chico. "I'm here to make sure you're registered to vote tomorrow. . . ."

The political commentator for PBS was saying, "You can see from Penn's presentation that he is using the King Arthur/Camelot scenario as a metaphor for all that he intends to achieve. He has locked on to this entire 'view from another era' to help clarify and lend a certain degree of validity to his unorthodox approach to politics and the issues at hand."

"This being so," the commentator was asked, "it comes down to the question of what Bittberg's motives could possibly have been in giving Penn such an opening? Did he really believe that Penn was actually the Arthur of legend?"

"Whatever Bittberg had in mind, I can only surmise that it backfired spectacularly. It's hard to say what sort of response he expected, but it could hardly have been what he got—namely, what observers are already referring to as the Camelot speech."

The commentator was on tape. It was now being viewed, for the hundredth time, by a fuming Bernie Bittberg. He sat in front of the VCR in his office, feeling his innards broil as he watched tape after frustrating tape. The rest of the debate, Bernie thought, including most of his exceptional observations and responses, had been totally overshadowed by Penn's performance in the first five minutes. A performance that he, Bernie, had helped to cue.

There was a knock at his door, and Bernie called unenthusiastically, "Come in."

Moe entered and looked around in distaste. Crumbled memos and newspapers were scattered everywhere, as were half-drunk cups of coffee and several stale doughnuts. When Bernie saw who it was, his mouth assumed the frown that came to it so naturally these days.

"So. It's the turncoat. I haven't seen you since the night of the debacle—oh, pardon me, the debate."

"Now, Bernie—"

"You can save the 'Now, Bernie' bullshit! You're outta here, Mr. Brilliance. You and your genius idea."

"You went a little far," said Moe reasonably. "When it became clear that he wasn't going to crack immediately, you should have backed off."

"Backed off? Now you're giving me backed off! I go in there with guns blazing, and you leave me with no ammo. You said he'd come out and say he was some long-dead king."

"Well, he did," said Moe reasonably.

"Yeah, but he came off smelling like a rose! He wasn't supposed to do that!"

"Obviously he didn't read the script."

Bernie sighed and sagged back in his chair. "So where does this leave us?"

"You're asking me? I thought I was through."

"Oh, come on. How could I do that to one of the top seven P.R. hacks I ever knew?"

"I thought I was one of the top three."

"You're sinking fast."

"Wonderful." Moe circled the table slowly. "Where we stand now is in the hands of the voters. But I've been reading the polls pretty carefully, and everyone who's predicting a landslide for Penn is off base, as far as I'm concerned."

"You think so? You're not just bullshittin' now?"

"No, I'm very serious. A lot of people were suspicious of the Camelot speech. The more perceptive voters sense that Arthur really does have a screw loose. Add to that that there are a hell of a lot of people out there who vote along a party line. Asking a Democrat to vote for an Independent can be like asking them to switch toothpastes."

"Maybe," said Bernie. "Still, I wish that Penn were the Republican candidate. I think people would be even less likely to cross party lines to vote for him. Why don't you think that Penn tried for the Democratic nomination? If it were just him and Goodwin, they could be putting his monogram on the welcome mat to Gracie Mansion right now."

"Because Arthur's an independent thinker. There's no way in hell that you'd convince him to go along any party line on earth."

"That might be his fatal flaw. If he allied himself more, he could have had it iced before the polls opened."

Moe shook his head. "Men like Arthur Penn always have to carve their own way in life."

"I've never understood that sort of thinking." Bernie leaned back too far in his chair. It crashed over backward, sending him tumbling to the floor with loud curses and bruised dignity.

"No, Bernie," said Moe, "I don't suppose you would."

It was several minutes before midnight.

Arthur sat in his dressing gown, staring out the window of his modest apartment, staring up at the moon. It was a cloudless night, and only a sliver of the new moon was visible, but there were many stars to make up for it.

Arthur chose a star and wished fervently on it, so fervently that he stood there for a full minute with eyes tightly shut. When he opened them he half hoped that his wish would be granted. But Merlin had not materialized in his living room.

He paced like a caged panther. It was an incredible feeling of helplessness, not even knowing where to start looking for the kidnapped seer. Was he in New York? New Jersey? The East Coast, the West Coast? Was he even in the United States? Arthur moaned and rubbed his temples. Merely contemplating the possibilities made his head hurt.

He turned and looked at the telephone. It sat there, inviting, so tempting. To talk to her for just a moment . . . That would be all he needed to patch together the relationship that had once meant so much to him. But obviously it hadn't meant anything to her, or she would not have made a mockery of it. But still . . .

He stood over the phone, the man decisive in all matters except those of the heart—a failing many men share.

In Queens a demon entered the apartment that Gwen De-Vere shared with an old college friend, Wendy Goldstein.

Wendy, fortunately enough, did not encounter the demon. She was off visiting her parents for a week. She did not know that a demon was going to come this night to attack her old friend. If she had, she might have stayed around to help out. Either that or she might have gone farther than to visit her parents in Pennsylvania—say, for example, her maiden aunt in Portland, Oregon. Either way, she was not home when the demon, clinging to a wall outside a window seven stories up in an apartment complex in Queens, paid his visit.

It was a different demon than the one that had abortedly stolen Excalibur. This one was about average height, with more humanoid features. It had several distinguishing characteristics however, such as dark green skin and fur, which covered its bottom half and back. It was baldheaded, with pointed ears and small twin horns projecting from its temples. And it had a grimly determined expression on its face as it pried its fingertips into the small space between the bottom of the window and the sill. The demon got a firm grip and pulled upward. The window slid up, rattling and shaking, and the demon winced at the noise.

It was embarrassing, breaking and entering like some sort of human. Transportation through time and space was within the demon's powers, but Morgan had been unsure of the exact physical location of the apartment where Gwen was staying. The demon could only transport to where it had already once physically been, and even that could be difficult. So skulking around was the only alternative.

But it had found her now. It could see Gwen lying asleep on the bed in the small spare bedroom. Her blanket was pulled tightly up to her chin; she was curled in a fetal position. Her breathing appeared ragged to the demon—clearly she was not sleeping well. It grinned and clicked its long fingernails together. Soon she would be sleeping forever.

It pulled its torso through the window, then one leg, then the other. It paused there inside the apartment, relishing the expected moment of the kill.

There was a single light cast from the hallway as it approached Gwen. Her lovely face looked drawn and harsh in the stark light. The demon crept toward here, careful to make not the slightest noise. As it passed the nightstand with the telephone, it thought eagerly of the blood that would soon be on its hands. It grinned, and the grin looked all the more hideous on that inhuman face.

The phone rang.

It froze. One eye was riveted on the phone, the other on Gwen. It was unsure whether to disappear or leap to the attack. That damnable phone!

The phone rang once again.

Miles away, Arthur paused. He'd changed his mind. He slammed the receiver back into its cradle, turned and looked outside at the moon again, wondering if he would ever understand (a) women, and (b) himself.

There was no further noise from the telephone. Slowly, bit by bit, the demon started to relax. The phone had rung twice, stopped, and not resumed. Probably it had been someone who realized abruptly that they'd dialed a wrong number and hung up quickly to avoid embarrassment. It was, after all, midnight. Midnight, when the powers of creatures such as it were at their strongest. Midnight, when Gwen DeVere, lover of Arthur Pendragon, would cease to exist. For she had not stirred in the slightest when the phone rang, which meant that she was definitely easy pickings.

It leaned over her bed, grabbed her shoulder, and rolled her roughly onto her back.

It had thought she was asleep. But she was staring at it with eyes wide open and bright with fury.

The demon's first thought was, Drat, this may be a little tougher than I thought. Just how tough, it was soon to realize.

Gwen's right arm shot up, grabbing the demon by the left horn. She pulled down quickly, and unsurprisingly, the demon's head and body went with it.

Her left hand appeared. It had the skull-shaped knife. The tip was at the throat of the demon.

"Want to whistle when you breathe?" asked Gwen.

The demon gulped. It had a large Adam's apple which bobbed up and down and bumped against the point of the knife.

"Please," whispered the demon urgently. "Don't kill me. Don't—"

Gwen's voice was hoarse with strain and tension. "If I wanted to kill you, I could have done that already."

"Then why haven't you?"

"Because, you ugly spud, I need you. I need you to take me to Morgan."

"Ohhhh, you don't want to go to Morgan," said the demon. The back of its head was pressed against Gwen's lap, its body twisted around. Its arms, however, were free. Gwen felt the tension in its body begin to build and she pressed the knife ever-so-more gently against its throat. A small trickle of greenish blood appeared. The demon gasped.

"Oh, yes," purred Gwen. "I do. I do want to go to Morgan. And you'll take me there."

"But she'll kill me! And then she'll kill you." The demon tried to strike a conversational tone. "Let's talk about this sensibly. We're both caught in circumstances here. No sense both of us dying, right? So let me kill you quickly and painlessly, and at least one of us can go on living."

"And what advantage would that be to me?" said Gwen.

The demon paused a moment, its thick eyebrows furrowing. "I'd . . . I'd never forget you." But even the demon didn't sound completely convinced by that. And Gwen certainly wasn't.

"Nice try," said Gwen. "Take me to her. Now!"

"All right! All right!" The demon suddenly started to breathe rapidly. Gwen looked down at it frantically. "What the hell is it now?"

"I'm—" The demon gasped repeatedly. "I'm hyperventilating."

"Oh, Christ."

The demon's chest continued to rise and fall rapidly. "A-hunh! A-hunh! A-hunh!"

"Oh, Jesus Christ in the foothills. Wait here."

Gwen rolled out of the bed, dashed into the bathroom, and came back moments later with some Valium and a cup of water. She leaned over the demon and proferred them, her hands trembling but her face a mask of intensity. The demon took the offerings, swallowed the tranquilizers and washed them down quickly. Then it lay back full on the bed and tried to calm down. "I'm . . . I'm sorry—"

"Be quiet. Just get yourself together." She shook her head. "All the demons in the world and she has to send me one who goes hyper in tense situations."

"Look!" said the demon. "There's demons and there's

demons. We're all pretty much alike to you mortals, like you're pretty much all alike to us. Some of us just handle tension better than others. If you'd just had the common decency to stay asleep and let me gut you like I'd planned, none of this would have happened."

"Gee, I'm sorry to have inconvenienced you," she said with as much sarcasm as she could muster.

"You're not exactly Miss Tough-as-Nails either. Look at you. Your hands are shaking. Your eyes are glazed."

"Of course they are," snapped Gwen. "I haven't slept for four days now. I was certain Morgan would want to make some sort of attack on me prior to the election, to demoralize Arthur. But I didn't know exactly when. I'm so loaded with uppers, I have to wear lead weights on my belt to keep my feet on the floor."

"Oh, dear."

"How do you think it feels, lying there at night, staring at the ceiling, waiting for someone or something—no offense—to come after me? I'd hoped it would be Morgan. So she sent a flunky. Okay, that's cool. As long as the end result is the same."

The demon regarded her with open curiosity. Gwen had pulled her strawberry-blond hair back in a tight bun. She wore a tight-fitting black sweater, black slacks, and black shoes. "You're not at all the way Morgan described you. She made you sound like . . . like . . ."

"Like a wimp?" She nodded. "Circumstances change people." She waved her knife. "Come on, up. Let's go. Let's move it."

The demon nodded slowly. "My name's Morty," it said. "You performed a service for me, helping me out when I was having my . . . my problem a moment ago. The rules say that means I have to serve you now."

"Great. Fine. Let's go."

Morty stood and weaved slightly from side to side. "Ohhhh boy," it muttered.

"What is it now?"

"That tranquilizer is reacting more powerfully than I expected. I'm feeling really woozy."

"Well, let's get moving before you get too woozy to do anything useful. Where's your car, or whatever?"

"We transport. Just give me a second." It squinted at her. "You got a compact?"

"In the nightstand. Why, you planning to freshen up?" she asked incredulously.

It went over to the nightstand, rummaged through the drawer, pulled out the round compact and tossed it to Gwen. She caught it and looked uncomprehendingly.

"I'll explain on the way," said Morty. "I'll fill you in on a little trick I taught a guy named Pericles. You'll love it."

The demon walked over to her, raised his arms and said, "Hold me around the waist."

Gwen complied. Her face against the demon's back, she said, "Is this necessary for me to be transported with you?"

"Not at all," said the demon. "But I get off on it."

Before Gwen could reply, they vanished in a puff of black smoke.

As they reappeared outside Morgan's New Jersey home, Morty had just finished filling Gwen in on the little trick it had taught Pericles.

Gwen looked up, saw the ominous house and shuddered. But something else took her attention more immediately. It was pouring rain. She hugged herself tightly and wiped the water from her face.

Morty was looking up in dismay. "Aw, nuts. It was so nice out earlier."

Gwen frowned. "Yeah. Yeah, it was. In fact . . ." Her eyes widened even as her clothes started to become plastered to her skin. "I heard a weather report earlier. It was great weather tonight in New York and New Jersey! They weren't expecting heavy rain until—"

She turned on him, grabbing him by the scruff of the neck. "You idiot!" she shrieked into his face. "It was supposed to rain like this tomorrow! Not today. You jumped us through time!"

"Impossible!" bleated Morty. "If I had, your watch would have been automatically recalibrated through the nature of the spell I use. Look at your watch."

She looked at her watch. It was a digital. It read eight-ten P.M., November seventh.

"It is! You moron! The polls just closed. The election's

already over. It's only a matter of counting the votes now."

"Then what's the problem?" shouted Morty over the sound of thunder rumbling in the storm. "Even setting Merlin free—"

"I don't know," Gwen shouted back. "But Morgan's going to try something. I just feel it. And the only one who could stop her is Merlin."

Chaptre the Eighteenth

The Colonial Room at the Roosevelt Hotel, near Grand Central Station, had been made over completely in preparation for election night. The walls and ceilings had been festooned with balloons and crepe paper. Three televisions had been set up to monitor the election returns on the local news stations and network affiliates. Tables had been laid with several tons of food, including chicken legs, meatballs, and countless other munchies. The room was already packed with supporters, apprehensive campaign workers, news people, and whoever else had even a near-legitimate reason for being there.

Arthur was not present, however. Up on the third floor, in a suite with a fully stocked bar, he was pacing like a caged panther. He looked at his watch: 8:15. He turned to Percy, who was sitting there with infinite patience, and demanded, "Where the hell is she? She can't have vanished into thin air."

"With all due respect, Arthur, you've made it more than clear to her that she is not your favorite person and you are just as happy when she's not around."

"Yes, but . . ." Arthur waved his hands in meaningless circles and then let his arms fall limply to his sides. "You're right, I suppose. Still, it's damned odd."

"Maybe."

"The polls are closed," said Ronnie, who was reclining on a

sofa. "Early word is that this is going to be a tough election to call."

Arthur turned to him. "To call what?"

"It's a bizarre phenomenon, Arthur," said Ronnie bemusedly. "All the stations want to be the first to announce a winner. So over the years they've started predicting who the winner will be earlier and earlier in the evening. Sometimes with as little as one percent of the vote tabulated."

"Really?" asked Arthur, fascinated. "One percent? But that sounds so insane. I mean . . . isn't that the equivalent of going up to a crowd of a hundred people, picking one person, getting his opinion, and assuming that the rest of the crowd can have their opinions guessed at from this one chap?"

Percy smiled. "It's more scientific than that, Arthur."

"Oh." Arthur nodded. "Science. Incomprehensible. Give me magic any day."

Morty walked quietly in front of Gwen, taking several steps, pausing and listening, then gesturing for her to follow. It was nervewracking, slow progress. Yet with this method they had managed to penetrate into the hallways of Morgan's house without detection. The demon had maneuvered itself and Gwen past the detection wards placed around the house, and now, as they crept through hallways dimly lit by candles along the wall, Gwen started to feel as if the corridor were closing in on her. "Oh, God," she moaned softly.

Morty turned to face her. "What?" it asked anxiously.

Her lips tight, Gwen hissed back, "I don't know. I'm starting to feel clammy. I'm sweating like the devil. My hands are trembling. . . ."

It nodded, its inhuman face etched with very human concern. "We have to get you out of here."

"No. Arthur needs Merlin. So that's who I came here to get. Which way?"

The demon paused, for they had reached a corridor with a fork. It looked off to the right and to the left, then pointed left and said, "This way."

They padded noiselessly down the hallway. At the end of the hall Gwen saw that it opened out and there was brighter light at the end. Morty drew up short and she bumped into it. Her hand brushed against its furred rump. It grinned maliciously. "I didn't know you cared."

"Shut up."

"Fine." It pointed toward the end of the corridor. "That's Morgan's inner sanctum. That's where she was keeping Merlin, I assume. She's never let me in there."

She nodded, and the knife was in her hand. Its tip glittered in the dim light. She only wished that she could have wielded Excalibur. Even so, she still felt herself an enemy to conjure with.

They got to the end of the corridor, Gwen straining her ears for some sound that Morgan was in the vicinity. And she did hear something. It was a television, and it was tuned to the election returns.

Gwen pushed past the demon now, and bold as brass, walked into the inner sanctum of Morgan Le Fey.

Morgan wasn't there. Morty came in behind Gwen and peeked over her shoulder. Its sigh of relief was audible.

Gwen's glance took in the large pillows, the black walls and tables, and then over on one side, as if it were a trophy, the column of crystal with Merlin embedded inside.

Gwen's breath caught. "Oh, God," she murmured, her fingers interlacing as if in prayer. "Oh, God, I'm so sorry."

She started across the room to Merlin, caution thrown aside. Morty was right behind her. "Gwen," it started to say, "I don't think we—"

Suddenly there was a dazzling flash of light and Gwen felt as if something had exploded behind her with concussive force. She rolled forward, the strength of the blast carrying her, and her left shoulder impacted with the crystal column that held Merlin prisoner. She rolled over and looked behind her, where the blast had originated, and squinted against the fading light.

Where Morty had been there was now a small pile of steaming ashes. Gwen moaned, deep in her throat. Then, her jaw set, she looked past the remains of the demon to see Morgan standing on the other side of the room. Her left hand rested affectionately on Lance's shoulder. Her right hand was still smoldering from the force of the spell she'd just unleashed.

Morgan looked at the mound of ashes and shook her head. "It's so hard," she lamented, "to get good help nowadays."

*   *   *

The desk clerk looked with great distaste at Chico and Groucho. "Sirs, I am afraid that Mr. Penn does not wish to be disturbed. I am not going to tell you what room he's in. My understanding is that he will be coming down to greet all his constituents—"

"Look," said Chico reasonably. "We knew this was gonna be a fancy hotel and everything. Percy said we should have ties and everything, and we did." He rummaged in the pocket of his beat-up duffel jacket and pulled out a wrinkled brown tie. He waved it in the desk clerk's face. "See?"

"Yes. I see." His brow clouded. "And I also see that I'm going to have to call the police unless you—"

Groucho leaned forward. "Now listen," he said intensely. "We're not, what you said before, constituents. We're knights. We're the first ones. Arthur said so. Arthur wouldn't bullshit us, the way you are. Now either you ring his room and tell him we're here"—and his voice lowered as he delivered the most horrendous threat he could pull to mind—"or we're gonna go into the middle of your lobby and take our clothes off."

The desk clerk picked up the phone immediately, his eyes never leaving the two unsavory characters. The phone up in Arthur's suite was picked up on the second ring, and the desk clerk said, "Sir, I hate to bother you, but two rather disreputable looking characters have—" He stopped talking as he heard something on the other end that he clearly had trouble believing. Then he nodded slowly and put the phone down. "Room three twelve," he said without looking at them.

"Thanks, man," said Chico. He headed over toward the elevator, but Groucho remained there, glowering at the desk clerk. Chico took him by the elbow and dragged him over to the elevator. One showed up almost immediately. They stepped in, and as the doors started to close, the desk clerk shouted, "I'm glad *I* didn't vote for him!"

Groucho lunged as the doors closed on him. The desk clerk grinned and went back to his work.

Minutes later Groucho and Chico were in the Royal Suite, helping themselves to the bar. The television was already on in the corner. Ronnie was saying, "Now in presidential elections, the polls were closing three hours earlier on the east coast than on the west coast. Then the networks started doing their predicting thing, saying that one candidate had won before thousands of people in the west had gone to the polls. So they didn't bother voting. Quite a brouhaha."

"I've had enough of this," said Arthur abruptly, heading for the door. "A true leader doesn't hide from his men when the final campaign begins. He's at their side. Why am I hiding up here?"

"Drama, Arthur!" said Percy. He sipped his seltzer. "The people expect it. They want it. They need to look forward to your appearance if the evening's going to build to any sort of climax for them. That's your one problem, Arthur." He finished his seltzer and poured another glass. "No sense of drama."

Ronnie suddenly said, "Arthur. First returns are in. Only one percent of the vote in. . . ."

Arthur looked at Ronnie, hunched in front of the set, and turned away. He stared at the drink in his hands. "Have they predicted a winner?"

"No. Not yet. Too early."

Arthur sensed the unspoken *but* hanging in the air, and voiced it. "But. . . ?"

"But at the moment—only at the moment, mind you—"

"Out with it, Ronnie."

"Bittberg's in the lead."

It's going to be close," said Morgan. "Make no mistake, little queen. It will be close. But Arthur shall lose."

Gwen's eyes never left Morgan. The sorceress had not moved from the spot where Gwen had first seen her. But Lance, dressed like something out of the *Road Warrior*, was already starting to creep in her direction. "You're wrong, Morgan. You're going to lose. Everything."

"My, oh my." Morgan looked down her nose at Gwen. "The little queen has become quite the bold one. I haven't forgiven you, you know, for that attack in the park." Her fingers drifted to her cheek.

"I figured you wouldn't. I banked on that being my eventual ticket here." Her gaze and the point of her knife momentarily flicked in the direction of Lance, who froze. "Don't try it, Lance. I swear I'll kill you."

"Why, Gwen," said Morgan. "You're positively a woman warrior, aren't you?"

"Not a wimp?" Gwen replied. "You don't understand, do

you, Morgan. All my life I felt like a nothing. Like everyone
always stepped on me. Then along came Arthur, and he made
me feel like someone. And now I've lost him. Lost him thanks
to you. Without Arthur I don't care what happens to me. I
don't care if I live or die. And when you stop caring, it means
you can become reckless. That, and I've been using my brains
a bit. I've watched what happens. I'm figuring out the limits
of your power."

"Are you now?"

Lance was creeping up on Gwen's right. Taking small,
careful steps, Gwen sidled to her left, keeping a large table
between herself and Lance. Still she continued to watch
Morgan, Morgan the unmoving. "Yes. For example, I've
figured out that when you are attacked mystically, you defend
and counterattack mystically. But when you're attacked
physically, the only way to ward it off is by physical means.
That's why they burned witches, isn't it?"

"Hanging was also popular," said Morgan dryly.

"That's why that demon could take Merlin with his bare
hands. That is why I could take you in the park. And that is
why," and her voice rose suddenly, "I'm going to take you
now!"

She drew her hand back, the skull-shaped dagger in her
hand now held by the point, and she hurled the dagger straight
at Morgan's chest. The dagger flew unerringly and plunged
deep into Morgan's breast, piercing her evil heart and putting
an end to her forever.

At least that's what Gwen had hoped would happen.

Actually she missed by a country mile. The dagger,
weighted completely improperly for throwing, spun erratically
in its flight and hit the wall behind Morgan a good three feet to
her right. It thudded to the ground, way out of Gwen's reach.

"Uh-oh," muttered Gwen.

Morgan raised her hand. "Oh, little queen," she said, "you
who are not afraid to die. Who are reckless. I'm going to show
you that there are worse things than death. Now . . ."

Back at the Roosevelt Hotel Arthur was watching the set intensely now. A mask of gloom had spread over his face. "I
don't understand," he murmured. "Don't they know what's
best for them? Look at that."

At that moment, with two percent of the voting in, Bittberg was at forty-six percent and Arthur was at forty-two percent with Archibald Goodwin and all the others left far behind. The newscasters were already intimating that Bernard Bittberg was the new mayor of New York City.

The phone rang. Arthur leaned over and picked it up while the others in the suite looked on. "Yes?" said Arthur.

"Bernie Bittberg here, Art!" said Bittberg on the other end. Audible over the phone were noisemakers, party music, and the like. Bittberg was shouting to be heard. "Ready to concede yet?"

"Concede?"

"Yeah. You know, quit. There's no need to be a sore loser, Art."

"I wouldn't know," said Arthur evenly. "I don't make a habit of losing."

He dropped the phone back into the cradle.

But he was not happy. Not happy at all.

It happened with incredible swiftness.

Gwen pivoted and leaped in the direction of Lance Benson.

Lance, thinking she was trying to escape, shouted, "Don't worry, Morgan! I got her!" And so saying, he grabbed for Gwen. He got a grip on her shoulders and made as if to hold her in place. It looked to all intents and purposes that he had a really solid grasp on her.

Morgan's hands were glowing. The power of the spell was already in existence, and once called into the world, the power had to be unleashed lest it backlash against the wielder. Morgan passed her hands through the air, the gestures shaping the nature of the spell, and the power was aimed right at Gwen.

At the last second Gwen suddenly twisted away from Lance, breaking his grip easily, fear pumping adrenaline through her body. She dropped to the ground, shielding her eyes. Lance only had the chance to open his mouth and start to frame a question before he was bathed in the light of the spell. There was a sudden sound, like a vacuum being sucked into a bottle instead of being allowed out. One instant Lance was there, the next he wasn't.

Actually, that was not quite true. There was a large, gray rodent skittering around on the floor, squeaking angrily.

Morgan looked down in dismay. She said, "Rats."

Her smoldering eyes turned to Gwen, and without saying another word, she gestured and a blast of eldritch energy blew from her hand. Gwen leaped out of the way, sure-footed in her black tennis sneakers. She felt the air sizzle around her, and looked around. Where the energy bolt had missed her, several large pillows and a good chunk of the floor were gone.

Her heart pounding like a trip-hammer, Gwen moved quickly in Merlin's direction, praying that somehow the trapped magician would be able to aid her. She reached the crystal column and clung to it like a life preserver, looking defiantly at Morgan.

"You think he can help you?" said Morgan disdainfully. "Don't kid yourself, my queenlette. But let's fine tune the spell, just for you, to make sure I don't accidentally release the little bastard."

She pointed and a single beam of lambent energy shot forth. Gwen threw her back against the crystal column, and the energy beam passed within a hair's breadth of her breasts.

"You can't win!" crowed Morgan.

"Get stuffed!" Gwen screamed back. She circled behind Merlin's prison, keeping the crystal column between the two of them. She felt terrible about putting Merlin in the middle of all this, yet what choice did she have? But she couldn't keep it up all day. . . .

Her hand trailed over the small bulge in her hip pocket, and she remembered what the demon had said. It was worth a try, because she sure as hell couldn't keep dodging all night.

Morgan advanced on her slowly. "Come out, little queen. I promise you it will be painless. . . ."

"Everyone is so concerned about my welfare," muttered Gwen.

Compact firmly in hand, Gwen suddenly leaped out from behind Merlin. Morgan shouted her triumph and let fly a bolt of energy.

Gwen flipped open the compact and held it between her and Morgan. The pencil-thin beam of light hit the mirror and bounced off. Gwen had hoped that it would bounce back and hit Morgan herself. Instead the beam shot off to the left and struck the crystal column in which Merlin was trapped.

"No!" screamed Morgan, but it was too late. Like a laser

cracking a diamond, the spell of disintegration pierced the crystal. A weblike pattern of lines appeared on the crystal surface, and Merlin's small body began to glow with power. Again Morgan cried *"No!"* but that was a split second before the crystal shattered into a million shards. Gwen shielded her eyes, but miraculously, or perhaps magically, not so much as a single piece cut her. Morgan, on the other hand, was unable to fend off what seemed like thousands of angry hornets ripping at her. She went down, pieces of crystal embedded in her dress and skin.

Merlin stood there. His eyes were smoldering with anger and power. His fists were clenched and glowing. "Morgan," he said in a dangerous voice, "you've kept bound forces with which you should not have tampered."

"You little fiend!" Morgan cried. "That's the second time you've done that. First you nearly get me cut to ribbons with my own television set, and now this. Well no more, I tell you. No more!"

Her body glowed. "You're in my place now, Merlin! You cannot win!"

"Gwen! Behind me!" ordered Merlin. Gwen barely had time to comply before Morgan's mystical attack was launched.

"And in a sudden reversal," the newscaster was saying, "returns from the upper Manhattan voting districts have tilted the balloting more toward Arthur Penn. . . ."

Arthur, up in his suite, could swear that he heard a roar of approval go up from the gathering room downstairs. He smiled as the newscaster said, "Once again this race has become so close that it has become impossible to call."

"Gentlemen," said Percy, "it looks like we're going to be putting in a long night."

Merlin had erected his mystical defenses barely in time. A sphere of pure energy surrounded Merlin and Gwen as Morgan's powerful spells bounced off the shields. Pillows imploded into nothingness. Walls began to melt into puddles. And Morgan's wrath grew.

Merlin, his face frozen in concentration, worked on maintaining the shields that were preserving their lives. Gwen crawled to him and demanded, "Now what?"

"You're asking me?" said Merlin desperately. "You're the one who came to the rescue. I assumed you'd figured a way out."

"I did," said Gwen. "You're it."

"Wonderful," replied Merlin.

Energy cascaded around them, dancing in little sparks. "I can't hold her back much longer," grated Merlin. "I'm too weak. I've been cooped up for too long."

"Then what are we going to do?"

"Will you stop asking me that?"

"All right," said Gwen angrily. *"All right!"* She started to stand. "Cover me."

Merlin looked at her, aghast. "What do you think this is, *Gunfight at the OK Corral*? What do you mean, cover you?"

"I'm going to get her."

"You're insane! There are forces being unleashed here you know nothing about."

"Good," said Gwen. "If I knew about them, I'd probably be more terrified than I am right now. See you next lifetime, Merlin."

"Gwen—"

Gwen DeVere leaped out from behind the protection of Merlin's shields. She rolled across the smoldering carpet as Morgan, blind with fury, directed her attack at Gwen's quick-moving form. Gwen, heart pounding with excitement, mind racing thanks to the uppers, moved with a speed that defied description. And Morgan, caught up in her anger, used her power wildly, recklessly. She did not take time to aim, or plan, or think. She was reacting on the most primal level—utter rage. Gwen broke right, broke left, leaped forward, then pivoted and dodged again to the right. Explosions of primal force bracketed her. A chunk of floor tilted wildly under her and she jumped off it, rolling that much closer to Morgan. A sudden instinct warned her, and she ducked to one side as a huge piece of plaster from the ceiling fell and shattered right where she'd been.

Morgan was grinning wildly. "You're going to die, Guinevere, you slut!" she shrieked. "My brother's whore! There'll be less than nothing left of you when I'm through."

Still two yards away, Gwen grated, "All talking, bitch queen, but no action. Hiding behind your spells and your pretty lights! When it comes down to the crunch, you just don't have what it takes.''

"You . . . you . . ." Raw energy flew between Morgan's palms and arced outward at Gwen. She leaped in the one direction Morgan had not anticipated—straight at her. Gwen came in low in a flying tackle, her arms wrapped around Morgan's legs, and the two of them went down in a tumble of arms and legs.

Merlin shouted from across the room, "Gwen! Don't look in her eyes! Not at such close quarters!" And Gwen, hearing his words, shut her eyes tightly, even as she and Morgan rolled, struggling hand to hand.

Then Gwen was on her back, Morgan straddling her. There was a triumphant gleam in Morgan's eyes that Gwen didn't see. "I don't need my magic to finish you, little queen." She brought her hand down, open, slapping it across Gwen's cheek. "That's just the beginning of paying you back for what you've done to me."

The pain raced through Gwen's face even as she brought her legs up from behind and wrapped her knees around Morgan's neck. The sorceress gagged, gasping for air, as Gwen turned and slammed her down on the ground. The impact stunned Morgan momentarily, and also caused Gwen to involuntarily open her eyes. Her gaze fell on the skull-headed knife with which she had missed her mark earlier. It was just out of her reach. Quick as lightning she released her hold on Morgan and hurled herself at the knife. Her desperate fingers curled around the hilt, and before Morgan could regain her senses, Gwen had thrown herself across Morgan's prostrate form.

She held the knife over Morgan's rapidly rising breasts.

"Finish her!" shouted Merlin.

Morgan, petrified, made no move. Her gaze shifted from the knife to Gwen, but Gwen was careful not to look at her directly. Her entire concentration was on the point of the knife, poised directly over her fallen foe's heart. Gwen's hand trembled. She bit her lip.

"Dammit, woman! What are you waiting for? Kill her!" Merlin screamed.

"I—" Gwen half sobbed, exhaustion overtaking her. "I can't! I can't just kill someone. We've beaten her. Isn't that enough?"

The air crackled around them. Gwen's head flew back, her

mouth open in a silent scream. And then, like a marionette, Gwen was hurled back, soaring through the air, her body twisted. She hit a wall with a sickening crunch and slid to the floor like a broken doll. A small trickle of blood ran down the side of her mouth. She did not move again.

"No," said Morgan, getting slowly to her feet. "It wasn't enough, little queen. Not nearly enough."

Arthur was in the men's room. Percy watched dismally as the latest tallies were reported. He turned to Ronnie, Groucho, and Chico and said simply, "The gap is widening. We may lose her."

Morgan started to laugh. She tilted her head back, her mouth opened wide, and she started to laugh. Then a mystic bolt hit her with full impact. Her instincts warned her barely in time to raise a most minimal shield. She fell back, terror in her eyes.

Merlin was standing there. His fists were glowing, smoke rising from them. His eyes were little more than white, pupil-less spots with energy crackling from them. Lance the Rat cowered in a corner.

"All right, Morgan." The voice of an old man rose from the throat of a young boy. "This ends here. Now."

The air exploded.

Ed Shukin on WNYW looked surprised. "And with new returns coming in, we see another swing in the direction of Arthur Penn. With ten percent of the votes tallied, it now appears that the Independent candidate and Bernard Bittberg, the Democratic candidate, are even at forty-six percent each. To be honest, I have covered many a political race and I cannot recall in recent history one that seesawed quite as much as this one has. But I would have to say that, at this point, it is far too early to call Arthur Penn out of the race."

Arthur stood up and slapped his knees. "I'm going downstairs."

"But Arthur—"

"Protocol be damned, Percy," said Arthur good-naturedly. "Those are my people down there. We started this together and by Uther we're going to finish it together. All of us."

"Not all of us," Chico piped up. "Where's Gwen?"

"Yeah. And the kid?" added Groucho.

Arthur sighed. "I'm quite certain," he said, "that if they could be here, they would."

Time lost its meaning, warped and twisted back on itself as the battle raged between Morgan and Merlin.

Neighbors of Morgan's in Verona looked out their windows, turning from their televisions in shock as unleashed elemental forces erupted from the old house. The ground started to rumble, narrow crevices opening in the weed-covered grounds. Windows glowed with wild, unearthly fires. And those who were of a more imaginative bent thought that bizarre black shapes, twisted and reeking of evil, emerged from the cracks and sideboards, from the chimney and the gutters, dissipating into the rainy night—dozens of them, creatures that had been Morgan's slaves, on whose energy Morgan had fed. Poltergeists, near-formless creatures that on their own created minor mischief but which, under the control of a master necromancer, could alter probabilities on a wide scale —and even effect election returns—vanished into the night. Morgan's control of them slipped through her fingers as she utilized every iota of mystical energy she possessed in her battle against Merlin.

Arcane shields hovered before her, cracking and splintering. She blocked Merlin's thrusts the way a fencer would, but more and more began to slip through. She began to weaken mystically. Her energy slipped away from her. Only her hate grew and grew, but hate is destructive force rather than constructive.

Merlin advanced on her, his face set. Morgan battered at his defenses, but he had had time to recuperate. The edge was his, and he was not for one moment permitting Morgan to recapture it. His lips were constantly moving, chanting, invoking the power of the gods, drawing strength from bands of mystic energy that hovered before him.

"Damn you, Merlin Satan-Spawn!" Morgan cried. She raised her hands above her head and abruptly dropped her defenses, pulling all her mystic reserves together. A solid black bolt of power sizzled through the air like a thing alive. And Merlin brushed it aside as if she'd tossed a feather at him. It

angled upward, blasting through the roof of the old house.
Sparks flew from it as it passed, caught on the shingle roof.
The roof began to blaze.

·· Neighbors on the sidewalk pointed at the fire and hurried to
call the fire department.

"Merlin." Morgan raised a hand. "We could rule together—"

"Go to hell," said Merlin. His hands formed the horns of
Satan, and eldritch power flowed from them. Morgan hastily
tried to create more shields, but Merlin's spell passed through
them as if they were not there. The power surrounded Morgan, bathing her in an unearthly light, and she clenched her
fists, beating at air as she screamed her fury. "You haven't
won yet! I still hate!"

Her body turned black, then pale blue. And then, with a
rush of air, Morgan's body exploded outward.

Merlin turned away as a wave of light and heat rushed at
him, and a foul stench that made him gag. When he looked
back, in the space where Morgan had been, there was nothing.

No, not quite nothing. A black cloud was there, hovering,
fuming. Merlin rushed to create a spell of containment, but
before it was fully formed, the black cloud slipped away and
vanished through the walls.

The ceiling overhead burst into flames. The fire had worked
its way downward, and the house was going quickly. Merlin
dashed over to the side of the fallen Gwen, fully expecting to
find a corpse. He knelt beside her, lifted her wrist and checked
her pulse. To his surprise he found one, strong and steady.

He took her face in his hands even as the room began to fill
with smoke. "Gwen!" he shouted. "Get up! I don't know if I
have enough power to get us both out of here! Gwen, speak to
me!"

Gwen snored.

"Oh, bloody wonderful," said Merlin. A sharp cracking
overhead alerted him, and he saw a flaming timber break off
and fall toward them. He spoke then, spellcasting faster than
he ever had in his life.

The timber crashed down.

"Repeat," said Edward Shukin to his viewing audience,
"we are projecting Arthur Penn as the winner of this year's
mayoral election—"

The repeat was not heard, for the cheer that had gone up when the announcement was first made totally drowned it out.

In the midst of the crowd Arthur was laughing, cheering, being pounded joyfully on the back. Nubile young women hugged and kissed him, and every man wanted to shake his hand. He was alternately pushed and pulled to the podium up front, and within moments he found himself facing a mob of cheering, enthusiastic fans and workers. He smiled and put up his hands to indicate that they should quiet down, which only provoked further cheering. Laughing, he just stood there and allowed the adulation of the crowd to wash over him, wave after wave of love. It filled his soul to bursting.

Finally the crowd started to calm down enough for Arthur to begin to say, "My friends—"

At that moment Ronnie ran up onto the stage and shouted, "Bittberg just conceded!" And that set off another round of cheering and applause. By the time Arthur finally got to say anything, it was past midnight.

"My friends," he said. "My dear, dear friends. It's been a long fight. It's been a difficult fight. We've had small victories along the way. We've had . . . small losses." He paused, searching for words. "The trust that this city—that you—have in me, a humble visitor from the past"—and this provoked some cheering—"has certainly been gratifying. I swear that I will uphold the trust that you have placed in me, and do the best job for New York City that any mayor has ever done."

Someone in the audience shouted, "When are you running for president?"

Arthur grinned as people applauded. "Well, let's give me a few years to get my feet wet. After all, it's a lot easier being king than being mayor or president. I have a lot to learn first." He waited for the laughter to subside. "When you're a king," he continued, "and you tell people to do something, and by God they do it. When you're a mayor, they ask you why. And when you're a president they bring it over to some house or somesuch where a group of men who don't give a damn what you say get together and decide that they're not going to do it at all."

"Arthur for king!" someone shouted.

Arthur raised a clenched fist in appreciation. "Now that's the kind of forward-looking backward thinking that I intend to make the hallmark of my career!"

The applause was thunderous.

Meanwhile in Verona, New Jersey, the house of Morgan Le Fey burned to ashes.

It was the early hours of the morning when Arthur finally arrived home and stepped into his modest apartment. He looked around and sighed. Merlin had advised that he keep the place, even after he moved into Gracie Mansion. He sighed. No matter where he lived, it would seem pale in comparison to Belvedere Castle. And yet, the castle itself would seem empty now that Gwen wasn't there.

"Congratulations, Mayor Wart."

Arthur spun. There, at his bedroom door, was Merlin. His hair and eyebrows were singed. He had removed his jacket and tie, but his shirt and slacks were blackened from smoke. And to Arthur he had never looked so good.

"Merlin?" He walked slowly toward him, not daring to believe it. "Merlin is it really you?"

"Yes, Wart," he said tiredly. "It's me."

Arthur touched his shoulder gently, tentatively, and then a grin split his face. "You got away, didn't you? You little fox. I should have known." Then his voice hardened. "Where's Morgan, Merlin? Where is she hiding? Tell me, because by Excalibur there'll be a reckoning—"

Merlin raised a hand. "No need, Arthur. There's already been a reckoning. Morgan is dead."

Arthur paused in disbelief. "Dead?"

"Yes. Her body, at any rate. It's hard to destroy her utterly. At the moment all that remains of her is a little discorporated cloud of hate. And I'll get that eventually too. I'd like to put it in a bottle on my mantel. Make a nice conversation piece."

Merlin sauntered across the room and threw himself full length on Arthur's sofa. Arthur followed him, shaking his head wonderingly. "You did it. You really did it. Morgan is gone."

"Well, I had some help. . . ."

"Help? How do you mean?"

Merlin told him. He told him everything—everything Gwen had said, everything that he'd done. And Arthur stood there, trying to take it all in.

"You're saying . . . you're saying that she really saved your life."

"No," said Merlin, positioning the throw pillow under his head. "I'm not saying that. I'll be double damned if I'd ever admit that I needed anyone's help to fight my battles. However, if you say it, I won't contradict it." He stared up at the ceiling. "I was wrong about her, Arthur."

"No, Merlin." Arthur sat across from him. "You were right. You said she wasn't trustworthy, and you were right."

Merlin shook his head. "Her actions were not dishonorable, Arthur. Merely unfortunate. Mistakes, if you prefer. But I've known you to pull one or two boners in your time. Everything that your precious Gwen DeVere did, she did out of a sense of loyalty to someone to whom she had once sworn loyalty. She was certain no lasting harm would come to you. She was betrayed by Morgan in that respect. As I recall, Morgan pulled the wool over your eyes more than one time. As a matter of fact, Modred would never have existed if—"

"I . . . gather your point, Merlin," said Arthur sheepishly. "So that horrid Lance of hers is gone?"

"Not at all. He's over there."

Arthur turned. A small rat was in a corner of the room, sitting under the television set. He was watching the two of them intently, his little nose quivering.

"What are you going to do with him?" asked Arthur. "Feed him to a cobra?" His eyes narrowed. "You're not going to restore him, are you?"

"Oh, Arthur, even if I could, I don't know if I would. But I have no idea what spell Morgan used to change him into a rat. It could take years to find." He sighed. "No, I'm going to keep him in a little cage. He'll be comfortable enough. He'll even have company—Gladys."

"What, the former receptionist?" Arthur looked surprised. "I thought you'd fed her to our new receptionist."

"What, and waste a perfectly good shrew? Phawgh. You never know when she's going to come in handy. No, she's safe and sound at home. And I'm certain she's going to adore her new little friend."

They were silent for a time, and then Arthur said, "Merlin? How can I trust her loyalty to me now?"

Merlin snorted. "Good God, Arthur, that woman went through all manner of hell, on the remote chance that she'd win your favor back. Even though her motives were, in a way, honorable, she was still remorseful over what she'd done. She risked life and limb to win you back by undoing the results of her handiwork.''

Arthur shook his head. "I can't believe some of the things she was capable of.''

"Neither can I," admitted Merlin. "Frankly, I suspect she couldn't either. I never thought, Wart, that I would be trying to talk you into taking that woman back. But I owe you my honest opinion, and I will tell you this, Arthur—I would stake my immortal soul on the loyalty of Gwen DeVere.''

Arthur sat there, square jawed, and then said, "Can I see her?''

"Of course. She's in your bedroom.''

Arthur got up and went into the bedroom. There, stretched out on the bed, was Gwen. There was an ugly bruise on her forehead, and her clothes had the same smoke discoloration as Merlin's. But she was there, and she was sound and whole. Arthur went to her side and took her hand. Her chest rose and fell steadily in sleep. "Gwen?" he said gently, shaking her shoulder.

From the doorway Merlin said, "You're wasting your time, Arthur. As near as I can tell, she was taking some sort of pills to keep herself going. You can only do that to yourself for so long before your body just says, 'Enough.' She's going to sleep for quite some time, I would say. There's not a single thing that you could say or do that would bring her around.''

Arthur glanced at Merlin and then back at Gwen. Then he sat next to her on the bed, squeezed her hand and said, in a voice full of love and affection, "Gwen, would you do me the honor of becoming my wife?''

Gwen's eyes fluttered open. "Yes.''

Merlin sighed and shook his head. "Women!''

Chaptre the Nineteenth

The horses thundered toward each other, hooves kicking up clods of dirt. On their backs the two armored knights, lances firmly in place, were intent on each other's approach. The sun glinted down on their shields, and the crowd roared as they met. The lance of the knight with the blue plume in his helm shattered against the shield of the other jouster, and a cheer went up. The other knight, in the red plume, was the good guy.

The horses reached the opposite ends of the field, and the blue-plumed knight was handed a new lance. He spun his horse, shook a fist at his opponent, and the crowd booed the unsportsmanlike gesture.

It was a beautiful day for a joust on the fields of the Cloisters. Standing within a mile of the jousting field was a castle that housed tapestries and pieces of lovely artwork. Stretched out around the Cloisters was parkland bordered by the Henry Hudson Parkway, and 183rd Street up to 210th Street. It was a little bit of another century staking a claim against the encroachment of this century.

The knights were members of a performing troupe that produced medieval fairs on a regular basis around the country. But this particular medieval fair was for a very special occasion—a celebration, a party to which all of New York City had been invited. And it was to celebrate the election of Arthur Penn to the high office of mayor of New York City.

A reviewing stand erected on the edge of the jousting field had been deliberately designed to look like something out of an ancient tournament. There was a box down front in which the royalty was supposed to sit, and Arthur had very cheerfully and willingly taken his place there, Gwen at his side. Gwen was stunning in a long white gown and a small crown with sparkling jewels on her head. Next to her sat Arthur, looking as if he'd stepped from another time. He was dressed in full chain mail. The main garment was called a hauberk, sort of a nightshirt made out of chain mail that hung to his knees, the skirt slit up the middle almost to the waist. Underneath the hauberk was a padded tunic to prevent the mail from digging into his chest. His leggings were mail tights called chaussures, tied just below his knee with a wide strip of cloth. Over the hauberk Arthur wore a white surcoat—a sleeveless white garment that had no collar or sleeves. It was split up the sides and laced up from the waist to the armpit. The long skirts fell free and were split up the middle the same as the hauberk. A roaring dragon was pictured on his chest.

Around his waist was Excalibur, visible thanks to Merlin, even though Arthur had not drawn it. Nor did he have any intention of drawing it. Of course, even the best of intentions are lost sometimes to the flow of events.

Gwen leaned over. "Arthur, aren't you hot in that outfit?"

"More than you'd believe. But look at them." He gestured to the excited crowds. "They love the entire concept of me as an ancient king. So occasionally I feel that we really have to give the people what they want, no matter how personally uncomfortable I might be. Let's just be thankful it's the end of November rather than the middle of July. Though it is warm for this time of year."

The two knights thundered toward each other once more, and this time in a beautifully choreographed move, they knocked each other off of their respective horses.

The knights, who were dressed in plate armor, turned toward Arthur expectantly. An announcer clad in a jerkin and possessing a considerable set of lungs, shouted, "The combatants request permission from the king to continue the joust on foot." It was the current mayor, all set to embark on his career, and more than willing to play a part in Arthur's show.

Arthur smiled and gave a thumbs-up gesture. The crowd cheered, as they knew they should, as the two knights drew their swords and began hacking at each other's heavy wooden shields. They took turns whacking at each other, wood chips flying from the shields as they moved back and forth, up and down the field. At one point the red-plumed knight went down to one knee and the blue-plumed knight came in for the kill. The red-plumed knight came in low, swung his sword, and caught the blue-plumed knight across the middle. The air rang with the impact of the blow, and the blue-plumed knight went down. The red-plumed knight was up in a flash and held the blade of his sword over the fallen knight. The crowd went wild as the downed fighter put up a hand in supplication and the announcer shouted, "The blue knight yields!"

Arthur applauded the outcome along with the rest of the crowd. There was a tap on his shoulder and he turned. Percy was there, smiling. Arthur looked at him reproachfully. "Percy, you're supposed to have dressed for the occasion."

"But Arthur, I did."

"I hardly think that a Dragon's Lair sweatshirt qualifies as knightly attire."

"Best I could do." He clapped Arthur on the shoulder affectionately and said, "I've seen Merlin wandering around. He looks suspicious."

"Merlin always looks suspicious. That's what he does best—be suspicious. Don't worry about it."

"Okay. You're the king. Is there anything I can get for you?"

"Yes. Something to drink. Anything liquid, short of motor oil."

Percy nodded and left.

Costumed actors wandered about, mixed in with the crowd. Young maidens shrunk in fear as amused tourists snapped their photographs—the lasses were concerned that pieces of their souls were being taken. Knights in armor looked gallant, assassins stalked, and a good time was being had by all.

Percy found a booth where cider was being served, and got a large mug of it for Arthur. He turned and bumped into a knight clothed similarly to Arthur, except that his surcoat was solid black. Not a spot of any other design on it. He held a barrel helmet under his arm.

"Excuse me," said Percy, trying to get around the knight.

But the knight took him forcefully by the arm. Percy looked up in surprise and said, "What do you think you're—" Then his eyes widened. "Moe!"

Modred's eyes smoldered with fury, and he said in a low voice, "Listen to me carefully. Are you listening, Percival?"

Percy stared deep into those angry eyes, and his own glassed over. Modred did not smile at his easy success. He held up a small packet with a green powder in it and said, "You will take this. You will empty the contents into the drink. You will give the drink to Arthur, and you will say nothing about it to him." Modred paused to allow the words to sink in. "Is that understood, Percy?"

Percy nodded, turned and left. He took several steps, then lifted the packet up, tore open the top with his teeth, and spilled the powder into the drink. The cider bubbled momentarily, and a thin wisp of steam rose from it. Then it settled down, changing to a slightly darker hue. Percy stared at it blankly and went on his way.

Modred smiled and turned, only to bump into two scruffy-looking individuals dressed as village idiots.

"Do I know you?" Chico asked him. Groucho, his fellow village idiot, inclined his head slightly and looked at Modred with passing curiosity.

"No," said Modred tightly. "I don't think so." He placed his helmet on his head and stalked away, patting the hilt of his sword eagerly. Chico and Groucho watched him and scratched their heads in thought.

Back in the reviewing stand Gwen was looking at a printed list of activities. "Arthur," she said, "that joust was the last thing. You think we can go soon? I love the gown, but I'd really like to get out of it." She smiled mischievously. "Would you care to help me?"

He laughed. "Ma'am, I'll have you know I'm betrothed."

Gwen rested her head on his shoulder, wrapping her hands around his arm. "It can't be soon enough for me, Arthur," she said.

"Nor for me," he said.

A cup was thrust under Arthur's nose. He looked up and saw Percy there. Percy was smiling, yet something about his expression seemed a little . . . he wasn't sure . . . off, somehow.

"Percy, is something wrong?"

"No, Arthur. Not at all. Here. Here is your cider."

Arthur shrugged and took the mug. He stared at it for a moment. There was something vaguely wrong. Something he could not put his finger on. But he could not for the life of him figure out what it was.

He shrugged and downed the poisoned cider.

It had a faintly acid taste and he frowned. "Needs more sugar," he said.

"Arthur, please," said Gwen. "Can we go now?"

"Yes. Absolutely, we'll—"

"Arthur! Arthur Pendragon the Coward, son of Uther Pendragon the Murderer! I challenge you!"

Arthur had half risen out of his seat, and now he sat down slowly, his gaze held by the knight in the black surcoat who stood before him. His loud words had attracted the notice of everyone within earshot. Crowds that had started to disperse began to gather once again. And Gwen, completely befuddled, paged through her program. This wasn't on the schedule.

Even though the other knight was helmed, Arthur recognized him. He smiled unpleasantly. "Hello, Modred. Come to wish me success in my new career?"

"I have come to put an end to you, Pendragon. You, and your damned notions of a New Camelot."

There was no doubt in the crowd's collective mind who the bad guy was in this little scenario. Modred was roundly booed.

It made no impression on him as he drew his sword and pointed it at Arthur. *"Well, Pendragon? Do you dare fight me? Or will you be revealed to all here as the coward that you are?"*

There were yells and catcalls as someone shouted out, "Teach him a lesson, Arthur! Clean his clock for him!" And the crowd, which thought it was watching another staged event, took up the encouragement.

Arthur started to rise and Gwen put a hand on his arm. "Arthur, please. Don't do this. You don't have to do this."

"Yes," said Arthur simply. "Yes, I do."

He reached down and picked up his helmet—similar to Modred's, but with a more rounded top. As he began to put it on, the crowd roared its approval.

Merlin, on the other side of the field, froze in horror as he saw Arthur descend from the royal box, Excalibur already drawn from its sheath. "Oh, no," he breathed. "The great fool. We can put all of that nonsense behind us, and he still insists on playing the warrior king." He started to make his way through the crowd, urgently.

Arthur carried a shield on his left arm, as did Modred. It was wood covered with leather, and it was formidable. Under the helmet his face was set in grim lines of determination. In his right hand he held Excalibur with such ease that you'd never expect it would take an exceptionally strong man to wield it at all with two hands, much less one.

They faced each other. The sun was overhead. Arthur circled slowly while speaking in a conversational tone of voice. "Modred, you haven't a prayer against me. You're a puppy. You were a puppy in your earlier life and you're a puppy now. You were probably a puppy in every other incarnation you've had in between. Please don't take offense. It's just the way you are. But I can live with it if you can."

"The only thing I can't live with is you!" snarled Modred, and he charged.

He took three steps forward and immediately staggered back, blinded by the glare of the sun. Arthur, who hadn't moved, grinned and said, "I could have killed you just then, son. First rule of battle—make certain that your opponent's eyes are in the sun, not yours."

Modred attacked again, barreling forward and swinging his sword. Arthur sidestepped the charge completely, and as Modred went past, swatted him on the rump with the flat of Excalibur's blade. The crowd roared. "Come now, Modred. Let's end this nonsense," said Arthur reasonably. "You don't have a prayer."

"No, Arthur. It's you who has no prayer. But you're too stupid to know it yet."

Modred came forward, sword swinging like a windmill. It bit deep into Arthur's shield. Arthur cut across with Excalibur, fully expecting to slice Modred's shield completely in half. Instead Excalibur glanced off the shield without even so much as making an impression.

Arthur was clearly taken aback by it. Modred enjoyed the small victory. "Found something your precious blade can't cut through? Here's something else." Modred's sword flashed and Arthur parried the blow directly, rather than taking the force of it on his shield. The two blades clanged together. Excalibur should have cut the other sword off at the hilt. It did not.

They separated and stepped back from each other. Arthur was now a bit more wary. His superiority to Modred in fighting skills was not at issue in his mind. But these weapons were on a par with his own, and that bore further investigation.

"You like my toys?" crowed Modred. "They're presents, Arthur. A legacy if you will. The last artifacts from Morgan Le Fey. She passed them on to me so that I could lay you low for all time."

His own armor was beginning to feel heavy on him as Arthur grated, "Come on. Are you planning on talking me to death or are you going to fight?" Fiercely, summoning all the power at his command, Arthur attacked.

Meanwhile Merlin made it to the reviewing stand, climbing in next to Gwen, who was wringing her hands. Percy was standing there, watching the proceedings as well. "Gwen," demanded Merlin, "what in hell is going on? How could you let Arthur get himself mixed up in some stupid fight?"

"How do you propose I stop him?" asked Gwen reasonably. "You think I want him out there? When Arthur gets an idea in his head, nothing can dissuade him."

"Tell me about it," said Merlin mournfully. "Still, I don't like this one bit. . . ." His voice trailed off, and Gwen turned to him in alarm. "Merlin, what's wrong?"

"There's magic in this box. I can sense it. Hell, it's Morgan, I can smell it." He turned slowly and faced Percy. Quickly he leaped up onto the seat of Arthur's chair, putting himself on eye level with Percy. Gwen looked on in surprise as Merlin grabbed Percy by the face and peered deeply into his eye. "Good God, no! He's been hypnotized."

The sudden clanging on the field alerted Merlin. He turned and watched in horror as the battle was truly joined.

Arthur was fully on the offensive now. He drove down hard on Modred, Excalibur pounding on Modred's shield again and again. *Wunk! Wunk! Wunk!* Huge chunks of the shield flew as Modred was not even able to mount a defense to slow Arthur for a moment. Back, back down the field Arthur sent Modred. And then he drew back Excalibur for another blow, brought down the sword, and totally misjudged the distance. Modred dodged and Arthur swung at empty air. The miss sent him off balance and he stumbled and almost fell. Only his warrior's reflexes saved him from tripping and hitting the ground, but by the time he recovered Modred was upon him. Modred swung hard and Arthur took the brunt of the blow on his shield. He felt the impact far more than he should have, the blow sending vibrations of pain along his left arm. Surprised, he wheeled back, and his breath came in ragged gasps. He was sweating so heavily it was pouring into his eyes. His vision was starting to fuzz over and he felt a ringing in his ears. He couldn't understand it. Lord knew the armor was heavy, but certainly he wasn't this out of shape.

Modred attacked and they alternated now. Modred slammed at Arthur's shield, Arthur hacked at Modred's. And this time, step by step as they exchanged blow after blow, it was Arthur who was beginning to retreat. The crowd shouted encouragement, roared its approval for Arthur's bravery and catcalled their disapproval for Modred. They were having the time of their lives, because after all, they knew the whole thing was rigged ahead of time and that Arthur would triumph.

It was knowledge that Merlin did not share. Staring into Percy's eyes, he spoke in low tones, then shook Percy's face once and said, "Percy! Come out of it, man!"

Percy Vale blinked slowly, the fog lifting from his mind. His eyes widened. "Modred! Where did he. . . ?" Then slow horror started to register on Percy's face. "Oh, God. Don't tell me." He looked out on the field and saw the two combatants, heard the ringing of metal on metal and the thud of metal on wood. "Tell me that Arthur didn't drink anything I gave him."

Gwen wasn't sure what was wrong, but she saw true fear in Percy's eyes, and she said, "Yes. You gave him some cider."

"It was poison," said Percy.

Gwen's mouth flew to her hands. "Percy, how . . . how could you—"

"It's not his fault," said Merlin quickly. "He was hypnotized. It was against his will—hell, I suspect that Modred didn't even tell you that you were putting poison in. You only realize now that you're fully conscious what it must have been." Merlin shook his head. "This is all my fault. I was the one who was so concerned about history repeating itself, and here I set us up for it and didn't even think of it."

"Merlin, what are you talking about?" asked Gwen.

Merlin chucked a thumb at Percy. "The fates can have a sick sense of humor. I know, I've met them. Percy here is an accountant."

"Yeah? So?"

"So . . . in his final battle Arthur lost because he was poisoned by an adder."

"Merlin, you can't be serious. You mean by a snake, right? Not by a person who adds."

"What can I say? Obviously Morgan decided to implement a little poetic justice."

"You mean Modred," Percy said.

"No. Modred's personality has been supplanted, locked away somewhere deep within him. Modred couldn't hypnotize you like that. Modred wouldn't be out there fighting like that. That cloud of hatred, that essence of Morgan that escaped me, has found a host in the body of Modred. Make no mistake, for things are not as they seem." Merlin leaned forward. "Arthur's battling Morgan Le Fey out there. And he's dying while he's doing it."

Arthur's right arm was starting to feel heavy. Lifting Excalibur became more and more of a burden. His legs were like two lead weights. Each blow from Modred's sword felt stronger than the one before. And then Arthur stumbled, falling back on one knee. Modred came in fast, swinging hard, and his sword sheered Arthur's shield in two. Quickly Arthur dropped the crumbling remains of his shield, gripped Excalibur with both hands, and using it as a crutch, drew himself to his feet. He swung Excalibur back and around with all the force he could muster. Modred parried the blow with his sword and it glanced off and struck Modred's shield, which shattered. Modred tossed it aside, gripping his sword with two hands as well.

They stood there facing each other, a moment frozen from time.

Modred feinted to the left, then brought his sword swinging in low to the right. Arthur tried to block the blow and failed. Modred's sword bit deep into Arthur's ribs. Arthur moaned and went down to one knee, and Modred stepped back, his blade tinted red. Gasping, Arthur clutched at the wound, his face deathly white beneath his helmet.

Instead of pressing the attack, Modred stood there, admiring the damage. "How does it feel, Arthur?" he crowed.
"How does it feel to take the pain instead of inflicting it for
once?"

Gasping for breath, Arthur looked up. His voice was a
harsh whisper as he said, "Morgan?"

"My, we are the perceptive one. Gaze on the face of the one
who hates you beyond death itself." Modred yanked off his
helmet, and it was Modred's face underneath, but the eyes, the
expression, was that of Morgan Le Fey.

"And I wonder," Modred continued, "if you've figured
this out. I wonder if you've realized that you've been poisoned."

Arthur grunted, the blood in his veins turning to fire. "Now
that you mention it, I do feel a little off."

"You're going to die, Arthur. The only question is whether
it's going to be from the blade or from the blood."

Modred gripped his sword firmly and swung at Arthur's
head.

Arthur blocked it.

Modred was visibly surprised. "I didn't think you had
enough strength left in you for that."

"You'll find I'm full of surprises," said Arthur, a grim
smile on his lips. And he rose. Slowly, agonizingly, he got to
his feet, holding onto his sword. Holding on to his life, not
allowing the release of either. His mouth curled back in a
sneer. "You're pathetic. You couldn't even beat me fairly,
you had to try and poison me. Well it didn't work."

"I—I saw you drink the poison," stammered Modred.

"Perhaps you did," Arthur said. "And perhaps I switched
the mugs." And without giving Modred a chance to think,
Arthur attacked.

Merlin watched in shock as Gwen said, "Do something!"

"I don't know what," said Merlin. "And I couldn't
anyway. This is Arthur's battle. He wouldn't forgive me if I
interfered in something as personal as this."

"Forgive you!" she shrieked. "He's going to die!"

"You haven't known him for as long as I have," said
Merlin.

Arthur pressed the attack. He did not allow himself to feel
the pain. He refused to acknowledge that his arms were dead
weight, that Excalibur had become unwieldly. He refused to

acknowledge that he was dying. He drove Modred back, back. The great sword Excalibur came faster instead of slower. The speed of Arthur's blows increased. The crowd went wild as Modred retreated farther and farther before Arthur's savage onslaught. Blood pumped furiously from Arthur's wound. The left side of Arthur's surcoat was stained red. And Arthur grew stronger.

"It's impossible!" screamed Modred.

"This is all impossible!" said Arthur. "We all are! And you'll never defeat me, Morgan. Even if you kill me, you'll never defeat me."

They spun in a semicircle and Modred squinted.

"Now what did I tell you about the sun?" said Arthur, and brought Excalibur down with every bit of strength he had left.

Modred's sword went flying from his hand.

The crowd went wild.

Modred made a desperate grab for his sword as Arthur swung Excalibur around. Modred dodged, and the weight of Excalibur pulled Arthur to the ground. He lay there, gasping, clutching at his wound. Under his helmet his features were twisted in pain. The poison running through his system, weighted down by his armor, his wound an agonizing pain in his side, Arthur could not rise.

Modred stood there for a moment, unable to believe his good fortune. "You . . . you lied to me! You did drink the poison. You are dying!" He laughed Morgan's laugh. "This is turning into a good day after all."

He turned to where his sword had fallen.

Groucho was holding it. Chico was standing next to him.

Their expressions were unreadable.

Slowly Groucho advanced on Modred. He held the sword with the same ease that he held knives. Slowly Modred started to back up. "Give . . . give that back to me, you hairy goon."

Chico darted around to the side. Modred didn't take his eyes off Groucho, and seconds later could retreat no farther because Chico was directly behind him. Before he could move, Chico had pinned his arms behind him.

"What are you doing?" bleated Modred. "What are you doing? Get off me!" He struggled in Chico's grip but was unable to break free.

Still Groucho said nothing as he walked right up to the terrified Modred. He brought the sword right up to Modred's throat and then, with a quick motion, wrapped one arm around Modred's head while Chico kept Modred's arms pinned back.

And the soul of Morgan Le Fey screamed, *"No!* I can't die *again!* Not *again!"* And with a scream of horror she leaped free of her host body.

And it was Moe Dredd who now screamed *"No!* Don't! D—"

Groucho dropped the sword and began rapping his knuckles repeatedly and furiously on Modred's skull. *"Noogies!"* he shouted. Chico laughed joyously.

A black cloud leaped skyward, and from across the field Merlin worked a spell of containment. This time he was fast enough off the mark, and a ball of energy formed around the pure hate that made up the remains of Morgan Le Fey. It enveloped her completely, and then in a bright flash was gone.

"What was that?" asked Percy.

"I transported her," replied Merlin. "She's back at my sanctum. And there she'll stay until I have time to attend to her. Right now I have something more pressing."

He was leaping out of the box, but Gwen was already out and halfway across the field. The crowd's cheering had been reduced to a confused buzz of conversation, because of the strange black cloud, the flash of light that made it disappear, and because Arthur was lying there, and boy, it sure looked like he was bleeding to death. It had to be part of the act, didn't it? But it seemed kind of tasteless. . . .

Modred blinked furiously. "Noogies?"

"Don't'cha remember us, man?" said Chico excitedly. "Remember the old days, the three of us? Chico, Groucho, and you, Harpo. We were a team, man. Don't you remember?"

"The sixties," said Groucho helpfully. "Remember the sixties?"

"Vaguely," said Moe, still trying to shake off the abrupt departure of Morgan. "I was doing some real weird shit back then . . . wait." He looked at them and frowned. And then he said, "Oh, my God. Wait. Chico and Groucho?"

They nodded eagerly. "You do remember!"

"I thought . . . I thought all of that was just some drug-induced hallucination."

"You disappeared one day, man. We never knew where you went."

"I'm not sure myself. I woke up in Thirtieth Street Station in Philadelphia. To this day I don't know how I got there. And that's when I decided to pull my act together."

"Geez." Chico looked at Groucho. "You think if the same thing happened to us, we'd have gotten our act together too?"

Groucho shrugged. "Could be. Philadelphia does weird shit to your head, man."

They pulled their newly-found third member of their group away even as a crowd started to gather around Arthur's fallen form. Gwen came to Arthur's side and dropped down next to him. She ripped off a piece from his surcoat and held it against the wound, and she looked up at the people standing around. "For God's sake, call an ambulance."

They stared at her. "You mean he's really hurt?"

"Get an ambulance, dammit!"

Three people ran off and one man stepped forward. He was a doctor and at that moment he didn't give a damn about malpractice suits. "I'm a doctor, miss. Maybe I can help."

He knelt at Arthur's side as Gwen pulled his helmet off. She gasped at the whiteness of his skin.

"Oh, God, Arthur."

He lifted a mailed hand to her cheek and stroked it, smiling sickly. "Gwen. Don't cry, my lovely Gwen. We gave them a real run for their money this time."

"Them? Who's them?"

"The fates. They have it out for me, you know. They hate happy endings, you know." He winced. "Now don't go crying for me, Gwen. It's unseemly."

Tears streamed down her face. "I don't want to lose you, Arthur," she sobbed. "I don't think I could go through waiting for you again for another fifteen centuries."

"You're not going to lose me," said Arthur. "I'll always be with you."

"I don't want poetic bullshit! I want you!"

He laughed. "That's my Gwen. Never could pull anything on her."

Merlin knelt down next to them. Gwen turned and said, "Merlin! Do something!"

And he said softly, "I'm a sorceror, child, not a doctor. A

curse on him I could handle. Poison and blood wounds, that's something else again. It's out of my reach."

She stroked Arthur's cheek as the doctor worked furiously on the gash in Arthur's side. "Merlin," said Arthur, and his voice sounded ghastly. "Promise you'll look after her."

Merlin nodded. There were no tears in his eyes, but they were glistening every so slightly. "It's not fair, you know."

"Life isn't fair, Merlin. You taught me that."

"I know," sighed Merlin. "Just once I'd like to be wrong."

Moments later the ambulance pulled up, driving straight across the green. The crowd melted from its path as the paramedics came rushing out. Plasma had already been prepared.

And the paramedics ran into a problem, as it took three of them to lift the armored king onto the stretcher.

"My God," murmured one. "How the hell are we going to get this stuff off him?"

Merlin handed one of the paramedics a pair of wire cutters. "This'll do it. They're special. Take the armor right off."

"Are you serious?"

"Trust me."

The paramedic shouted back to Merlin as he leaped into the ambulance. "You must be a Boy Scout, right?"

"Right," said Merlin.

Gwen started toward the ambulance. "I want to be with him!" she cried. But Merlin held her back. "It's going to be busy enough back there without another body to interfere."

She dropped to her knees and wrapped her arms around Merlin, sobbing piteously on his shoulder. "Oh, Merlin, I want to be with him!"

Uncertainly, he stroked her back gently. "You are, Gwen. You are."

"But you at least had him for one lifetime. I can't lose him after barely a year. I can't."

He held her close to him and let her cry. A single tear ran down his face as the ambulance roared off, siren screeching.

Directly outside the emergency ward of Lenox Hill Hospital, Arthur Pendragon, Son of Uther, King of the Britons, and mayor-elect of New York City, died.

Chaptre the Twentieth

Gwen DeVere sat out on the stretch of private beach outside the rented cottage. Getting a beachside cottage at this time of year in Avalon had been a snap. Avalon, a small resort community near Atlantic City, didn't get all that many people looking for that sort of accommodation in the dead of winter.

Gwen pulled her heavy sweater around her and looked out at the crashing waves. She exhaled her breath and watched the little puff of white steam hover in the air in front of her.

There was a crunch of a footfall on the sand behind her. She turned, looked up, and smiled. "Hello, love," she said. "Enjoy your nap?"

Arthur sat down next to her and draped an arm around her shoulder. "Feeling quite refreshed, thank you."

They sat next to each other, basking in the warmth of each other's presence. Finally Arthur said, "I'm glad I came back."

"What, from your nap?"

"No, from the dead. This was certainly worth returning for."

"Arthur, I wish you'd stop putting it that way." She sighed. "I keep telling you, you were only dead for under a minute."

"Is that all?" He laughed.

"Look, they bring people back from the dead all the time. Your heart stopped and they got it started again."

191

"Simple as that." He shook his head. "I'll never understand how so many people consider magic too unbelievable, but they accept as commonplace things that I would have once considered inconceivable."

They stared out at the ocean for a while longer. Then Gwen rested her head on his shoulder. "I like being married to you," she said.

"The local news people liked it too." He laughed. "Marrying me in my hospital bed. It must have looked delightful on the evening news."

"It did."

"You in your wedding dress, me in my gown with the string openings down the back. Very dignified."

"Look," she said in all seriousness, "I let you get away once. I'll be damned if I let you get away again."

She kissed him lightly. He smiled. "Let's run away," he said conspiratorially. "Right after I'm sworn in, I'll make Percy deputy mayor, and then we'll run off."

"You make it sound so tempting."

"It's meant to be."

"You can't. You know we can't. You have a destiny to fulfill."

"Oh, bugger destiny. You're starting to sound like Merlin." He lay back on the sand. "I suppose we'll have to return to it all soon. Merlin. Percy. Ronnie."

"Chico, Groucho, and Moe—sorry, Harpo—have vanished," said Gwen. "The last anyone's heard from them is a postcard of Philadelphia City Hall with a little note saying, 'Wish we were here.' She laughed. "Maybe they're going to stop being the Marx Brothers and become one large W. C. Fields."

She curled up next to Arthur as they lay back on the sand. "I did so many things wrong the first time around, Gwen," said Arthur after a time. "I had so many expectations to which no one could live up. I've been given a second chance—hell, a third chance. I desperately don't want to make a muddle of it."

"You won't," she said confidently. "You're Arthur. You're my husband, and you're a good man, and you'll always do what's right. Even if it's wrong."

"Thank you." He shivered slightly. "Getting chilly. Want to go in?"

"We could. There's an old movie on TV I always wanted to see. A Bing Crosby film."

"I don't know the fellow, but I'm game."

"Good. It's *A Connecticut Yankee in King Arthur's Court*."

He stared at her. "Let's stay out here a while longer."

"But you said you were getting chilly."

"Then," he pulled her close to him, "we'll just have to find some way to keep warm."

Somewhere in New York Merlin looked at the TV screen and smiled in spite of himself. "I suppose I was wrong about her. It is nice to be wrong every once in a while. But not too often."

He reached over, turned the channel selector. The image of Arthur and Gwen on the beach vanished, to be replaced by another. Merlin settled back with a box of popcorn to watch Bing Crosby.

Oddes and Ends

The description of armor was lifted from a book on armor by Sean Morrison, entitled, unsurprisingly, *Armor*. It was published by Crowell in 1963.

The following historic landmarks mentioned in this book really exist—Belvedere Castle, the Cloisters, the Camelot Building on Twenty-eighth Street off Broadway (at this writing the home of—honest to God—the Lady Guinevere Theater), and Arthur's Court, a men's clothing store near Central Park. Tell them I sent you. They don't know me from a hole in the wall and you'll probably get a blank stare, if not embarrassed coughs.

Other people and places mentioned in this book are entirely fictional, except where they're named after real people and places.

Lastly, the election depicted in this book is not at all meant to be representative of an actual mayoral campaign in New York City. Unless, of course, Arthur ran for mayor, in which case it would all turn out exactly as has been laid out here.

About Ye Author

Peter David is also known for his work at Marvel Comics, including *The Incredible Hulk*, *Spider-Man* and *Merc*. He lives in New York with his wife, two children, and countless stuffed animals.

Magikal mirth'n mayhem from the creator of Thieves' World™

Make no mythstake, this is the wildest, wackiest, most frolicking fantasy series around. With the mythfit Skeeve and his magical mythadventures, Aahz the pervert demon, Gleep the baby dragon, and a crazy cast of mythstifying characters, Robert Asprin's "Myth" series is a guaranteed good time. Join the world of deveels, dragons and magik—and join the wacky adventures of fantasy's most fun-loving mythfits.

_02362-2	**Another Fine Myth**	$2.95
_55521-7	**Myth Conceptions**	$2.95
_55529-2	**Myth Directions**	$2.95
_33851-8	**Hit or Myth**	$2.95
_55276-5	**Myth-ing Persons**	$2.95
_48499-9	**Little Myth Marker**	$2.95

Available at your local bookstore or return this form to:

ACE
THE BERKLEY PUBLISHING GROUP, Dept. B
390 Murray Hill Parkway, East Rutherford, NJ 07073

Please send me the titles checked above. I enclose _____ Include $1.00 for postage and handling if one book is ordered; add 25¢ per book for two or more not to exceed $1.75. CA, NJ, NY and PA residents please add sales tax. Prices subject to change without notice and may be higher in Canada. Do not send cash.

NAME_____

ADDRESS_____

CITY_____STATE/ZIP_____

(Allow six weeks for delivery.)

The Ebenezum Trilogy
BY
CRAIG SHAW GARDNER

On a road fraught with
peril and dark magic, the mighty
wizard Ebenezum and his hapless
apprentice Wuntvor search for the City of
Forbidden Delights.

"A lot of fun! I could hardly wait to find out
what was going to happen next!"
—Christopher Stasheff, author of
THE WARLOCK IN SPITE OF HIMSELF

"A fun romp! The field needs more humorists
of this calibre."
—Robert Asprin, author of the MYTH series

___ A MALADY OF MAGICKS	0-441-51662-9/$2.95	
___ A MULTITUDE OF MONSTERS	0-441-54523-8/$2.95	
___ A NIGHT IN THE NETHERHELLS	0-441-02314-2/$2.95	

Available at your local bookstore or return this form to:

ACE
THE BERKLEY PUBLISHING GROUP, Dept. B
390 Murray Hill Parkway, East Rutherford, NJ 07073

Please send me the titles checked above. I enclose _____ Include $1.00 for postage
and handling if one book is ordered; add 25¢ per book for two or more not to exceed
$1.75. CA, NJ, NY and PA residents please add sales tax. Prices subject to change
without notice and may be higher in Canada. Do not send cash.

NAME_____

ADDRESS_____

CITY_____STATE/ZIP_____

(Allow six weeks for delivery.)

Fantasy from Ace
fanciful and fantastic!

☐ 53721-9	**MOONHEART** Charles de Lint	$3.95
☐ 51662-9	**A MALADY OF MAGICKS** Craig Shaw Gardner	$2.95
☐ 67919-6	**THE PRINCESS OF FLAMES** Ru Emerson	$2.95
☐ 76674-9	**SILVERLOCK** John Myers Myers	$4.95
☐ 10264-6	**CHANGELING** Roger Zelazny	$2.95
☐ 89467-4	**WIZARD OF THE PIGEONS** Megan Lindholm	$2.95
☐ 51944-X	**MARIANNE, THE MAGUS AND THE MANTICORE** Sheri S. Tepper	$2.95
☐ 77523-3	**THE SONG OF MAVIN MANYSHAPED** Sheri S. Tepper	$2.75
☐ 52552-0	**MERLIN'S BOOKE** Jane Yolen	$2.95
☐ 31759-6	**THE HARP OF IMACH THYSSEL** Patricia C. Wrede	$2.95
☐ 58634-1	**THE NORBY CHRONICLES** Janet and Isaac Asimov	$2.95

Available at your local bookstore or return this form to:

ACE
THE BERKLEY PUBLISHING GROUP, Dept. B
390 Murray Hill Parkway, East Rutherford, NJ 07073

Please send me the titles checked above. I enclose _____. Include $1.00 for postage and handling if one book is ordered; add 25¢ per book for two or more not to exceed $1.75. CA, NJ, NY and PA residents please add sales tax. Prices subject to change without notice and may be higher in Canada. Do not send cash.

NAME_____

ADDRESS_____

CITY_____ STATE/ZIP_____

(Allow six weeks for delivery.)

COLLECTIONS OF SCIENCE FICTION AND FANTASY

☐ 52567-9	**MERMAIDS!** Jack Dann & Gardner Dozois, eds.	$2.95
☐ 05508-7	**BESTIARY!** Jack Dann & Gardner Dozois, eds.	$2.95
☐ 85444-3	**UNICORNS!** Jack Dann & Gardner Dozois, eds.	$2.95
☐ 20405-8	**ELSEWHERE** Volume III Terri Windling & Mark A. Arnold, eds.	$3.95
☐ 51532-0	**MAGICATS!** Jack Dann and Gardner Dozois, eds.	$2.95
☐ 48184-1	**LIAVEK: THE PLAYERS OF LUCK** Will Shetterly and Emma Bull, eds.	$2.95
☐ 16622-9	**DRAGONFIELD AND OTHER STORIES** Jane Yolen	$2.75
☐ 06977-0	**BODY ARMOR: 2000** Joe Haldeman, Charles G. Waugh, Martin Harry Greenberg, eds.	$3.50
☐ 22564-0	**FAERY!** Terri Windling, ed.	$2.95

Available at your local bookstore or return this form to:

ACE
THE BERKLEY PUBLISHING GROUP, Dept. B
390 Murray Hill Parkway, East Rutherford, NJ 07073

Please send me the titles checked above. I enclose _____ Include $1.00 for postage and handling if one book is ordered; add 25¢ per book for two or more not to exceed $1.75. CA, NJ, NY and PA residents please add sales tax. Prices subject to change without notice and may be higher in Canada. Do not send cash.

NAME_____

ADDRESS_____

CITY_____ STATE/ZIP_____

(Allow six weeks for delivery.)